THE SLAVES OF NEW

by

SUSANNA HUGHES

CHIMERA

The Slaves of New York first published in 1999 by
Chimera Publishing Ltd
PO Box 152
Waterlooville
Hants
PO8 9FS

Printed and bound in Great Britain by
Caledonian International Book Manufacturing Ltd
Glasgow

THE SLAVES OF NEW YORK

Susanna Hughes

Chapter One

In the black stretch limousine he'd made her kneel on the thick carpet in front of him. She had been totally obedient. She'd slipped onto her knees, and even grasped her hands behind her back and bowed her head in the correct position before he'd ordered her to.

'I've never done this before,' she whispered, nervously.

'I know,' he replied. 'But it's what you want, isn't it?'

He'd picked her up in a bar on W48th Street and Fifth Avenue. Her name was Lisa. She was young with beautiful blonde hair, so long it almost reached to her buttocks. That is what had first attracted him. Her hair swung and swayed as she moved her head this way and that, catching the light.

'What do I have to do?' she asked.

'Whatever I say.'

Jake Ashley leant forward and touched her cheek. He could see the apprehension in her eyes. But there was also lust. He'd picked up at least two dozen women like this and it was always the same. He seemed to have a sixth sense when it came to recognising the signs.

'Take your dress off,' he said.

Immediately she took hold of the hem of her dress. The back was trapped under her thighs and she had to raise herself on her haunches to free it. She pulled the red shift over her head. She was wearing a lacy red bra, her big spongy breasts spilling out over its low cut cups, matching tiny red panties and champagne coloured hold ups. She was dressed to undress, out for a night that would end in a man's bed.

Jake reached into his pocket and took out a long strip of white silk. Lisa started as he wrapped the silk around her eyes. 'What are you doing?' she asked, though the answer was obvious.

'You have to be blindfolded,' in a tone that suggested that everyone knew that and he couldn't understand why she didn't. He knotted the silk tightly at the back so it pressed on her eyelids, then reached forward and pulled the left cup of her bra down, tucking it neatly under her breast. He stroked her breast briefly with his fingers, the nipple hard as stone.

'You know who I am, don't you?' he said.

'Yes. You wrote those books.'

'You've read them.'

'Yes.'

'So you know what will be required of you?'

'Yes.' Her voice was vibrating with excitement.

It had taken thirty minutes to drive to his apartment and she had remained there on her knees with the white silk banding her head, her left breast exposed and her hands clasped firmly behind her back. She hadn't moved except to sway from side to side as the car cornered. His chauffeur had helped him take her in the back entrance of the apartment block and up in his private elevator. In his apartment he'd taken her straight to his bedroom.

'Stand where you are,' he said. 'You are not to move.'

'What are you going to do?' Lisa asked with a note of alarm.

He did not reply but unclipped the clasp of her bra and gently slipped the cups off her breasts. They quivered. She had small nipples that were puckered and hard. He pinched them and watched as they knotted themselves even tighter.

'I want you to lie back on the bed.'

'Where is it?'

'Three steps forward.'

He watched as the girl edged forward until her knees touched the edge of the bed. She turned, sat down, then pulled herself across the white counterpane.

'What are you doing to me?' she asked, her voice breathy and thin.

He could have taken her right there, stripped those slutty little red panties down her long slender legs and fucked her. She would have screamed with delight whatever he had done with her. But Jake wanted a great deal more from her than that.

He was sure from the way her whole body seemed to be trembling with excitement that she had often fantasised about being treated like this, and used it over and over again in her masturbation rituals. That's why she'd read his books. She used them to supply the details, the trappings and paraphernalia that she could not have imagined for herself. She was a natural.

'Stay exactly where you are,' Jake said.

There was a video camera in the corner on a tripod. He took a quick look through the view-finder, adjusted the position slightly so the lens took in every detail of the big double bed, then locked it off and started the mechanism rolling. Tomorrow, in his study, he would play the film back. He would carefully note down everything that happened, everything she said. If there was anything unusual he had not written about before it would appear in one of his books.

'Take your panties off,' he ordered.

The girl did as she was told, a little awkwardly, as she could not see what she was doing.

'Lie back and don't move, Lisa.'

He walked out of the bedroom. He returned five minutes later. He was not alone. The woman at his side was wearing a shiny red PVC body with a halter-neck, its legs cut so high they exposed most of her flanks. Two cut-outs in the front of the garment revealed her small round breasts. Her left nipple was pierced with a gold ring. The gusset of the body had also been cut away to reveal her sex. It had been shaved and was completely hairless. Her head was covered by a red rubber helmet, stretched so tight that it fitted the contours of her face like a second skin. There were holes for her mouth and her eyes. Her wrists were bound with metal handcuffs out in front of her, and she had a thick leather collar around her neck attached to a long metal leash by which Jake led her over to the bed.

'Undo her blindfold,' he ordered. He had taken off his clothes and was naked now except for a dark blue silk robe.

The woman in red knelt on the bed beside Lisa, rolled her over onto her side, and unknotted the white silk. Lisa blinked as she got accustomed to the light, her eyes trying to focus on the woman.

'Meet April. Have you ever been with a woman?'

'No. Don't make me do that.'

'I thought that's what you wanted, sweetness. I thought you came here because you wanted to obey.'

'Please,' she said. 'Don't make me.' But her body language betrayed her. Jake could see her whole body seemed to be angling itself towards the other woman.

'April's going to be good to you. Real good.'

'No.'

'You know what to do,' he said, unclipping the leash from the leather collar. He looked across at the video camera. The little red light on its right-hand side indicated it was still rolling. The tape would run for two hours.

April leant forward. She gathered one of Lisa's big breasts in both hands and shaped it into a pyramid. Then she sawed the edge of her teeth across the nipple.

Lisa gasped. 'Please don't let her do that,' she said.

Jake sat on the bed beside her. 'But you like it, sweetness. I can see you like it.'

'No,' Lisa insisted.

'Yes.'

April's mouth moved to her other breast. He watched as her fingers sunk into the flesh. A little dribble of saliva ran over her lips and trailed down Lisa's breast as her teeth worked on the nipple. She followed it with her mouth, licking it up. Her lips ran down over Lisa's flat belly, her fingers playing with the girl's blonde pubes.

'I want you to spread your legs apart, sweetness, just as far as they'll go.'

'I can't,' Lisa said.

'You have to, sweetness. You have to obey, remember? That's what you've always wanted, isn't it? To obey. To be a slave. Isn't it?'

'Yes,' Lisa whispered as if it were a secret.

'Then obey me now. If you don't open your legs then April can't go down on you. And if April can't go down on you I wouldn't be able to see you come. Don't you want to please me?'

'Yes.' The girl looked lost and confused. He'd seen that before too. Slowly she scissored her legs apart. He looked at her sex, her soft blonde pubic hair already plastered against her labia by her juices.

'Wider,' he ordered. 'I want you to pretend they're bound there and you're unable to move them. Will you do that for me?'

She stretched them across the bed. Later he would tie her like that, bind her with soft white rope. He'd tie her tits and put a rope up between her legs so she could work her clit against it. But she had to prove herself first. Bondage was a privilege, not a right. A good slave should be bound by the words of command just as tight as by any bonds. Like April. April was a very good slave. Lisa may have fantasised about being a slave but fantasy and reality were two different things. If she wanted to be his slave she had to prove herself first.

April squatted between Lisa's legs, then dipped her head and pressed her lips to the blonde's hairy sex. She parted the bush of her pubes and poked her tongue into the slit of Lisa's labia.

'Oh God…' Lisa moaned. 'Please.' She turned to face Jake, pleading with him, 'please get her to stop.'

'Stretch your arms up above your head,' he ordered. 'As far as they'll go. As if they were bound.'

Lisa obeyed at once. Her slender body was stretched out across the white counterpane, her ribcage visible and her belly almost concave.

April's tongue worked at her clit.

'No,' Lisa sighed, but she made no attempt to close her legs or pull April away with her hands. Jake smiled. As if they were bound: she'd already learnt that lesson.

April's tongue circled Lisa's clit, as her bound hands moved up between her legs. The handcuffs clinked as she pushed three fingers into the girl's sticky wet cunt.

'Oh God,' Lisa whimpered, quivering.

'Don't move,' Jake said.

He saw her fingers spread out and her whole body shudder almost as if she'd been punched. Then her mouth opened wide and she let out a low, keening moan, and pushed herself down on April's mouth, grinding her hips from side to side to extract the last ounce of sensation from the first orgasm she'd ever had with another woman.

'Stay as you are,' Jake warned.

She did just that. As April raised her head, her chin and lips glistening with Lisa's copious juices, the blonde remained stretched across the bed, the blonde hair of her pubes plastered back against her sex.

'Come on April.'

April knew what to do. She straddled Lisa's body, facing her feet, so her sex was immediately over her mouth. Her labia smooth, hairless and glistening wet, were framed by the red PVC. Immediately she dropped onto her haunches and pressed her sex down on April's mouth.

'Does that feel good, sweetness?'

Lisa's reply was muffled by April's sex. 'Oh yes,' she gasped.

He could see Lisa's body gently undulating on the bed. He congratulated himself on his perspicacity. His sixth sense never failed him. She needed this. She had needed it all her life.

Jake opened his robe. His cock was erect, a little drop of fluid leaking from the slit. He moved around behind April. He grasped her hips and pushed himself forward, so his erection slotted between her legs, April's sleek labia on the top and Lisa's hot wet mouth beneath.

'Suck it.'

He felt Lisa's lips purse around his shaft, sucking the fat tube that formed his urethra. He ran his hands around April and cupped her breasts, pinching both her nipples at the same time and feeling her squirm with the pain. He pulled on the nipple ring and her whole body shuddered. Slowly he began to move his cock back and forth, all the way back until it was almost out of reach of the girl's mouth, then all the way forward until his balls were nudging against her face. Normally he would not allow himself to come so soon, but there was something special about this girl. He felt his spunk rising as he pumped his cock back and forth. He could feel April's labia throbbing against it too, the wetness from her vagina leaking over the upper surface.

'Suck,' he ordered. He stopped moving and concentrated on feeling the blonde's mouth sucking hard at the underside of his cock. His phallus jerked and his spunk jetted out over her naked breasts, big fat hot gobs of it.

He pulled away, slightly annoyed with himself that he'd let her get to him. Not that it mattered. The night was young. He would come again. He'd take her into the punishment room next door and have April string her up on the vertical rake and see how she responded to being whipped. He was sure she'd fantasised about that too. If she responded well, tomorrow he would ask her if she wanted to come up to the house in New England. There he could make all her fantasies come true. There she could become a slave – a slave of New York.

Kim Holbrook sat in the window seat of the Boeing 747 watching as the plane dipped its left wing and banked over the city of New York. There was a good view of Manhattan and she could see the lake in Central Park. Further south the Staten Island Ferry left a white wake as it ploughed across the Upper Bay.

It had been an uncomfortable flight. Her editor on the

Sunday Post was not prepared to pay for club class travel on what he regarded as a wild goose chase, so she had been crammed in economy, the seats so close together they provided little room for her long legs. The flight was crowded too, which made it impossible to stretch out, or do much other than stay put and try to read and catnap.

At least the woman in the seat to her left had not invaded her space, and had seemed content to keep conversation to the absolute minimum. And she had the advantage of the window. She had watched the plane approach the Eastern seaboard and now was able to pick out all the familiar landmarks of Manhattan; the Chrysler building and the huge *Metro Life* block – better known in its former incarnation when it bore the logo of *PanAm* – sitting squarely in the middle of Fifth Avenue.

Kim packed her book away in her bag, the woman in the next seat giving her a quizzical look. In the last four weeks she had set herself the task of reading all eleven books in the *Slaves of New York* series by Jake Ashley, and *The Disciple* was the last.

'Are you enjoying it?' the woman to her left said, catching sight of the cover. It featured a brunette with a dusky complexion kneeling with her hands raised in an attitude of prayer, her long hair flowing down over her shoulders. Her wrists were handcuffed together by thin steel bands and she was naked, though her elbows hid her breasts.

'Sorry?' Kim said.

'*The Disciple*, are you enjoying it?' The woman nodded at the book. She had short layered light brown hair streaked with blonde. Her legs were crossed, her nylons very sheer and shiny. Her accent was a soft East Coast American.

'It's work, actually,' Kim explained. 'I've come to New

York to interview him.'

'Jake Ashley? Really?' The woman arched a delicately plucked eyebrow.

'Yes.'

'How fascinating. I've read a lot of his stuff.'

That surprised Kim. Jake Ashley was almost a cult figure in the world of S&M, his books highly prized among the cognoscenti of such practices as being the most outrageous but perceptive of the many titles that had flooded the market. It was not the sort of material she would have expected the rather elegant woman to her left even to have heard of, let alone read.

'And what do you think?' Kim asked.

'What do I think?' She thought for a moment. "I think he makes it easy to understand how a woman could get involved in that world, how it could be extremely attractive and exciting, even if never fantasised about it. He makes me believe it's relevant to even the most independent of woman.'

'Relevant?'

'Yes. Like something that affects you, personally. Come on, don't tell me you haven't got off on it?'

Kim felt herself blushing. Since she'd first had the idea to do a story on Jake Ashley a few weeks ago his books certainly had affected her, though she did not like to admit it to herself. She had no idea that the total domination his heroines were subjected to, progressively reduced from strong independent women to sex obsessed slaves willing to obey every whim of their virile and demanding master, would have any appeal to her, but it had.

'I suppose so.'

'And he's attractive, isn't he? That's part of it, I suppose. Those eyes, they're sort of hypnotic.' She nodded towards

Kim's bag.

The colour photograph on the back jacket of the book was peaking out from Kim's bag. The eyes seemed to be looking directly at her. Jake was an attractive man. He had a rugged, craggy face, and dark black curly hair that flopped over his forehead. His mouth was firm and sensual and he had a long straight nose. But it was his eyes, large blue eyes, that caught and held the attention.

'Look, we're perfect strangers, honey. We're never going to meet again in a hundred years so it isn't going to make a blind bit of difference what you tell me. Fact is they're a huge turn on for a lot of women. Sex is a whole barrel of worms. That's why Ashley is successful. It's not just weirdoes on the Upper East Side, whipping their naked buns. He makes it available to everyone. He makes you believe in it. He makes you believe that crawling around on the floor in a garter belt and stockings with your tits in nipple clamps could really be a turn on. Am I right?'

Kim hadn't thought of it that way before. She had been rather embarrassed about her reaction to the books and had thought it was something particular in her that she wasn't very keen to discuss.

'Yes, yes you are,' she said. 'To tell you the truth I was finding it hard to come to terms with.'

'Right. I mean, it's not something you really want to admit, is it? Doesn't mean you can't have fantasies though, right? I've read every one of his books and I can tell you some of those scenes I know by heart.' The woman grinned. Her whole face was animated. 'Actually, I have a theory that the more up-front and independent a woman is the more likely she is to be attracted to the submission thing. You know there's that old cliché about the most powerful men always being the ones who go to hookers to be treated like shit. Perhaps it's the same with women.'

'Could be, I suppose.'

'But I thought Jake Ashley never gave interviews.'

'He doesn't. I'm just hoping to persuade him.'

'Christ, just talking about it makes me go all squirmy right here.' The woman pressed her fingers into her belly. She was wearing a white blouse and Kim noticed her nipples had suddenly hardened, their contours outlined under the material. 'Do you think it's all based on his experiences?'

'That was going to be my first question,' Kim said. The plane began to descend. The pilot announced that they were going to be landing in approximately ten minutes. 'But it might just be in his imagination. That's what a writer is supposed to do, after all; imagine things.'

'I don't believe anyone could write like that unless they've experienced it. All the detail, all the equipment the master uses…' She shuddered, her eyes turned inward for a moment accessing a private memory.

'But he writes about the women's emotions as accurately as what the masters feel. That's pure imagination. He's not a woman.'

'You're right. He certainly knows women. He knows exactly what makes them tick sexually. But I guess that's because he's been there, he's had them as his slaves. He just couldn't write like that otherwise.'

'So what, you think he's got a chateau?' The eleven books that Ashley had written all feature the same male protagonist, a rich businessmen who had built a French chateau in New England.

'Possible, I suppose. But he's certainly got punishment rooms. And he's certainly done most of the stuff he writes about.'

'Perhaps he tries it all out on his wife, or a willing girlfriend?'

'Could be. It's a funny thing, isn't it?'

'What is?'

'Fantasy. Sexual fantasy. I mean, there's lots of stuff in his books – bondage, whippings, nipple clamps – that would be really painful. But when you read about it you don't think about the pain. Only the pleasure it seems to bring.' The woman licked her upper lip very slowly with the tip of her tongue. 'Have you ever tried it?

'No. Never.'

'But you have fantasised about it?'

Kim turned to look at the woman. 'Yes, I suppose so,' she said vaguely. The truth was that she had masturbated at least three or four times imagining herself as one of Ashley's heroines, tied and bound with a large dildo forced into her sex as the master applied a whip to her buttocks. But she didn't want to admit that – even to herself.

'Have you ever thought of going further.'

'Further?'

'There're contact magazines in New York. There's a lot of ads for submissives.'

'I'm not sure I'd really enjoy it.'

'You never know until you've tried.' Her eyes turned inward again.

'And you? Have you tried?'

'That's a long story.'

'Which sounds like you have.'

'I got scared.'

'Scared of getting hurt?'

'No. Scared because I'd liked it too much. Actually I was always into all sorts of sex. I used to be married. But my husband was very conservative when it came to sex.

He doesn't even like it if I wear stockings and a garter belt. Thought that was kinky. He'd have gone apeshit if I told him I wanted to be tied to the bed and whipped. It was easier to get a divorce.' She laughed. 'Hey, we're nearly down.'

Kim had a feeling there was a lot the woman was not telling her. There was a grinding noise as the landing gear was lowered and a few minutes later the plane landed on the tarmac with a squeal of rubber.

'Ladies and gentleman,' the stewardess said over the tannoy, 'welcome to New York.'

Kim paid off the yellow cab she had taken in from the airport and allowed the doorman to take her single suitcase into the Monument Hotel on W45th Street. The hotel was a five-storey nineteenth century building with a huge forty-storey skyscraper on one side and a vacant lot on the other. It was not particularly salubrious but again Kim had to be careful with her expenses. When she got home they would be minutely examined.

She was tired after the flight and as soon as she had been shown up to her tiny room, with a small en suite shower cubicle, and unpacked, she stripped off all her clothes, took a quick shower, and got into bed. Though it was eight o'clock in New York her body clock was set to London time where it was two in the morning.

But sleep did not come. The room had a primitive air conditioning unit poking through the lower half of the window, but it was too noisy to have on all night. Without it however the room soon become muggy and hot. As she lay listening to the wailing sirens that seemed to be as frequent as the subway trains rumbling below her, she thought about what the woman on the plane had said. Jake

Ashley's writings had certainly got through to her. She seemed normal enough, whatever normal meant, but behind that smartly dressed elegant facade she was actually entertaining fantasies about being a sexual slave and had hinted that she'd tried it in reality. She wondered how many other women felt the same way. Perhaps that explained why the books were so popular. They certainly had a market well beyond the small core of devotees of such outré practices, which is why she'd suggested to her editor that an interview with the reclusive Jake Ashley would be a good idea.

But her own reaction to what she had read was more ambiguous. *The Disciple* was about a Dolores Salgardo, a young secretary who had started to work for one of Piers Blanchard's companies. Piers, the master featured in every book in the series, had noticed her immediately and set about introducing her to the arcane world of submission and domination. Soon Dolores was being bound and whipped for the entertainment of the master's friends, and discovering that her sexuality blossomed under such treatment. She was also expected to have sex with the other female slaves to please her master, and found that though she had never been with a woman before, it too turned her on. If Kim were absolutely truthful with herself she was appalled at the idea that any woman should want to be totally and absolutely submissive to a man. On the other hand, the descriptions of the emotions that Dolores had felt as she dressed in incredibly tight satin basques and glossy stockings, had her feet strapped into dauntingly high heels and her sex shaved in preparation for meeting her master, were undoubtedly arousing. At the 'chateau' the slaves were subjected to a punishing regimen. All their choices were removed; what they wore, what they did, even when they were allowed to eat, and there was something exciting about that too. It was a world where nothing else existed but the nexus of sex.

Kim realised her hand had slipped down to her belly and was clutching the curved mound of her mons, her middle finger slipping into her labia. Her labia were wet.

'Damn,' she said aloud.

She pulled her hand away and rolled onto her side, but it was too late. Kim always slept in the nude, and her nipples tingled with excitement. She moved an arm across her breasts, pressing them back against her chest to try to calm the feelings they were generating, but this only made matters worse. She felt her clitoris throb and her vagina squirm. She rolled onto her back and stared up at the ceiling as a siren wailed out across the city, so close it might have been right outside.

'No,' she said to herself.

But she stripped the single sheet off and turned on the bedside light. She looked down at her naked body. Kim was slim with a narrow waist, a flat stomach and long sculptured legs, their firm muscles toned up by weekly sessions in her local health club. Her complexion was olive-skinned and her mons was covered with a thick bush of black hair that she trimmed regularly into a perfectly neat triangle.

She reached over to the bedside table where she had left her makeup case. Flipping the top open she reached inside. Carefully hidden under the little plastic wallet where she kept her lipsticks, nail varnish and eye shadow, was a large flesh-coloured dildo. She pulled it out. She had left *The Disciple* on the bedside table too, and picked it up. She held the book open with her right hand and pushed the dildo between her legs with her left.

Dolores was trembling as Monica fitted the leather blindfold over her eyes. It was padded on the inside and moulded around the bridge of her nose, cutting out the slightest hint of light. They had cinched her into a waspie girdle in red satin, lacing it so tightly she was having trouble breathing. Its long ruched satin suspenders pulled the glossy sheer black stockings taut. She wore long red satin gloves and her arms had been drawn behind her back, her wrists bound there with two thin leather straps, one at her wrists and the other just above her elbows. This pulled her shoulders back and her chest out, her big pear-shaped breasts hanging over the front of the corset, each nipple circled by a black clamp, the puckered flesh so tightly squeezed by the jaws it was white. The clamps were joined by a thin gold chain.

Monica stood back to admire her work. She was a short woman with razor cut black hair who looked as if she spent hours in the gym pumping iron, her muscles hard and well defined, almost like a female bodybuilder. She was wearing a leather bra and leather shorts, though the bra was totally unnecessary as her breasts were almost completely flat. She took Dolores's arm and pulled her out of what the girl had come to think of as her cell. She pinched spitefully at Dolores's flesh. In the days since she had arrived at the chateau Monica had never missed an opportunity to make her life, and the life of all the other slaves, uncomfortable. And as the master's overseer, charged with looking after the slaves, she had plenty of opportunity to do just that. They walked along the corridor, then turned into another room.

'Very pretty.' It was the master's voice.

'Do you want her gagged?' Monica asked.

'No. I don't think that will be necessary, will it Dolores?'

'No, master.' The word still made her shiver with excitement.

'Walk forward a few steps, child,' he ordered.

The girl tottered forward on her high-heeled shoes, still, after a week at the chateau, unaccustomed to their height. She stopped, sensing she was right in front of her master, the musky cologne he wore filling her nostrils.

'Tonight we are going to try something new.' *She had long black hair that had been washed and brushed out over her shoulders by one of the other slaves. He stroked it gently as if he really cared about her. The gesture of tenderness made Dolores's heart beat faster.*

Kim trapped the vibrator between her thighs, enabling her to turn it on with her left hand and not put the book down. She gripped the shaft again and forced it hard against her clitoris.

Dolores felt his hand slip down to her belly. Briefly it dallied with her sex, a single finger pushed into her labia. She was shaven every day now, strapped onto a specially designed table with her buttocks raised and her legs splayed so far apart she thought she might be split in two. One of the other slaves shaved her over and over again until her labia and the whole plain of her sex was as smooth as the nap of a rose. She knew he would be able to feel the sticky juices that had escaped her vagina.

'I want you to stand with your legs apart.'

She did what she was told immediately. After a week at the chateau she had learned that any hesitation was punished severely. Six bright red weals criss-crossed her buttocks as proof of that.

Monica was slotting a metal bar under her arms, so it

rested across the back of her shoulders. She clipped the ends of the bar to two chains hanging down from a complicated gearing of pulleys overhead. She wound a leather strap around Dolores's body just under her breasts and over her arms so the metal bar was trapped in place. Then Monica pulled down another metal bar attached to the pulley arrangement by a single chain. There was a thick leather cuff at each end of the bar, which she buckled tightly around Dolores's ankles.

Suddenly there was a whirr of electric motors and Dolores felt the metal bar under her arms hauling her into the air. She gasped in surprise. As she dangled in mid-air she heard the motors whirr again, and this time her ankles were raised, pulled up behind her until her body was horizontal, her breasts pointing at the floor. She felt her body swaying slightly from side to side. She had never felt so completely powerless, her body bound more tightly than it ever had been before. The sensation made her hot with excitement.

Kim managed to hold the book in front of her face and rub her upper arm against her right breast at the same time. Her nipple tingled. The humming of the vibrator filled the air, her clitoris pulsing with delicious sensations.

Dolores heard something being moved, its feet scraping the floor. Then there was the odd clicking noise that the ratchet of the crank made, and she felt herself being lowered. When the movement stopped she was sure she could feel hot breath fanning her thighs, her sex suspended above someone's face.

She felt a hand seize her head and pulled it forward onto a large, pulsing erection. Though she had never been allowed this privilege before she knew instinctively it was her master, and gobbled it deep into her mouth, wanting to show him how eager she was to please. Almost immediately she felt another sensation that made her gasp. A tongue, hot and wet, was forcing itself into her vagina, as hands wrapped themselves around her nylon-sheathed thighs, to steady her.

'How pretty,' the master said. He took her cheeks in his hands and pulled her head back until the ridge at the base of his glans was held between her lips. She felt his cock throb.

'Take the blindfold off, Monica,' the master said.

Dolores blinked as the blindfold fell away. She saw the master standing in front of her, his thickly haired body naked but for a purple silk robe that was draped from his shoulders. She looked down. Lying on a bench under her body was one of the slaves. She was naked, her face buried between Dolores's thighs, her tongue working on Dolores's clit.

'No,' Dolores tried to scream, the word muffled on her master's cock. She had never even been touched there by a woman, let alone had a woman kissing and sucking at her so intimately, and the idea had always revolted her. She tried to struggle and pulled herself away, but the master's hand at the back of the neck, and the girl's hands on her thighs, held her firm.

The master nodded at Monica, who immediately moved forward, stooped down and took Dolores's left breast in her hand. She unclipped the nipple clamp and replaced it with her mouth.

'Does that feel good, child?'

Dolores managed to pull her mouth off his cock. 'No, master, please no. Don't let them do this to me.' Of course

24

*she'd always known this moment would come, and hoped
that somehow she would be able to control her
repugnance. All she wanted was to serve her master, to
obey his commands, but she couldn't stand this.*

Kim spread her thighs apart and moved the dildo down
between them. She found the mouth of her vagina. The
vibrations made the wet flesh oscillate wildly, providing
a whole new raft of sensations.

'You have to obey.'

'Please, please...'

*But as she struggled to push herself away from the
invading tongue something happened. Instead of the
revulsion that had been making her skin crawl, she
suddenly felt a hot flush of pleasure. Deep inside her
vagina she could feel a new flow of juices running down
the velvety walls and her clitoris throbbed violently. She
found herself pressing down against the bonds, hoping to
get the tongue to go deeper. Her nipple too, clamped firmly
in Monica's mouth, was delivering the most exquisite
sensations. The master took hold of her hair and pulled
her face up to look at him.*

'Well, child?' he asked.

*'Oh master, master...' was all she could say. The girl's
tongue was flicking her clit artfully from side to side.*

*The master smiled. He pushed her mouth back onto his
phallus. She sucked it eagerly, trying to make sure the
soaring pleasures that were seizing every part of her body
were somehow concentrated in her mouth, so he would
feel her passion. She wanted him to come. She wanted to
feel his spunk and swallow it greedily. She had never
wanted anything more in her life.*

'I'm coming,' she tried to tell him, her lips moving against this hard flesh, the words barely audible. Her body shuddered. Her cunt contracted. Her clitoris pulsed as the girl's tongue pressed it back against the underlying bone.

'Master…'

Kim dropped the book and used her left hand to cup the mound of her pubis, her finger pressing her clitoris. She thrust the dildo deep into her sex, feeling the hard phallus drive right up into her soaking wet vagina. She was coming before it was fully embedded, her whole body trembling. As the feelings cascaded out of her she saw, in her mind's eye, the woman on the plane, the way her fingers had pressed into her belly, her hardened nipples under the white blouse and the way her tongue had licked the upper lip of that fleshy, sensuous mouth. And she saw Jake Ashley's eyes staring up from the cover of the book, watching them both.

'Hi, can I speak to Candy Brook please?'

'This is she.'

'Oh hi, my name's Kim Holbrook. You don't know me. I'm a friend of Johnny Danton.'

'Hey, great, how is he?'

Though the idea for a story on Jake Ashley had come from her, she would never have put it up to her editor without being able to tell him that she had at least some prospect of tracking Jake Ashley down. But a few weeks after first coming up with the idea she had interviewed the film director Johnny Danton about his new project. The subject had turned to Ashley and it turned out that Danton had been trying to get distribution companies interested in filming the first of Ashley's books. They had shied away from the idea, however, despite his insistence that it would not be pornography but a genuine attempt to look at human sexuality. When Kim had mentioned that she wanted to interview Ashley, Danton thought it would be a good idea and would help generate interest in the film project. He, unfortunately, had never met the man and had only communicated through his agent, but had employed an actress in his last film who claimed to have been one of Ashley's slaves. He had given Kim her telephone number and told her to use his name, but warned her not to be too direct. If she wanted Candy to give her information about Ashley she would have to do it subtly.

'He's fine,' Kim said. 'He's doing a film in London for the next three months.'

'So, what can I do for you?' Candy said.

'I just wondered if we could meet up. I'm doing a piece on Johnny and I'd really like to get a prospective on what it's like to work for him.'

'Hey, it's real great.'

'Do you think we could get together?'

'Sure. Why don't you come over here? What are you doing tonight?'

'Tonight would be fine.'

'Great. See you around eight. Did Johnny give you the address?'

'No.'

'It's in the village. Got a pen?'

Kim wrote down the address and they said their goodbyes.

Chapter Two

The brownstone was on 8th Street just around the corner from Washington Square. It had a traditional stoop with a flight of stone steps leading up to double panelled doors. There was a small brass Entryphone to the left of the entrance.

Kim rang the bell for Apartment 3.

'Hi.'

'It's Kim.'

'Come up. Top floor.'

The lock on the door buzzed and Kim pushed her way in. There was a large straight staircase to the left of a wide hallway, its stripped wood floor highly polished. She climbed the stairs. At the top of the second flight the door at the far end of the corridor opened.

'Hi, I'm Candy,' the girl in the doorway said.

Candy Brook was young and short and slim, and had a waif-like quality. She had a rather wide face with sharp hollow cheekbones, and her heavily permed hair was blonde. She was wearing a loose fitting black silk T-shirt over tight and very shiny white lycra leggings and high-heeled satin slippers.

'Kim Holbrook,' Kim said, extending her hand.

Candy shook it. She had long bony fingers with rings on almost every one. 'Come in.'

The apartment was small and cosy with a living room overlooking the street. It was cluttered with stuff; antiques, objet d'art, pictures and books. The two small sofas and a large armchair were all covered with ethnic throws providing a riot of colours; oranges, reds and gold. A large film poster dominated the room. It featured a picture of Candy in a tight black dress. The dress had been ripped in such a way as to expose most of her thigh, which was sheathed in a glossy black stocking supported by a taut black suspender. UNNATURAL ACTS it announced, starring Candy Brooks and Ralph Polombo.

'Would you like a glass of wine?' Candy asked. There was a large coffee table in front of the sofas, and among the clutter of books, magazines, and what looked like pre-Colombian artefacts, there was a bottle of California Chardonnay and two glasses.

'That would be nice,' Kim said.

'Sit down, please.' Candy poured the wine. 'You're real pretty.'

'Thank you.' Kim sat on one of the sofas.

'Love that accent. I guess everyone in New York's going wild for it. We love the way you Brits speak.'

She handed Kim the wine, then sat on the sofa opposite and stared at her.

'It's that long hair, I think,' she said thoughtfully. 'I'm a sucker for long black hair like yours.'

Self-consciously, Kim combed some of the hair out of her eyes. 'Every brunette wants to be a blonde and vice-versa, isn't that what they say?' Then in an effort to change the subject she nodded at the poster. 'How long ago was that?'

'Last year. It's what they call art porn. That means you get screwed and buggered just as hard but some guy tells you he's doing it because it's a way of expressing the human condition, or some bullshit like that.'

'Have you done a lot of that?'

'Sure. That's how I bought this place. Matter of fact it's how I got the job with Johnny, too. He's really into porn. Did he tell you that? He's got quite a collection.'

'No, he didn't mention it.'

'Well don't tell him I told you, in that case.' She sipped her wine, her eyes roaming Kim's body. 'Real pretty,' she said, almost to herself.

Kim was wearing a black skirt and a cream blouse. It had been too hot out on the streets to wear her jacket, so she carried it over her arm.

'So I wondered if I could ask you a few questions about Johnny?'

'Sure.' Candy sat up straight. 'Do you want to know if I slept with him to get the job?' Before Kim could say anything she continued. 'Well I did.' She laughed. 'There's a scene in that,' she nodded up to the picture, 'where these two guys are having a go at me. You know, a double-decker?'

Kim looked blank.

'Hey, honey, don't you do that stuff in England? You know, when one guy's in your pussy and the other's in your arse?'

Kim felt herself blushing. She remembered a scene in one of Ashley's books where this had been described in some detail. 'Oh, right... I just didn't know what that was called.'

'The first time hurts like hell, but once you've got used to it, it's one hell of a ride.' She wiggled her bottom against the seat.

'Anyway, Johnny was crazy about this scene. He wanted to fuck me while he watched it. Naturally, I was only too happy to oblige. He's some guy, right? And hey, I got the part.' She grinned broadly.

Kim noticed a bookcase behind the sofa. Though the books were spilling out of it in no particular order, she noticed several of Jake Ashley's titles.

'He's certainly a very attractive man,' she agreed, though she wasn't sure she had been attracted to him.

'That's so great,' Candy said. 'I mean, the way you say that. Sounds so classy.'

'So what was he like to work with?'

Kim pulled out her little tape recorder and set it on the coffee table, then worked her way through the questions she had prepared, not wanting Candy to guess the true purpose of her visit. Only when she'd spent nearly half-an-hour on how they'd got on during the shooting of the film in which Candy played a small but important part did she allow herself to glance over at the bookcase.

'I see you're a fan of Jake Ashley. Did you know Johnny wants to make the first book as a film?'

Candy looked surprised. 'Hey, is that right? Christ, that would be great, wouldn't it?' She wrinkled her forehead. 'The first book. Yes, I remember. Have you read it?'

'Yes.'

'There'd be a great part for me. You remember the blonde who's been at the chateau for a year and who gets to instruct the new slaves?'

'Yes.' Kim had only read it three or four weeks back and it was still vivid in her mind.

'She's a blonde, and real kinky. That's typecasting.'

'Have you read all the books?'

'I've done better than that, baby. I've been there.'

'Been where?'

'Been at the chateau. Been with Ashley. Been one of his slaves.'

'I don't understand,' Kim said, being deliberately slow.

'The chateau's all fiction.'

'Sure, that's what everybody thinks. But Jake lives it all out. Everything. Of course there's no eighteenth century French pile in the middle of Connecticut, but he's got a big house up there and he's got at least six slaves behaving just like the ones in the book. I was one of them.'

'Really?' Kim tried to look astonished. 'What was it like?'

'It was no picnic, honey. You have to be into pain. But I reckon it was the best fucking time I've ever had in my life, bar none. Literally, I mean. You know, by the end of my time there I was so turned on I could come just by having Jake look at my snatch.' She shuddered. Kim could see the points of her nipples sticking out from under the T-shirt.

Kim had carefully rehearsed what she was going to say next if the conversation got this far. 'Can I tell you a secret?'

'Sure.'

'I've always thought... well, I mean... I've always had these fantasies about his books. I had no idea they were based on fact.'

'Are you into all that?'

'I don't know. I think I might be.'

Candy leant back, examining Kim closely again with a new eye. 'Jake would really go for you; that cut-glass accent, that hair. Have you noticed all the best characters in the books always have long black hair?'

'No.'

'Yah, he's really into it. The brunettes always got the best share at the house. Not that I had anything to complain about.'

'You mean, he'd actually take me to his house?'

'If he thought you were good material.'

'So how do I meet him?'

Candy laughed. 'You don't. He meets you. There's places he goes to trawl for girls; clubs, bars. If he takes a fancy to you he'll approach you. If he doesn't...' She shrugged her shoulders. 'But let me tell you, sister, you can't fake it. It doesn't matter if you've never done it before – in fact, he prefers it that way. But if you're not really into it he'll know. He's got like this sixth sense.'

'I never have done it before. But I've read the books...'

And masturbated over them, she thought but did not say.

'Believe me, if you're into it he'll know, even before you really know yourself. So maybe you'd get picked. Christ, this is making me incredibly horny.' Suddenly she took hold of the hem of the T-shirt and pulled it up over her head. She had small round breasts that were held high on her chest. Her nipples were large and erect, and the left one was pierced by a gold ring. She saw Kim staring at it. 'Souvenir of my stay chez Ashley,' she said. 'So you want to play around?'

'I'm sorry?'

'Come on honey, let's have some fun. I've got all sorts of little tricks I can show you.' She got to her feet, her little breasts bouncing.

Kim didn't know what to say. This was the last thing she'd expected. 'Look, I didn't mean that I... I mean, I'm not...'

'You're not a dike. Hell, neither am I. Doesn't mean you can't drink from both sides of the cup. Listen honey, if you really want to get it on with Jake you're going to have to find out real quick whether you're into all sorts of things. I can help you out with one of them right now.'

'But, I've never...'

'I can see that in your eyes. Let's cut the bullshit, shall we Kim? I know why you're really here.'

'What do you mean?' Damn, Kim thought, she'd seen through her.

'You're here because you want to get to Jake. Believe me, you're not the first. Half the women in New York are wetting their pants to meet him.'

Kim was relieved. Candy had not guessed the truth. 'I really do work for a paper,' she said.

'Sure, sure. I don't give a shit. But here's the deal. I'm into S&M, honey. Really into it. And I love getting it on with women. We have a little scene here tonight – you and me – and tomorrow I take you to a club where Jake likes to hang out. Otherwise, it's good night. You decide. I'll be in that room over there. If you don't get your arse in there in the next five minutes you can let yourself out. Okay?' Candy turned on her heels and marched over to the door in the far corner of the room. She opened it, then closed it behind her.

Kim stared at her wine glass. She took a sip, then looked up at the poster on the wall. She hadn't the faintest idea what she was going to do. She'd hoped to persuade Candy to let her have Jake Ashley's address, or a telephone number, and was relying on her gift of the gab to talk herself into an interview. But Candy wanted something in return for her help, and Kim was not at all sure it was something she was prepared to give. She had never been anywhere near the S&M scene, and if she hadn't read Ashley's books she wouldn't even know it existed. Nor had she ever been to bed with a woman. She had never even thought about having sex with another woman. Or was that true? She remembered last night. Wasn't it true that thinking about the woman on the plane had made her climax that much more intense? Whether she liked to admit it to herself or not, she hadn't conjured up that vivid image for any other reason but to enhance her excitement. And the reason for that was undoubtedly to do with Ashley's books. She'd been excited by what was happening to Dolores, and imagined herself being made to do the exact same things.

If she walked out of the front door now the trail to Jake Ashley would be cold. She had no other leads. She would have to go back to London with her tail between her legs to face an irate editor.

She told herself that was the only reason she got to her feet, finished her wine, then walked over to the door in the corner of the room.

The room was small, with no windows. It was lit by a bar of spotlights set into the ceiling, which had been dimmed. The walls and ceiling were painted white and the floor carpeted in a thick cream wool. The only furniture was a tall metal cupboard, rather like a medical cabinet in a doctor's surgery, a plain wooden chair and a small double bed. The bed had a wooden frame and a thin mattress, and was covered with a black sheet. At each corner, attached to a rope knotted around each leg, were four padded leather cuffs.

In the centre of the room was a thick square wooden post. On three of its four sides, at one foot intervals all the way down its length, metal rings had been screwed. Hanging from some of these were white nylon ropes.

Candy had stripped off her white leggings and was naked apart from her high-heeled slippers. Her pubis was completely hairless and Kim could see the folds of her labia. She had clipped a steel chain into her nipple ring and it hung down her body.

'Glad you could join me,' she said. 'Guess this is going to be an education for you.'

She walked up to Kim and touched her fingers against Kim's neat mouth.

'You ever kissed a woman?' Candy asked.

Kim shook her head.

Candy moved her face forward. She put out her tongue and licked Kim's lower lip. Then she moved the tip of her tongue into Kim's warm mouth, though their lips were still not touching.

Kim suddenly wanted to take the initiative. She wrapped her arms around the girl's naked body and kissed her, pushing Candy's tongue aside with her own. She felt a wave of excitement course over her as she pressed her body into the other woman's and felt the heat and wetness of her mouth.

'Nice,' Candy breathed, when the kiss ended. 'Why don't you let me see what I'm getting?'

Without wanting to think too much about what she was doing, Kim unbuttoned her blouse and pulled it off. She unzipped her skirt and let it fall to the floor, then stooped to pick it up.

'Real pretty,' Candy said. She kissed Kim lightly on the lips while her hands snaked behind Kim's back, unhooking her bra. She stepped back and pulled the white lace away. 'Great tits.' She cupped one in her hand as if trying to guess its weight. 'I'd just love these, honey.'

Kim was standing in her white thong panties and high-heeled shoes. It had been too hot to wear tights.

'What do we do now?' she asked meekly.

'Don't look so worried; this is my scene, not yours. Come over here.' She walked to the post. 'See those ropes up there? Tie my wrists. You can stand on the chair.'

'You really want that?'

'Sure I do.'

Bondage had been an everyday occurrence in Ashley's books. The 'chateau' was full of what he called punishment rooms where the slaves, male and female, were strapped into a variety of positions, some on simple arrangements like this post, and some on much more complex contraptions.

'Did he do this to you at the house?' Kim asked, collecting the chair and placing it by the post.

'And how. But I was into it before that. I used to do modelling for this bondage photographer. Christ, he'd tied me so tight I couldn't move an inch, and it used to make me come. He got some great shoots.'

Candy stood against the side of the post that had no rings, then raised her hands above her head, placing them against the two rings on the left and right-hand sides. White nylon rope hung from both.

Kim stood on the chair. She wound the rope around Candy's wrists and tied it securely to the metal rings.

'Good,' Candy said. 'Now, pull the chain around the post and clip it into the nipple ring.'

Kim picked up the steel chain. It was just long enough to stretch around. A snap-lock was fitted to either end. One was already clipped to the nipple ring. She quickly opened the other and hooked it to the ring as well.

'Jake wanted me to have my pussy pierced, too. Each side of my labia, so he could padlock me shut.'

'But you didn't?'

'He changed his mind. Go to the cupboard; there's leather straps in there. Strap my waist to the post, then my legs. Get the picture?'

Candy's body was pressing into the post. Though she was slim she had an apple-shaped bottom that stuck out prominently from her back. On her right buttock Kim noticed a round blue tattoo, the letters J A elaborately scripted within the roundel.

She opened the cupboard. It was ranged with shelves. There were dildos, coiled leather straps, rubber and leather gags, rubber and satin blindfolds, and several whips. She picked up three leather straps, went back to the post, and wrapped one around Candy's waist, one around her legs just above her knees, and one at her ankles, cinching them all securely so not only were her legs bound together but she was tied tightly to the post.

She could see Candy was trembling with excitement. But curiously the sight of her body, bound so tightly, also excited her. Tentatively, she ran a hand down the girl's back. Her skin was hot. She smoothed her palm over the rounds of her buttocks and felt an immediate desire to push her fingers up between her legs. But she stopped herself. She wasn't yet ready to take that step.

Candy squirmed against the post, deliberately struggling against her bonds. 'I can't fucking move,' she said through clenched teeth.

'I thought that's what you wanted,' Kim said.

'It is. Do you know what to do now?'

'No.'

'Don't you remember? In the book, the one Johnny wants to film. The two girls together while the master watches…'

Kim remembered the scene vividly. Even though she had read so many of Ashley's books, a lot of the scenes were lodged in her memory. As much as she tried to hide it from herself, they had aroused her when she read them,

38

so she guessed she should not have been surprised that they had the same effect in reality.

'Is – is that what you want?' she asked uncertainly.

'Yes, it is what I want.'

Kim went back to the cupboard. If Candy wanted to enact the scene Ashley had written, Kim was determined to do exactly that. She took out a gag; a large rubber ball that had been drilled through the centre so a leather strap could be passed through it.

'Open your mouth,' she said, pulling Candy's head back. She could see the excitement dancing in the blonde's eyes.

'You're as turned on as I am, you little bitch,' Candy hissed.

Kim forced the gag between her lips. It was so large her mouth was held open, her lips pursed around it. She buckled the strap tightly around the girl's head.

The fact that this was so unexpected and so far removed from anything she had ever done before, combined with being in New York in this strange room, gave the whole experience a dreamlike quality. That didn't mean it was any less arousing. Her nipples were knotted into little peaks and the crotch of the white lacy panties was distinctly damp.

Back at the metal cupboard Kim took out a large dildo. It was made from rubber and moulded to resemble the veining on an erect male phallus. She took out one of the whips, too. It resembled a pony's tail tied into a braided leather handle.

Returning to the post Kim lightly flipped the lashes of the whip against Candy's side, then tucked it under her arm. Very slowly, measuring her own reaction as she did so, she ran her hand down over the girl's fleshy rump. She allowed her hand to curl inward, pushing between the girl's thighs until she felt the soft rubbery labia of the girl's sex. She had never touched a woman here before. Tentatively she pushed her fingers deeper, immediately feeling the wetness and heat of her vagina. She thrust one finger into the silky wet tube. Candy's sex seemed to be sucking it in.

Candy made an exaggerated moaning noise and pushed her bum back as much as the bondage permitted, so Kim's finger was driven deeper. Her sex clenched around it strongly.

The extraordinary thing was that Kim's sex reacted in exactly the same way. She felt a jolt of arousal that plucked at her clitoris and her vagina clenched exactly as if it had been penetrated. This had all happened so quickly she'd not had time to develop any expectations, but she certainly hadn't expected this. As she felt the velvety interior of Candy's sex throb, her own throbbed too. Emboldened by her arousal she pushed another finger in alongside the first, then screwed them both around and pushed them deeper until her knuckles were hard up against the blonde's hairless labia. She had done this to herself many times, and the interior of Candy's vagina felt exactly the same, the flesh wet and pliant.

Kim pulled her fingers out and replaced them with the tip of the phallus she was holding in her other hand. She thrust it forward and watched as it sunk so deep into Candy's sex that only the butt end was visible. Again she felt her own sex react exactly as if it was the recipient of this penetration. In the book, in the scene Candy wanted to act out, the girl had been whipped while she was made to hold a large dildo in her cunt.

'Hold it there,' Kim said breathlessly. She saw Candy clench the cheeks of her bottom and her thighs together, the flesh folding around the end of the dildo. She stood back. There was no doubt in her mind that the sight of Candy tied so tightly to the post, the leather straps and white rope biting into her soft flesh, was terribly arousing. Ashley had conjured up this image in his books time and time again, and she had never failed to respond to it. But the reality made her realise exactly what she was responding to. She knew the image was exciting because she was imagining herself in that position, bound and powerless with a big gag filling her mouth, and that realisation shocked her.

She plucked the whip from under her arm and tried to concentrate on what she was supposed to be doing. She raised the whip and sliced it down onto Candy's buttocks, but the stroke was ineffectual and made little impact. Kim raised the whip again. This time she swished it down harder. There was a loud thwacking noise and Candy's buttocks trembled. The blonde moaned and wriggled her buttocks as far as her bondage would permit.

Kim cut the whip down again and again. Every time the whip landed Candy's reaction to the sudden surge of pain made her unclench her buttocks and allowed the dildo to slip down her greasy vagina. She saw Candy struggling to keep the dildo in place, trying to push it back up by squirming her thighs together. As she could not bend her knees this was proving difficult.

Each stroke had reddened her white flesh and Kim could feel the heat it was generating. She moved around to the front of the post and looked into Candy's eyes. They were blazing with excitement. The blonde pulled her body back as far as she could, so the chain attached to her nipple ring made her nipple stretch taut, her breast elongated too. She threw her head back and tossed it from side to side, pushing her belly against the post and frotting her pubis against it. Kim could see she was coming, every muscle in her body suddenly locked and rigid. She shuddered and gave a long low moan, before she went so completely limp that if she had not been tied to the post she would have fallen to the floor.

The effect this had on Kim was just as dramatic. She thought she might come too. Her nipples knotted, and deep inside her vagina a new flood of juices was running down the inner walls. She moved behind Candy and raised her hands to undo the gag. It was dripping with saliva.

'Christ, you've got hidden talents,' Candy panted. 'That was real good. Every time that dildo slipped down it was so fucking frustrating because I wanted it jammed right up in me, but the frustration's all part of it. Jake's a clever bastard. This was all his idea. See, he knows exactly what drives women wild.'

Kim unbuckled the belts.

'Guess it's your turn now,' Candy said. 'Look at you, you're aching for it, aren't you?'

'I don't know what I feel,' Kim said. But it was a lie. She mounted the chair and untied the white ropes that bound Candy's wrists. Finally she unclipped one end of the chain from the single nipple ring.

The blonde moaned as she lowered her arms, rubbing her wrists to restore the circulation. Then she bent her legs and extracted the dildo from between her thighs, half of the shaft still buried in her sex. She brought it up to her mouth and licked off the juices enthusiastically.

'Hey, I taste real good,' she said, grinning. 'So what are we going to do with you now?'

She unclipped the other end of the chain from the nipple ring and threw it aside, then pulled Kim into her arms and kissed her full on the mouth. Her whole body was hot to the touch and her flesh seemed to mould itself to Kim's body. Kim felt a wave of wonderful new sensations as her breasts were crushed against Candy's. She could feel the ring on her nipple buried deeply in her own malleable flesh.

As Candy's tongue probed her mouth, her hand worked down between Kim's legs, smoothing over her buttocks. They delved into the cleft between them and were soon exploring lower. Kim gasped as the fingers touched the mouth of her vagina. Instead of penetrating her she felt them slowly circling the opening. She hadn't realised this area was so sensitive, and gasped as a rush of feelings rippled through her, the sound gagged on Candy's tongue.

'Come over here,' Candy said, breaking the kiss and taking Kim by the hand. She led her the few steps to the bed. 'Wait here.'

Candy opened the metal cupboard. She came back with a silk sleeping mask with elasticated sides. 'Put this on,' she said.

'Listen, I'm not sure…'

'Trust me woman, I know what you need.'

Kim fitted the mask over her eyes. It was padded on the inside so it pressed down on her eyelids, cutting out all the light.

She felt Candy's hands pulling her down onto the bed. 'That's it,' the blonde said. 'Lie on your back.'

Kim lay on the bed. Immediately she felt her left wrist being pulled over her head. Something soft was being wrapped around it. She knew what it was.

'No,' she said at once. But even though her mind was screaming that this was a very bad idea, that being spread-eagled helplessly across the bed in the apartment of a total stranger who had already demonstrated a penchant for kinky sex, was a very bad idea, her body appeared to have other ideas and refused to protest, remaining absolutely passive. It allowed her other arm to be drawn across to a corner of the bed, then both legs to be splayed out and bound into the leather cuffs at the bottom.

'Very pretty.'

The blindfold was perfect. Without it Kim would have felt terribly self-conscious. But the odd thing was that being unable to see herself tricked her mind into thinking that she could not be seen either. The blindfold guaranteed a kind of anonymity.

The leather cuffs stretched her right across the bed, and there was no play in the ropes attached to them. The position of her arms held spread above her head lifted her pectoral muscles and pulled at her breasts, which seemed to be tingling all over. Her sex too, completely exposed by having her thighs forcibly spread apart, was alive with sensation. All the feelings that Jake Ashley had ascribed to the female slaves in his books as they had been bound and rendered helpless, the extraordinary mixture of aching pain and cramps and the overwhelming passion this position seemed to produce, were racing through Kim's body, turning it into a seething mass of nerve-endings. She was unable to keep still, wriggling and squirming against her bonds, undulating her hips in a slow but unmistakably erotic rhythm.

Kim felt Candy's weight moving on the bed beside her.

'So needy,' the American whispered.

'Yes,' Kim agreed. There was no point in lying now.

She started as she felt Candy's fingers touch her neck. They trailed down between her breasts to her flat belly, then began fingering her thick pubic hair. 'Jake would have you shaved,' she said.

'I know,' Kim said breathlessly. She knew that any second now the girl would move her hand lower. There was absolutely nothing she could do to stop her. No female had ever touched her down there.

The girl's weight shifted again. Kim sensed she was leaning over her. She felt hot breath blowing against her right nipple, then Candy's lips were surrounding it, sucking it gently into her welcoming mouth. Kim moaned. The blonde pinched the hard bud of flesh between her teeth, then drew it up until the whole of Kim's generous breast was suspended by it. Then quite deliberately she opened her mouth and let the breast fall back, the heavy flesh bouncing against her chest and causing a huge jolt of exquisite sensation.

Candy moved her head across to the left. She clamped her teeth around the nipple there and pulled it up until Kim's breast was stretched taut, then let it go. Again Kim felt a rush of pleasure.

Exactly at that moment the American pushed her hand down over Kim's sex. At first she covered the whole area, pressing down firmly, squashing the labia, the tip of her middle finger touching the hole of her anus, the copious juices of Kim's vagina smeared against her palm. Then very slowly she moved her hand up, crooking her middle finger so it was dragged into the slit of Kim's labia. Kim moaned loudly as the finger butted against her clit, and louder still when Candy flicked the little bundle of nerves from side to side.

'Is this what you want, honey? Candy whispered, lowering her face to Kim's ear. 'Is this what you've always dreamed about?'

Kim didn't know. Before she had ever picked up one of

45

Jake Ashley's books she'd never dreamt of anything so outré. What he had written, the ideas and images he had created, had undoubtedly affected her, but until she'd stepped into this strange room – a replica, she remembered now, of one of the punishment rooms in the books – she hadn't realised exactly how profound that effect had been.

Candy's fingers took hold of her clit and pinched it. Then they moved away. Kim felt something cold replacing them. It nudged down into the whole length of her labia, spreading them apart. She knew what it was, of course. Candy had picked up the dildo. A humming noise filled the air and strong vibrations seized Kim's vulva, her clit pulsing violently as it oscillated against the rubber phallus.

'Oh God…' Forgetting she was bound Kim tried to close her legs, but the sharp jerk of the ankle cuffs reminded her that she had no such freedom, and that in turn provided her with a new jolt of pleasure. Deliberately this time, she tried to wrestle her arms down, the total constraint of the cuffs winding her feelings ever tighter.

'You remember what I was saying about frustration?'

'Yes…' Kim gasped huskily.

'Well…' Candy pulled the vibrator away.

'No!' Kim screamed.

'There's where Jake is so good. Anyone can just get fucked. But he knows that the real art is to give a little – then take it away. The more you're denied the more you want, the more you want the more you're denied.' She jammed the dildo into Kim's wide open vagina, thrusting it right up as far as it would go. Kim's momentary frustration was instantly relieved. The vibrations were deep inside her sex now, spreading out from the neck of her womb. She felt her cunt clench around the phallus as strongly as any fist.

46

'Oh yes, *yes*...' she moaned, tossing her head from side to side, her orgasm beginning to well up inside her.

'Oh no...' Candy said, pulling the vibrator out.

'No!' Kim cried.

'You see?' Candy said proudly. 'The frustration is terrible, but it only makes you want it more.'

'Please...' Kim had never wanted anything more in her life. She arched off the bed in the vain hope of making contact with the buzzing vibrator. The blindfold made it worse, concentrating all her feelings on her cunt.

She felt Candy's body moving again. For a moment she thought she was going to get off the bed and leave her there. That caused a sensation of panic that raised her tortured nerves to a new pitch.

'Please...' she repeated earnestly. She wriggled and writhed against her bonds, trying to sit up, trying to bring her hand down to her sex to relieve the incredible aching frustration she was feeling, trying to do anything to achieve her thwarted pleasure. She rolled her hips and strained to bring her thighs together, hoping she would be able to close them enough to put pressure on her clitoris. It would not take much. But her legs were much too far apart to attain this goal.

Candy pressed the dildo into her labia again and Kim sighed with relief, the vibrations hard against her clit.

'Oh God, that's... that's...'

She felt her whole body tense, every nerve focussed on her sex.

Laughing, Candy pulled the dildo away for a third time.

'No...' Kim pleaded again. Now she was angry. 'Put it back, you bitch. Put the damn thing back.'

'Oh, now we're turning nasty. Say please.'

Kim tried to twist herself free. It was useless. The leather cuffs gave not an inch. 'Please,' she begged, in a more conciliatory tone.

'Pretty please.'

'*Pretty* please,' Kim moaned grudgingly.

'When I was with Jake, when I was one of his slaves, he liked to watch me do this. He said I had a penchant for torturing and teasing the female slaves. I think it was because I loved being tortured and teased myself. Do you think that could be it?'

'Please, Candy.'

'Didn't realise how desperate you could get, did you? If you meet Jake it gets much worse than this.'

Every nerve in Kim's body felt as though it was stretched like piano wire. On the blank screen of her mind she suddenly saw an image of the master; sitting, watching, staring at her naked and exposed body. It added a new twist to her excitement. But she still needed that last touch.

Candy nudged the tip of the dildo into the mouth of Kim's glistening wet vagina, but did not press it home. Kim tried to strain down onto it. Then suddenly Candy dipped her head forward and pressed the flat of her tongue hard against Kim's clit, ironing it back against her body, then dragging it from side to side. At the same time she thrust the large vibrating dildo deep into Kim's cunt, as deep as it had been before.

Kim was overwhelmed with sensation. The jolt of pleasure from her clit as Candy's tongue wormed against it combined with the huge wave of sensation from the vibrations in her vagina and the two danced together, weaving themselves into an orgasm that seemed to pull her up off the bed like an invisible hand, her limbs stretched against the bonds as though on some medieval rack.

She heard herself screaming with pleasure, though the noise seemed a long way away. It felt as if her sex had been opened and a set of raw nerves exposed. At the centre of it all she saw a man, his eyes staring into her sex, his expression sardonic and knowing, one thick eyebrow slightly arched.

It was Jake Ashley's face.

'So where is this club?'

They were in Candy's sitting room again, drinking another bottle of white wine.

'Upper East Side.'

'So when can we go?' Kim asked.

'Tomorrow night. But you'll need something to wear.'

'It's all right, I've got a couple of good cocktail dresses.'

Candy laughed. 'That's not what I mean.' She got to her feet and walked across the room. She had put the black T-shirt back on but not the leggings, and as she stooped to pick something off an old antique desk, Kim could see her shaven labia nestling between her legs. The sight gave her an odd sensation, somewhere between lust and interest. She was having trouble accepting that less than half-an-hour ago she had not only been kissed and touched by a woman for the first time, but had allowed herself to be bound and rendered helpless, experiencing a whole new set of sexual feelings as a result.

Candy walked back. 'Here.' She handed Kim a neatly printed business card. 'You'll need to go and see them. You've got to wear something special. You'll see.'

The card read: *Velvet Tongue*. It had an address in the garment district and a telephone number.

'What about you?' Kim asked.

'Don't worry, I've got lots of stuff. Give me the address

of your hotel. I'll swing by and pick you up.'

'Thanks,' Kim said, and then asked, a little uncertainly, 'What sort of place is it?'

Candy grinned. 'Don't look so worried,' she said. 'It's fun, you'll see. And judging from tonight, you'll thoroughly enjoy it.' She sipped her wine and gave Kim a long and searching stare.

Chapter Three

She took the bus down the twenty blocks to W37th Street, got off at the corner of 8th Avenue and walked to the east. The street was littered with the trash of the garment industry, big empty cardboard cylinders that had once held reams of material, cardboard boxes bursting with 'cabbage' from the cutting room floors, and broken mannequins, their arms and legs shattered and deformed.

The number on the card was 1270 and she found it on the left-hand side, one of a block of identical looking buildings that had once been tenement houses. Puzzled, since she had been expecting some sort of shop, she climbed the stone steps to the front door and rang the bell under a neat plaque, the name *Velvet Tongue* spelt out in highly stylised lettering.

'Yes?' a female voice, distorted by the speaker, asked querulously.

'I, um, I wanted to see some of your clothes.'

The lock on the door buzzed immediately. Kim pushed it and walked inside, finding herself in a narrow hallway with as much rubbish as she had seen out on the street. All the doors in the hall were firmly closed, with no indication as to where visitors should go. There was a staircase in front of her, its steps covered by a carpet that had been worn threadbare. The noise of electric sowing machines buzzed all around her.

'Yes?'

A woman had appeared at the top of the stairs. She

appeared to be in her thirties, and was tall and slender. She was wearing a smart black suit over a tight white body. Her long legs were sheathed in very sheer, almost transparent nylon, and she wore black high heels.

'I – I wanted to see some of your clothes,' Kim repeated uneasily. 'A friend sent me.'

'May I have your friend's name?' the woman said.

'Candy... Candy Brook.'

The woman smiled. 'Of course. Come up, would you? You are supposed to ring and make an appointment.'

'Sorry, I didn't realise that. Candy didn't say.'

Kim reached the top of the stairs.

'Not your fault,' the woman said. She had a rich voice with a soft New England accent, and close up she had fragile and rather haughty looks. Her blonde hair was cut short and framed her face in waves. She extended her hand, her fingers glistening with three large and expensive looking rings. On the lapel of the suit she had a small gold pin, its motif resembling a tiny tongue; this same motif was repeated on the toes of her shoes. 'I'm Lucinda Black,' she said.

Kim shook her hand and introduced herself.

'Well, Ms Brook, perhaps you can tell me what you are looking for? Top or bottom?'

'Both, I think,' Kim said.

The woman arched a black pencilled eyebrow. 'You're English, I guess. Perhaps you don't have these expressions in England. Over here we often refer to dominants as top and slaves as bottom.'

'Oh, yes, silly of me.' Kim felt herself blushing under the woman's studious gaze. What Candy had meant by 'special' was becoming abundantly clear. No wonder she hadn't thought her cocktail dresses would be suitable.

'Well?' the woman asked.

She remembered the bizarre costumes Ashley had described in his books. If she wanted to attract his attention she was clearly going to have to be dressed as a slave.

'Bottom,' she said determinedly.

The woman smiled. 'I would have guessed as much. I can usually tell. Come this way.' She turned and walked along the corridor. 'We have a design service if there's anything you or your master want specially made.'

'It's for tonight,' Kim said.

The woman reached a door at the far end of the corridor and opened it. 'This way,' she said, and ushered Kim inside. The room was decorated like a modern and minimalist clothes shop with plain white walls and a large square geometrical abstract painting of three dimensional blocks in prime colours like a deconstructed Rubik's cube. A large rectangular window looked out onto the rooftops, and Kim could glimpse the trees of Madison Square Gardens in the distance. There were three tubular metal clothes racks on wheels arranged on either side of the room, and an elegant long low tan leather bench with pocketed upholstery running down between them.

On the left-hand side the first two racks held clothes made from leather. The third rack featured rubber clothing. On the right the racks were adorned with a much wider range of materials; silks, satins, delicate lace, georgette, tulle and jersey. The various garments were presented in sections on the racks; dresses, suits, skirts and blouses nearest to the door, and lingerie, bras, corsets, suspender belts, slips and panties furthest away.

There were two women already in the room, and one man. The man was immaculately dressed in a sleekly tailored navy suit, a white silk shirt and a dark blue tie.

His nails were manicured and his shoes so highly polished they reflected the light. He sat on the leather bench with his legs crossed, reading a copy of the *Wall Street Journal*. He was facing the doors of two changing cubicles, set into the corner.

'Just help yourself,' Lucinda said. 'If there's anything you'd like to try on...' She gestured towards the changing cubicles.

'Thank you,' Kim acknowledged, and began browsing the racks on the left, inhaling the strong odour of expensive leather. The clothes were beautifully made and looked fairly conventional, the suits tailored, the dresses mostly short and tight. It was only when she reached the lingerie that she could tell there was anything outré about their design. The leather corsets were boned and laced, some with a platform bra, others with no bra at all. There were panties with no crotch, and others that looked more like hot-pants but with no covering for the buttocks. A lot of the garments were no more than leather harnesses, some decorated with thick shiny chains, that clearly encircled the body but did not hide it.

The rubber garments on the next rack were all outrageous. The dresses were figure hugging but had large cut-outs in various places designed to expose the female anatomy. Some were totally backless apart from thick straps stretching like a ladder all the way down the spine. Others had holes for the breasts or the buttocks. There were catsuits too, with the whole area of the crotch removed. The lingerie included old-fashioned looking full-length girdles, and there were even stockings made entirely of rubber. Like the leather, the colour range was restricted to black, white and red.

Kim glanced at the other two women. One was short

and rather chubby. Her curly hair had been dyed orange and one nostril was pierced with a small gold stud. She wore a mini-dress short enough to reveal her plump legs, which were dimpled with cellulite.

The other was taller with dark brown hair that looked as though it had been shaved then grown back. It hadn't grown back very far and stood on end. She was wearing a tight catsuit made from brown lace. Her small breasts were visible under the thin material but she was wearing a brown satin G-string that hid her pubes. As she turned around Kim could see the narrow string of the panties emerge from between her buttocks, her bottom itself only veiled by the lace.

As Kim walked across the room to the other racks, the door of the changing cubicle opened and a young girl emerged. Like the girl in the lace dress her hair had been cropped, though hers was even shorter, hardly more than a reddish-brown stubble. She was wearing one of the rubber corsets, a tight garment in red, with thick shoulder straps, that ran from her breasts to the top of her thighs, completely encasing her body. She had red rubber stockings hitched to the stubby suspenders of the corset, and red rubber full-length gloves. Only her shoulders, the top of her arms and a thin band of her thighs above the top of the stockings were bare, the white flesh in stark contrast to the smooth red rubber. She stood in front of the man, with her eyes cast to the floor.

'I think she looks charming,' Lucinda said, walking over to the girl and putting an arm around her shoulders. 'It fits her beautifully.'

'Pandora, get over here,' the man said, looking at the girl in the lace dress and folding his paper. 'Stand by her side. I want to see the two of you together.'

The willowy girl stood next to the one in the corset, bowing her head in the same way.

'A nice contrast,' Lucinda said. 'If we find Pandora something in black.'

'Yes,' the man concurred thoughtfully. 'But I'm not sure about the rubber.'

'The rubber sounds wonderful,' Lucinda enthused.

'Sounds?'

'Yes,' she nodded. 'Are they fully trained?'

'Of course,' the man replied.

'Then if I may demonstrate.' Lucinda walked over to the side of the room. Kim had not noticed an elaborate umbrella stand of a Chinese design; a large dragon curled around the cylindrical pot. It contained two or three canes with curled handles, looking like they had once been used in schools. She took one and came back to the girls.

Seeing what she had in mind, the man smiled. He had a fairly handsome face with a shock of white hair, and sat with a ramrod straight back, though Kim guessed he was well over sixty. 'Over,' he said, looking at the rubber-clad girl.

Immediately, seemingly unconcerned about Kim and the other woman, the girl turned around so her back was facing the man, spread her legs apart and bent to grasp her ankles. Though the corset was long and covered most of her buttocks it did not hide her crotch, which was completely exposed. Like Candy, the girl's labia were hairless. To Kim's astonishment, on either side the labia had been pierced by tiny gold rings. Hanging from each of these rings was a larger ring, through which a heart-shaped padlock had been threaded and locked in place. This clearly prevented anyone gaining access to the girl's vagina. What's more, the padlock was clearly heavy and

56

stretched the delicate flesh downward. Lucinda put one hand on the small of the girl's back and raised the other, then cut the cane down across her rubber-covered buttocks. The girl yelped, but did not move.

'You see, a pleasing sound,' Lucinda said proudly, smiling at the man.

'Yes,' he agreed, uncrossing his legs and getting to his feet. He took the whip from Lucinda's hand. 'I see your point.'

He ran the end of the cane up the girl's leg, over the rubber stocking, and onto her bare thigh. Then he raised it and cut down viciously, aiming for the narrow strip of bare flesh above the stockings. The girl yelped again and a long red weal appeared across both thighs.

'All right, you've convinced me,' he said.

Kim could see that a bulge had appeared in the front of his trousers.

Lucinda noticed it too. 'Don't feel shy, Grenville,' she said, her eyes smiling, 'if you want to do something about that. We're all friends here. These two are both bottoms,' she said, gesturing towards Kim and the blonde. 'They'll not object.'

'No wonder I spend so much money here,' the man said thickly.

'It's what makes my job so interesting,' Lucinda replied.

She took two steps forward and casually ran manicured fingers down his front to his tented trousers. She smiled at him, unzipped the fly, and fished inside. Her forearm moved rhythmically a couple of times, and then she extracted his burgeoning penis. Kim could actually see it growing in the confident woman's fist.

'Which one do you want?' Lucinda asked.

He nodded at Pandora.

'Come on girl, come here and serve your master,' Lucinda ordered. She gave the man's erection a final squeeze, then let it go.

Pandora sunk to her knees. She reached up, took the base of his cock in one hand and fed it into her mouth. She sucked it so avidly her cheeks dimpled.

'Is she good at that?' Lucinda asked casually. They all watched as the girl began to pump her mouth up and down on his gnarled phallus.

'Mmm... not bad,' he croaked.

Kim saw him shudder.

'How long have you had her?' Lucinda continued conversationally.

'Four months. But she was with Eric before me. He comes here, doesn't he?'

'Yes, of course.' Lucinda took the cane from his hand and moved to stand beside the girl in the rubber corset, who was still bent over and exposed. She ran her free hand over her buttocks and grasped the padlock, pulling it from side to side. The girl gasped.

'Do you want the key?' the man asked.

'No,' Lucinda said coolly. 'This is for your benefit. I thought it might excite you even more.'

'It does.' He put his hands out and gripped Pandora's head, pulling her further onto him until her lips and nose were buried against his pubic hair.

'And this?' Lucinda dropped the padlock and positioned herself behind the kneeling girl, and sliced the cane across her buttocks. The girl jerked, but stoically maintained her position.

'Oh yes,' he said, his voice sounding strained. Kim saw his fingers grip the girl's head more tightly, not allowing her to pull back.

Thwack!

The sound echoed across the large room. The girl cried out, but the sound was muffled by the man's cock.

Thwack!

Kim saw the man shake as he thrust his hips up and threw his head back, his fingers holding the girl's head like a vice. Pandora's cheeks dimpled and she swallowed several times.

Lucinda was smiling. 'I like to see that,' she said softly.

'You should be running your own stable,' the man said. 'You're so good at knowing just the way to treat them.' He pulled away from the girl's mouth. She had swallowed most of his sperm, but a trickle escaped and ran down her chin and dropped onto the man's shoes. Immediately she dipped her head and licked it off.

'I don't have that sort of money, Grenville,' Lucinda said. 'Anyway, I prefer doing what I do now.

'The leather outfits you ordered are ready, too,' she added, her businesslike manner restored. 'Shall I send them over with the corsets?'

'Please do,' he confirmed. 'And perhaps you'd like to come over to dinner next week. I'm sure we could find a way to keep you entertained.'

'That would be delightful,' Lucinda accepted his offer, smiling beautifully.

Pandora zipped up his fly. He waved her to her feet and sat down again, opening his paper. The other girl went back into the changing room.

Kim began to examine the other clothes, trying to concentrate on what she was doing there. Clearly, the world Jake Ashley conjured up in his books was less of a work of fiction than she had thought. Grenville was obviously a master, like the one in the books, and Lucinda had described the chubby blonde as a 'bottom', which meant she probably had a master too. Grenville had also referred to a man called Eric, who made a third. And then there was Ashley himself. And from what the man had said, it sounded as if they all knew each other.

Kim searched the rack of dresses. They were all designed to reveal a great deal more than they hid. Some had necklines split to the waist, others were completely backless. There were skirts so short they hardly covered the legs at all, and others with splits that went well above the thigh. The silk, satin and lace lingerie was no less exotic, with tight panels of satin inset with lace, panties so high cut the waistband rested on top of the hips and bras in styles that either left the breasts exposed or lifted and squeezed them into an alluring cleavage.

'Can I help?' Lucinda said, walking up to Kim's side.

'I was thinking of this,' Kim said, holding up a dress in a shimmering silver material. It had a halter-neck but no back, the dress cut so low that it would reveal the upper curves of the buttocks and probably a little glimpse of the cleft between them. The skirt too, though full length, was split to the top of the thigh. Kim had never worn anything like it before, but she was sure it would attract Jake Ashley's attention.

'A good choice. It comes with this.' Lucinda pulled out another clothes hanger from the rack. Hanging from it was a thick silver choker made from a hinged piece of solid metal. There were two D-rings on the front of the choker, extending from which were two thick silver chains. Attached to the ends of these were two manacles, also in silver. The choker and the manacles were inset with diamanté.

'I'm sure your master would approve. Is he taking you

to an auction?'

'An auction?'

'You're very new to this, aren't you?'

'Yes.' Kim suddenly felt embarrassed and naïve.

'An auction is where you get sold to another owner,' the chubby girl interrupted. 'I've been sold twice,' she said proudly. Then she took a tight satin tube dress and walked into the changing cubicle.

'Actually,' Kim said, 'I just want to impress him.'

'Oh.' Kim was surprised to detect a look of disapproval sweep across Lucinda's face. 'Well, I'm sure that will do the trick,' the woman added. 'Try it on. You won't be able to wear anything underneath it but tights. We have some lovely crotchless ones, of course. I'll get you a pair.'

'Crotchless?'

'You must know you are not permitted to wear anything that covers your pussy.'

'Oh yes, of course,' Kim said, blushing, smiling weakly. 'I forgot.'

'My, you *are* new,' Lucinda said, with a distinct note of disapproval.

Kim glanced at the price of the dress. It was the most expensive garment she had ever considered buying, and she prayed it would be worth it. But if she got the interview with Ashley it would be syndicated around the world, and she would very soon get her money back.

Candy pecked Kim on the cheek as she squeezed into the grimy interior of a yellow cab. 'Hi, you look sensational,' she said enthusiastically.

'Thanks,' Kim replied quietly, not quite so sure of her appearance.

'What's in the bag?'

Kim was carrying a small carrier bag. She opened it and showed the slave collar to Candy. 'I thought I'd put it on when we get there.'

'Yah, I guess that's sensible.'

Unfortunately the June heat in New York was breaking all records, and it was much too hot to wear anything over the revealing dress. As she'd suspected, the dress exposed an inch or two of the cleavage between her buttocks as well as the generous outline of her unfettered breasts, the backless design making it impossible for her to wear a bra, the soft flesh dangerously close to escaping its snug confines. There wasn't a single man who hadn't stopped and stared as she'd walked through the hotel foyer and out to the street. The cab driver too, with a grimy beard and a T-shirt that looked as though he'd slept in it for weeks, couldn't stop eyeing her in the mirror, adjusting it so he could see her legs, the split in the skirt revealing the whole of one thigh.

Fortunately, he didn't appear to speak much English and didn't react when Candy said to Kim, 'Christ, looking at you is making my pussy juice up. You sure you don't just want to go back to my place?'

'Perhaps later,' Kim said. She hadn't gone to all this trouble for nothing.

'It's a date,' said Candy excitedly. 'So, what did you think of *Velvet Tongue*? Did you meet Lucinda?'

Kim nodded. 'I didn't realise what went on. Are there a lot of... of masters, like Jake?'

'Sure. There's lots of slaves in New York, so I guess that means there has to be masters too. But Jake is like the number one. Everyone wants to be with him.'

Kim remembered what the man had told Lucinda. 'Were you with another master first?' she asked.

'No. No, Jake picked me up in a bar. I was just totally into it. I'd read his stuff. It just turned me on. When he came over to me I was like knocked out. And he's got these real hypnotic eyes. Christ, I'd have done anything he told me to do. And he told me to do some real weird things when we got to the house.'

'That's the place in Connecticut, right?' Kim probed. 'That's the model for the chateau?'

'You speak so strange,' Candy said, without answering the questions. 'Sounds real posh.'

'But is it?' Kim persisted.

'Yah, I guess so, though it ain't no chateau. It's just like a big house with a basement.'

The cab had crossed Fifth Avenue into the East Side and was heading towards the river. It's tired suspension could do nothing to absorb the bone-shaking holes in the road.

'So, is this club where you met him?' Kim continued.

'No. But he took me there two or three times before we went up state. He likes to show off his new slaves, I guess. You'll see, it's quite a place.'

Ten minutes later they pulled up outside a nondescript apartment building that backed onto the river. On one corner of the building, away from what was obviously the main entrance, was a large front door with a circular porthole type window. The uniformed commissionaire standing outside was the only indication that it was the entrance to a club.

'Help me, will you?' Kim asked, the chains of the slave collar rattling as she took it out of the bag.

Candy helped her snap the collar around her throat, then circled her wrists with the silver manacles. All three were locked with a small key, which Kim then slipped into her evening bag. The chains were long enough to allow her to reach to her waist, but no further.

The driver watched in his rear-view mirror.

'Good evening.' The commissionaire had stepped forward and opened the car door.

Candy paid off the driver.

'Evening, Phil,' she said, climbing out. She was wearing a black PVC body with full sleeves and a high neck. But in the middle of her torso a large circle of the material had been cut away to reveal her belly button and glimpses of the undersides of her breasts. Over the body she wore a white wrap around skirt in the same material, which came to about mid-thigh, and white patent leather ankle boots with a spiky four-inch heel. 'This is my friend, Kim from England.'

'Pleased to meet you, miss,' the doorman said politely, opening the main door. 'Have a nice evening.'

Kim found herself in a small foyer with a scarlet carpet, the walls draped with scarlet velvet curtains. In front of her was a gilt table, behind which a young brunette sat. She was extremely pretty, her long hair pinned up in a complicated chignon which allowed sight of her neck and bare shoulders. She was wearing a tight gold leotard, with high-cut legs and a boned strapless bodice that pushed her ample breasts into a deep and shadowy cleavage. Her legs were sheathed in gold fishnet tights. Kim noticed that she had a little gold tongue dangling from a gold chain around her neck.

'Evening Ms Brook,' the girl said. 'Would you sign in please.'

Candy signed a large leather-bound book. The girl stood up. She had spectacularly long legs, shaped by high-heeled calf length gold boots. As she turned around Kim saw that the cut of the leotard revealed most of her very round buttocks, the gusset of the garment cutting down deeply between them.

'This way.' She pulled aside one of the curtains to reveal a door. There was a steep staircase leading down into the basement.

'Bryony will see you to your table,' she said, smiling warmly.

Exactly on cue an identically dressed girl appeared at the bottom of the stairs.

The two girls went down. Bryony also welcomed them with a broad smile, then opened another door. Immediately a wave of heat, expensive scent, and music flooded them. The music was modern jazz and the scent a powerful combination of many different perfumes. The room was large, and there was a long bar with black leather and chrome bar stools. Opposite this, black leather armchairs had been arranged around low tables. At the far end Kim could see steps leading down to a small dance floor, and a rostrum where a four-piece band played.

The club was busy. There were men and women standing by the bar, and others sitting around in the armchairs. Several couples were dancing to the music, their arms wrapped around each other. The men were all dressed perfectly normally, most in suits and ties, while the women, without exception, wore the type of clothes Kim had seen at *Velvet Tongue*. There were tight rubber and leather catsuits, with cut-outs to reveal breasts, buttocks or genitals. There were leather basques laced so tightly the girls' figures were reduced to wasp-like proportions, their suspenders hooked into stockings, and girls who wore little more than a platform bra, a G-string and hold up stockings. More subtly, there were slinky dresses in satin, silk and lace, though all, like Kim's, revealed tantalising glimpses of voluptuous bodies. Though their choice of footwear was different – thigh boots in patent leather or black suede, ankle or calf length boots, or shiny leather court shoes – there wasn't a female who wasn't wearing needle thin four-inch heels.

Plying between the tables were waitresses in the gold leotards. The legs of these garments were cut so high that at the back only a thin ribbon of material emerged at the top of their buttocks, leaving most of their bottom sheathed in the gold coloured fishnet.

'Would you like a table?' Bryony asked, 'or do you want to sit at the bar?'

'A table,' Candy said.

Bryony led them to a small table to the side of the dance floor. 'Have a nice evening,' she said.

A waitress approached immediately. 'Hi, I'm Tiffany, can I get you a drink?'

'House champagne,' Candy said curtly, barely looking at the girl.

The waitress walked away. Kim found herself staring at her large oval buttocks, swaying from side to side as she walked.

'Is he here?' she said, seeing that Candy was scanning the room.

'No. But he may be in back.'

A tall man in a black suit was walking up the stairs from the dance floor. The girl on his arm was wearing a red PVC halter bra, matching bikini briefs and stockings in the same material. Her breasts were heavy and swelled against the tight bra.

'Candy, hi there,' he beamed.

'Hi, Clint,' Candy said, with a bored expression.

'And who's this lovely little lady?' he asked, turning to Kim.

'Kim,' Candy said, with little enthusiasm, 'meet Clint Bernet.'

'Howdy, little lady,' he said. His cowboy inflections matched the snakeskin boots he was wearing.

'Hello,' Kim said politely.

'Say, she's from England!' the girl said enthusiastically.

'Long way from home,' the man noted. 'Hope I might get to see a little more of you later on. Angel here likes a bit of class.'

'Sure do, sweet thing,' the girl grinned. 'And you're real classy.' She winked suggestively at Kim, and then they walked away.

'I thought slaves weren't supposed to wear knickers,' Kim said, watching them go.

'They're not. But she's not a slave. She's just a want-to-be. She comes here hoping she'll get picked up by one of the masters.'

'So isn't the cowboy a master?'

'No way. He just likes the scene. You have to be loaded to be a master. You've got to have a real big place and security, and that costs big bucks. It's a very exclusive club. Most of the men here are losers, but they need them to make up the numbers.'

'The numbers?' Kim frowned, getting a little confused.

Candy grinned. 'You'll see.'

The waitress brought a bottle of champagne in a wine cooler and two glasses. She opened the bottle without a word and poured the wine.

'Shall I open a check?' she asked.

'Yah, do that,' Candy said.

The girl swung away again.

'See that guy over there, on the left?' Candy asked. She nodded at a man on the dance floor wearing a cream suit with a bolero jacket and tight trousers, their seams decorated with a satin band. He was no more than twenty-five, with blond hair flowing down over his shoulders. A long-haired redhead in an almost entirely see-through turquoise tulle dress was dancing with him, her arms wrapped tightly around his body. The girl was clearly not wearing panties. 'He's a master,' Candy stated, when Kim nodded to confirm she saw him.

'But, he looks too young.'

'Daddy was rich,' the blonde went on. 'He inherited everything, including his father's penchant for domination.'

As they watched, the man stopped dancing and pulled the girl towards a door at the back of the dance floor. They both disappeared through it.

Kim reached for her wine, forgetting the slave collar. Her hand was jerked back by the chain. She had to edge herself to the front of the leather armchair and bend her head forward slightly before she could reach the glass. 'Cheers,' she said, slightly sheepishly.

'Cheers. Welcome to New York.'

They both sipped their wine.

'So, what do we do now?' Kim asked.

'That really depends on what you want.'

'I want to meet Jake Ashley.'

'Okay, so that means we have to go out back. See, the way it works is he has scouts. If they see a new girl, one they think might interest him, they give him a call. His apartment's only around the corner from here. He'll come running. That is if he's not here already. So you've got to put yourself around, let everyone get a real good look at you. Hey, looks as though there's going to be some action, right here.'

The music had stopped and the lights dimmed, a follow spot dancing on the rostrum in front of the band. A tall slender woman, seemingly in her earlier fifties, stepped into the pool of light. She was wearing a long black strapless dress that was split almost to the waist, the rangy leg it revealed as she stepped forward sheathed in champagne coloured nylon.

'Ladies and gentlemen, welcome to the *Cul D'Or*. As usual we have a little entertainment for you now. Tonight we are featuring Master James.'

The woman stepped back and a large white screen dropped in front of the band. A picture appeared on it almost at once. It showed a small room, its walls painted in pink, with a black carpet. In the centre of the room were two pillars, attached to which were a series of metal rings. Behind it, against the far wall, was a double bed covered in a black silk sheet. For a moment nothing happened.

'What is this?' Kim whispered, her eyes glued to the scene.

'Just a taster. It's to encourage people to go out back. That's where the action is. And the club takes a cut.'

'A cut?'

'The men pay big bucks to go back there. Don't worry – for women it's free.'

On the screen the young blond man Kim had seen on the dance floor stepped into the picture. He was wearing a pair of black silk briefs and had a sinewy athletic body, though it was a little on the thin side. If he was aware the camera was on him, he paid no attention to it.

Three women entered the shot. Kim recognised the

redhead with whom Master James had been dancing. The two other women were manhandling her into the room, both dressed in black leather catsuits. Both were large, their meaty thighs and buttocks bulging, their bosoms spilling out of the plunging neckline of their clothing. They both wore black leather helmets laced at the back, their long hair pulled through the laces in a sort of ponytail. The helmets had holes for their eyes, ears, nose and mouth.

The redhead was manoeuvred between the two pillars. She was still wearing the tulle dress, but thick leather cuffs now banded her wrists and ankles. The two women busied themselves binding these cuffs to the pillars so that the girl's body was spread-eagled and facing the camera. Kim could see her breasts and her mons through the veil of material and, since the latter was completely hairless, also glimpsed the first inch or so of her labia.

'Do you want her gagged, master?' one of the women asked.

'No.' He came up to the redhead and very tenderly touched her cheek. He kissed her on the mouth and she responded eagerly, squirming her lips against his and trying to press her body forward.

He stepped back and took hold of the V-neckline of the dress with both hands, tearing it all the way down to the hem.

'Thank you, master,' the girl said in hushed tones.

She had small breasts and tiny nipples. He rolled one between finger and thumb and she moaned, grinding her hips as far as the bondage would allow.

'What do you want?' he asked.

'To be whipped, master,' she said.

'Why?'

'For your pleasure, master.'

70

'Then your wish is granted,' he announced. He turned and nodded to the two women. They disappeared out of the shot, only to reappear immediately, both carrying riding crops.

Kim looked around the club. Though there were a couple of tables still deep in conversation, most faces were riveted to the screen. Several of the men had either slipped their hands up between their partner's legs, or were having their own genitals massaged, or both.

Master James kissed the girl once again. His cock had engorged and was now sticking out of the front of the briefs.

'Come on,' he said. 'Let's get on with it.'

Both women positioned themselves behind the redhead. The one on the left raised her arm and cut the riding crop down hard on the girl's right buttock. The thwack of leather on flesh resounded from the speakers. Kim saw the girl's face contort, but almost before she had time to react to the first stroke the other woman had cut a second down onto her left side. With almost balletic precision the two women alternated their swingeing strokes, hardly a second between them, while the helpless redhead writhed against her bonds, struggling to pull herself away from the rain of blows.

The camera angle changed. Now the scene was viewed from the back, the camera closing in on the girl's buttocks. As the lashes fell the taut flesh trembled, the whole area already bright red, with several long diagonal stripes decorating each cheek. To the side of the pillars the master had pulled his briefs down and was stroking his erection.

The girl had started to grunt with each strike, the noise getting louder and louder.

'That's enough,' the master said. 'What do you say, girl?'

'Thank you, master,' the redhead intoned.

The women stopped. They looked at the blond expectantly, waiting for their orders.

'Cheryl,' he said.

Despite the helmets Kim could see that one of the women's faces had broken into a broad smile. She dropped the whip. The leather catsuit had a long zip running from the low neckline right the way down between her legs and up into her buttocks. Cheryl grasped the tongue of the zip and pulled it all the way down. When it was open to her mons she bent over, turning her back so the camera would have a full view of her rear, reached her other hand around down between her legs, and unzipped the garment so it gaped open between her legs. She was not wearing anything under the catsuit and the camera closed in on her sex. It was not shaved, though the hair that covered her labia was short and sparse. Kim could see that, like the girl in *Velvet Tongue*, her labia had been pierced, but this time only with a single ring. A thin gold chain ran from the ring just under her fourchette, down the whole length of her sex to her arsehole. There it was fastened into the butt of what was obviously a phallus that was plugged into her anus. With her body still bent Cheryl pulled the phallus out so it dangled from the chain, swinging slightly between her legs.

'Ready, master,' she said eagerly.

Kim looked over at Candy, who was leaning back in the armchair with her legs crossed. She suddenly felt a wave of desire, her clitoris throbbing so strongly it was as if it were trying to force its way out between her labia. The sight of Cheryl's pussy in close up on the large screen, the view of the dildo being pulled from her rear, made Kim realise she was capable of feeling real lust for a woman. That was an avenue of endeavour that Candy had opened up for her.

The camera angle changed again, so the screen was filled with a frontal view of the redhead. Her eyes were dancing with excitement, her whole body squirming from side to side against the leather cuffs.

Cheryl came around to the front of the posts and immediately dropped on her knees in front of the master. She took his cock in her hands and fed it greedily into her mouth, making appreciative noises as she gobbled it up, working her tongue against the ridge at the base of his glans. The other woman came around to the front too. With a nod from the master she raised the whip and slashed it down on the redhead's breast, the leather loop at the tip of the riding crop landing squarely on her nipple. The girl gave a little whimper of pain, but it was laced with excitement. Kim could see her straining to rub her thighs together so she could put pressure on her labia. Her legs were bound too far apart, however, to have any success.

The master pulled Cheryl's head back, his cock slipping from her mouth with a plopping sound. It was coated and glistening with saliva. He pulled her to her feet. Apparently she knew what to do next. She walked out of shot for a moment, then came back carrying what looked like a trapeze bar. It was hanging at about waist level from two white nylon ropes that disappeared out of shot. Cheryl bent herself over the bar with her back to the camera, and opened her legs wide, grasping them just below the knees. In the position her sex was framed by the black leather catsuit, each of her big pliant buttocks bisected by the tight black leather.

The blond master came up behind her. He grasped the dildo that was still hanging down between her legs and

73

inserted it into the mouth of her vagina. The camera closed in, lingering on the intimate details as the smooth black dildo slipped into the glistening flesh. Cheryl moaned.

Pulling the dildo out the master let it drop. The wrench on the chain and the ring it was attached to made Cheryl cry out, but the note of pain changed, mid-flow, to a much more melodious moan as the master gripped her hips and sunk his cock deep into the recesses of her cunt.

Holding himself in that position without pulling out again, he nodded to the other catsuited woman, who immediately slapped the whip down on the redhead's right breast, again aiming at her nipple. The girl yelped.

'Squeeze it,' the master ordered, slapping Cheryl's buttock. He moaned softly as she clearly obeyed.

Thwack! The whip landed again on the redhead's right breast.

The master had his back to the camera, but was clearly staring right at the girl. Whether at a signal from him or not, the woman changed her aim and brought the next stroke down on the inside of the redhead's thigh. The girl whimpered loudly, trying to twist to the side to protect herself.

Thwack! The next stroke landed against the delicate inner flesh of her labia.

Kim felt her own sex pulse as if in reaction. Her nipples were already stone hard. Her emotions at this spectacle were confused. She was undoubtedly attracted to the women, particularly to Cheryl, her large voluptuous body so lewdly exposed. But if she were honest with herself it was more than that. She couldn't help imagining what it would be like to be tied there, like the redhead, completely helpless and vulnerable as she had been in Candy's room, and to feel the whip cutting across her body. Whipping was a punishment most of the slaves in Jake Ashley's books had to endure, and he described the emotions it generated so vividly that though Kim had never experienced it, she thought she knew exactly how it would feel. And to be made to watch while her master used another woman in preference to her was another form of torture Ashley frequently invoked. Kim could see how much the redhead wanted the master, and how the whipping had only increased that desire. It was a lesson in frustration and, as Candy had said last night, frustration was the essence of Jake Ashley's work. Frustration and relief. Pain and pleasure.

On screen the camera angle changed again. There was another camera positioned to get a sideways shot of the master. He was beginning to pump into Cheryl's sex, his fingers gripping her hips more tightly. The redhead yelped twice in quick succession as the leather loop of the whip was flicked against her pussy. Suddenly the master's body went rigid, his sinewy muscles locked. He pulled himself out of Cheryl's body, his big cock glistening wet, and pushed it against her buttocks. His phallus spasmed twice in quick succession, then an arc of spunk jetted into the air, spattering all over the back of the leather catsuit.

'The come shot,' Candy whispered, leaning forward.

'The – the what?' Kim was feeling hot and bothered.

'In blue movies, it's always called the come shot. To prove the guy really got it off.'

The audience in the club applauded as the lights went up and the screen retracted into the ceiling. The band began to play again.

Kim looked around. Four or five of the girls were deeply involved in satisfying the lust the performance had created in their partners; two or three on their knees using their mouths, the others busy using their hands. The rest of the crowd watched with interest, occasionally urging them on.

'Was that a blue movie then?' Kim was confused.

'No. It was live.'

'What do you mean, live?'

'It's a direct feed from the back. I told you, it's to encourage the punters to go back there.'

'Back where?'

'See for yourself.'

Four or five men and their partners were waiting at the door at the back of the dance floor. Kim could see the woman in the long black dress checking everyone through and getting them to sign a clipboard.

'They're going in there to have sex?' she asked. It was certainly not like any club she'd been to in England. 'What about the health risk?'

Candy smiled. 'That's why this club is so exclusive. There's a doctor and a lab behind that door. No one gets in before they've had blood tests.'

'But, that takes days.'

'They've got all the latest equipment, really sophisticated stuff. It takes about fifteen minutes.'

'Really?' said Kim incredulously.

'So now the question is, do you want to join in?'

'Join in?'

'You saw what's expected of you. It's your choice. Jake may be in there already. Or, like I say, you might be seen by one of his scouts.'

'Can't I just stay here?' Suddenly Kim wasn't feeling too confident.

'You could. But you're not as likely to get noticed.' Candy finished her champagne and got to her feet. 'It's your choice, sister – no pressure. But if you don't mind I'm going to get some action. That show's made me *hot*.' She wriggled her bottom as if trying to get more comfortable in her clothes, the crotch of the PVC body no doubt cutting into her sex. 'Well?'

The word hung in the air.

Kim took a deep breath.

'Let's go,' she eventually said, the slave chains rattling as she got to her feet.

Chapter Four

Kim walked across the dance floor at Candy's side. The queue had gone down slightly and they reached the door in a couple of minutes. If they'd had a longer wait perhaps Kim would have changed her mind. Her pulse was racing and her heart was beating so hard she could feel it in her eardrums.

'Hi, Candy,' the woman at the door said.

'Hi Wanda. This is my friend, Kim. She's from England.'

'Hi, Kim. Can you vouch for her, honey?' Wanda was looking at Kim critically like some cinema usherette trying to judge whether she was old enough to be admitted to an adult movie.

'Sure,' Candy confirmed. 'She's really into it.'

'Sign her in then,' Wanda said, handing Candy the clipboard.

Candy signed, handed it back, and Wanda held the door open for them.

They walked through into a small room, its walls lined with folding wooden chairs. At the end of the room were a metal desk and a computer screen. A chunky nurse in a white uniform sat viewing the screen.

'Anders?' she said.

There was one man and three other women sitting in the room. The man got up.

'You're clear,' the nurse said. She handed him a thin metal chain, hanging from which was a filament of metal. He hung it around his neck then walked through the door behind her.

'Name?' the nurse said curtly as Candy and Kim walked up to her.

The medical checks did indeed take fifteen minutes, at the end of which the nurse handed them both the thin metal chains that reminded Kim of the sort of dog tags she'd seen soldiers wearing in films. They hung them around their necks and walked through the door behind the desk.

Beyond was a dimly lit corridor, along the whole length of which, on both sides, were doors; perhaps twelve in all. To the side of each door was a small window covered with a dark blue velvet curtain. There were three men in the corridor with women at their sides, each peering through one of the windows. The men were all wearing white cotton robes while the women still had the clothes they'd worn in the bar.

'The men change over there,' Candy said, nodding towards a door to the right of the entrance. 'The women wait to get stripped later.'

'What do we have to do?' Kim asked, a little bewildered. She now had a real feeling of apprehension, her bravado melting away. Of course she was desperate to meet Jake Ashley, but she knew that was not the only motive for her agreeing to take this wild step into the unknown. Like Candy, she was hot. Watching the young blond master sink his throbbing phallus into Cheryl had churned her insides to jelly. She wanted sex.

But despite her previous experiences with Candy and all the entirely new sensations that had created, and her brush with the arcane world of bondage and domination that morning at the *Velvet Tongue*, she was still not sure how she would respond faced with the reality of a man wanting to whip her or do any of the other things Jake Ashley wrote about so graphically. Her pulse was still racing, but now she wasn't too sure whether it was from excitement or fear.

'Look at this,' Candy whispered conspiratorially. She walked to the nearest little window and pulled the curtain. 'You just choose which room you want to go in. Or you can just watch.'

Kim gazed through the glass. Beyond was a room identical to the one she'd seen on the screen in the club a few minutes before. It had the two pillars and the bed. A man was lying on his back on the black silk sheet, with a woman astride his hips, her hand grasping his erection and feeding it into her sex. She was naked apart from a pair of white leather thigh boots. Another woman with the sort of short-cropped hair Kim had seen in the *Velvet Tongue*, and wearing a tightly laced black leather waspie, its long suspenders supporting black stockings, was standing at the side of the bed. Her breasts were so large and pendulous that they overhung the front of the corset. As Kim watched the woman climbed onto the bed, threw one thigh over the man's shoulders and straddled his face. She cupped one of her breasts and pulled it up to her mouth, so she could suck and bite at her own nipple.

'No Jake,' Kim observed quietly.

'Come on.' Candy moved along to the next curtain, which had just been vacated by one of the men. Again, Kim peered through. Here, very much as in the performance they had seen earlier, a naked woman was tied between the two pillars, her body spread-eagled. But instead of being whipped a man was busy inserting two dildos into her, helped by a woman in a bright orange rubber minidress. Two other men stood watching, their erections jutting from their loins. Candy took Kim's arm and led her a little further down the corridor. Instead of gazing through one of the curtains, this time she opened a door and ushered Kim inside. The room beyond was small and dark, with a line of armchairs facing the same wall. On this wall was a large glass panel, through which yet another red room could be seen.

'One way mirror,' Candy whispered.

There were four other people in the room, three women and a man. The women had arranged themselves around the man, one kneeling at his feet, the other two on each arm of the armchair. It was too dark to make out exactly what they were doing, but it looked as though each of them had a hand on his erection, which had been pulled clear of his clothes, and were rubbing and stroking it enthusiastically as he watched the scene beyond the glass.

'Candy, is that you?' the man in the armchair called, without taking his eyes from the scene before him.

'Hey, Tony, you look like you're having a good time.'

On the other side of the mirror a woman had been bound to one of the pillars, exactly as Kim had bound Candy last night, her hands stretched over her head, her ankles tied tightly together. Thick leather straps had been wrapped around her body and secured to the post at her shoulders, waist, the top of her thighs and her knees, making it impossible for her to move at all, the leather cutting deeply into her soft flesh. She had obviously been whipped, her neat, apple-shaped bottom marked with horizontal weals. Despite her bonds she seemed to be trying to wriggle her bum from side to side as if to fan air over them.

There was a man on the ubiquitous black-sheeted bed, and a woman knelt at his side, taking his cock into her mouth.

'Have you seen Jake around?' Candy asked.

'Jesus, Candy, you still got the hots for him?'

'Just wanted to introduce him to a friend.'

'He was here an hour ago,' Tony said, at last looking over his shoulder at the two girls, his eyes settling on and devouring Kim. 'But he's gone now,' he added, his hedonistic thoughts clearly evident in his expression.

Candy nudged Kim and they left the room.

'What do we do now?' Kim asked. 'If he's left—'

'Doesn't mean he's not watching,' Candy interrupted. 'Like I said, he's got scouts…'

'Hi, there.' A really tall, barrel-chested man suddenly appeared in front of them. He had a craggy, weather-beaten face, dark brown curly hair, and was accompanied by a shorter man. 'Now, you're just what I'm looking for,' he added, his eyes bulging.

'Good evening,' Candy said, her eyes registering approval as they roamed both men. They wore the white cotton robes provided by the club.

'You two want to get it on?' he asked, his companion saying nothing, but staring intently.

'That's why were here,' Candy said.

'There's a free room just there,' the shorter man at last piped up, holding one of the curtains open and peering inside.

'Sounds good to me,' Candy said, smiling broadly. She took hold of the bigger man's arm, then turned to Kim. 'Coming?'

Kim looked at both men. Though Jake had gone she could still kid herself that she was there for purely professional reasons; if what Candy said was true, she wanted one of Jake's spies to report back that there was a new and interesting girl in town. But even without that excuse the effect of what she had witnessed so far had twisted her sexual need to new heights, and she would have found it hard to leave.

'Y-yes,' she said, her mouth suddenly dry.

'So, I'm Duke, and this is Tom,' the tall man said, once they were all in the small room.

'Candy and Kim,' Candy replied.

'Well, let's get started, ladies.'

The room was warm and perfumed with a musky scent. What the camera had not shown on the screen was a large mirror on the left-hand wall behind which, Kim knew, the club's voyeurs would soon begin to watch the action.

Candy had turned to Duke and wrapped her arms around him. She reached up on tiptoe to kiss him, crushing her lips to his.

Tom took off his robe and hung it on a hook at the back of the door. To Kim's astonishment both his nipples were pierced, and he wore a silver chain between them. He also had a black leather strap around the base of his cock and under his balls. He said nothing to Kim and made no attempt to approach her.

Duke broke the kiss. Immediately Tom moved close to him and began to untie the belt of his robe.

'No, you get her ready,' Duke said, indicating Candy. 'You know what I want.'

Tom nodded. Under the mirror was a white chest of drawers. He went to it and began searching for something.

Duke took off his robe. He had a hairy body with well-developed muscles. His cock was semi-erect, its glans still covered by its foreskin. Candy unbuttoned her wrap around skirt and took it off. To Kim's surprise the gusset of the PVC body had been cut away, so her sex was exposed. The black stockings she wore had lacy hold up tops. 'So

83

what's he going to do with me?' she asked.

'I think I know what you want,' Duke said. 'But you,' he was looking at Kim. 'I'd guess you're the new girl on the block. Am I right?'

Kim blushed, but nodded.

'You know all the women here are slaves?'

She nodded again.

'Come here then.'

Kim hesitated, and then walked over to him, her pulse racing again. The shadow of Jake Ashley and his books fell across the proceedings. The fantasies he had created, and which she had responded to so unequivocally, were about to come true.

'On your knees,' Duke ordered gruffly.

She knelt down, her eyes lowered. Without waiting to be told she grasped his now fully erect cock, and pulled back his foreskin. She licked the tip of his glans.

'Very good,' he murmured appreciatively.

Kim sucked the pulsing stalk deeper. She tried to swallow it all, forcing it to the back of her throat, while her fingers played with his balls. A surge of excitement ran through her, any apprehension she had felt wiped away by sheer desire. Her insides melted as she imagined how wonderful it would be to feel the hot hard rod of flesh pressing into her cunt.

Out of the corner of her eye she saw that Tom had lowered a nylon rope from a pulley set in the ceiling between the two pillars. On the end of it was a metal hook. He was busy strapping a pair of leather cuffs around Candy's wrists.

'All right, up now,' Duke said.

Kim allowed the cock to slip from her mouth, and rose a little unsteadily. She watched as Tom led Candy to the pillars and hooked the central link of the cuffs over the large metal hook that was hanging just above head height.

'Now her,' Duke said.

Tom picked up another pair of cuffs. 'Hands out in front of you,' he said. As Kim obeyed he buckled the cuffs over the silver manacles that already banded her wrists, then took her to the hook, stretching her hands up so they too were secured above her head, the two girls facing and moulded against each other. The pulley was operated by an electric motor. When Tom turned a gnarled switch on the wall, the hook began to ascend, pulling the girls' hands up with it. It stopped when they were stretched up on tiptoe. The chains from the silver manacles on Kim's wrists to the collar were short, and forced her head back.

'Well, that's more comfortable,' Duke said. He moved behind Kim and managed to pull the halter-neck of the silver dress down under the silver collar. He unhooked the three eyes that held it in place and wriggled the front of the dress down between their bodies. 'Very nice,' he said, as the dress fell to the floor and he examined Kim's figure. She wore the flesh-coloured tights Lucinda had provided, the bottom and the whole area of the crotch and most of the belly cut away. His hand smoothed against her buttocks.

'Do you know, Tom, I don't think this one's ever been whipped. Her arse is real smooth. Is that right, hon?'

The incredible tension prevented Kim from saying anything, but he clearly took her silence as a yes.

'Then we're very privileged, aren't we?' He moved around to Candy. The PVC body had a thong cut back that left most of her buttocks exposed. Duke caressed them. 'This one, on the other hand, is very experienced in that department. Tom here likes to take a beating too, don't you Tom?'

'If it pleases you, master,' Tom said.

'Good answer.' Duke chuckled. 'Get me a cock strap.'

Kim looked at the smaller man with renewed interest. She had not realised until that moment that he too was a slave. There were male slaves in Jake Ashley's books of course, but he was the first example she'd seen.

Tom went to the chest of drawers and pulled out a small leather harness. He sunk to his knees in front of the taller man and strapped the harness around his erection. It lifted and separated his balls, and made the veins on his shaft stick out prominently.

Duke walked around both girls, then moved behind Kim again. He ran his hand over her hips and pulled her back onto him, his cock buried in the deep cleft of her arse. Kim felt it throbbing. He forced his hands between their bodies and cupped both of Kim's large breasts. She held her breath.

'All right,' he whispered softly in her ear. 'It's time we got you warmed up.'

He stepped away and sat on the edge of the bed, taking his cock in his hand and wanking it gently. Kim saw him nod to Tom, who had picked a whip from the bottom drawer of the chest and was standing at her side. It had a brass pommel at the end of its braided leather handle and a long thin lash that was knotted at the very tip.

'Give the new girl a taster,' Duke ordered.

Before she could even ready herself Tom had raised the whip and slashed it down on her buttocks. It was as though a line of needles had been driven into her flesh; a very thin, very straight line. She heard herself scream, her whole body shuddering, the way it was stretched so taut seemingly making the pain worse, like a note played on a highly tuned string. Before she could even catch her breath the whip whistled through the air and landed again, a new stripe of intense pain searing into her an inch above the first.

'No…' she cried, trying to wrest her bottom away from Tom's arm, pushing Candy around in her place.

But Tom merely took one step to the side and raised his arm again, slashing the whip down with all his strength, the lash cutting diagonally across the first weal, the pain greatest where the two lines intersected.

'No! No!' Kim screamed, struggling furiously against her bondage. But suddenly something inside her changed. The burning sensation that had set her whole bottom on fire, the countless needles of pain that were burying themselves deeper and deeper into her buttocks, making every nerve raw, seemed to transform themselves into an overwhelming sensation of pleasure, as profound as anything she had ever felt before. She realised with a shock that it was precisely the emotions Jake Ashley had ascribed in his books to a girl who was whipped for the first time.

She gazed mistily into Candy's eyes. The blonde was staring at her, wanting to see her reaction. And she was sure she could see exactly that, as her face slowly broke into a wry smile. 'Good, isn't it?' she whispered.

Thwack! Tom delivered another stroke. This time Kim's reaction was completely different. There was pain, searing pain, but it was pain that was on the same frequency as pleasure, and could not be distinguished from it. She found herself undulating against Candy, subtly rolling her hips so their bellies and thighs ground against each, the nylon that sheathed their legs rasping slightly. She could feel Candy's nipple ring buried between their breasts.

'Well, look at that,' Duke enthused. 'She's a natural.'

Tom's cock was now fully erect as well. He moved behind Candy. He raised the whip and cut it across her much less ample buttocks. Candy breathed out sharply but did not make any other sound. Kim felt her tense.

'Did I tell you to do that?' Duke admonished sharply.

'No, master,' Tom mumbled meekly, 'but I thought.'

'Don't think, just do. Haven't I told you that before?'

'Yes, master.'

'You just wait till I get you home. Now cut the new one down.'

Tom did as he was told immediately. He operated the switch that lowered the metal hook, released Kim from it, then wound it up again until Candy was once more stretched on tiptoe.

'Come here,' Duke said.

Kim walked over to the bed.

'Turn around and bend over so I can get a closer look.'

The whole area of Kim's buttocks had been tenderised and was throbbing strongly. Each pulse sent a direct message to her sex, some of them so powerful, like bubbles of pleasure bursting inside her, that she was having trouble not to gasp as they did so. As she bent over the skin was stretched taut and created a whole new panoply of feelings.

'Look in the mirror,' Duke said.

Kim looked up. With her hands still chained to the collar she could not rest them on her knees, and the position was uncomfortable. In the mirror she could see there was a cross-hatching of lines on her backside. Some of the lines were pink and others red, but there was one, the last stroke she was sure, that was a dark scarlet colour. She had forgotten that other members of the club were probably watching the spectacle of her being whipped for the first time. But the idea that there were people behind that glass seeing her like this fuelled her excitement.

Duke caressed the plump flesh. The feeling of his palm's coolness against her superheated buttocks made Kim moan. She knew he would not only be able to see the marks on her arse but the whole slit of her sex. She was sure it was already soaking wet.

'All right, hon, let's give the crowd in there a show.' Duke lay back on the bed, his big erection jutting up from his belly. 'Climb on board,' he said.

Kim knelt on the bed. In the past she had always selected her lovers carefully, often waiting weeks before agreeing to go to bed with them. She'd had so few one night stands she could count them on the fingers of one hand. Even then she had at least spent most of the evening with her partner before tumbling into bed. Duke was a complete stranger. She didn't even know if Duke was his christian or surname. And yet she was prepared to straddle his body and sink down onto his hard, hot cock. That fact, the idea that this represented something she had always forbidden herself, added yet another twist to her spiral of arousal.

The nylon of the crotchless tights grated against his hip as she positioned herself above him.

'Tom,' Duke said.

But Tom had already anticipated what was required and knelt on the bed beside her. With her hands still bound together by the leather cuffs and chained to her collar, there was no way she would reach down to guide Duke's cock into her vagina, but she felt Tom's hand moving between her legs. It gripped the shaft of Duke's erection and positioned it in the slit of her sex, her copious juices testimony to her extreme arousal.

The male slave slid his master's glans forward until it knocked forcefully against Kim's clit, so forcefully it made her gasp. Then he pulled it back and inserted it into the mouth of her vagina, his head bent forward so he could see what he was doing. She felt his other hand pushing her thigh down and allowed herself to be lowered onto the waiting phallus.

'Oh, God.' It felt wonderful. It was burning hot and steel hard. She felt the silky walls of her sex parting to admit it, and ground down until his glans was poking into the neck of her womb. For a moment she was simply overwhelmed with feeling, her sex clutching convulsively around him. She threw her head back, the slave chains rattling as her wrists were jerked upward as well.

'Jesus you're wet, you little bitch,' Duke grunted. 'I can feel it running down my cock.'

She could too. She spread her legs further apart and tried to grind down on him even further, her clitoris rubbing against his pubic bone.

'Yeah, let me see it,' Duke panted.

Thwack!

In the transport of ecstasy she'd experienced she hadn't noticed Tom leaving the bed. She strained her head back to see that he'd taken up a position behind Candy again, and was raising his hand to deliver another stroke.

Thwack!

Candy made an odd hissing noise; air expelled through clenched teeth. Duke's cock jerked powerfully inside Kim in reaction to Candy's exclamation. Kim's sex reacted strongly too, pulsing wildly.

'Again,' he ordered.

Tom struck again. Once more the thwack of leather on flesh echoed across the room. Again Candy hissed. Again Duke's phallus jerked against the tight confines of Kim's sex and Kim felt her own reaction; her clit and her vagina both exploding with sensation. The sight of Candy's body shuddering, and the expression on her face, the particular mixture of agony and ecstasy that Kim had now experienced for herself, conspired with all the other extremes of provocation she was experiencing and Kim orgasmed, her whole body locked around the hard rod of flesh buried so deeply inside her.

But her orgasm did not slake her desire. The moment the feelings had ebbed away she realised she wanted more.

Duke made a sign to Tom, who immediately dropped the whip and went to the chest of drawers. Kim couldn't see what he took out as at that moment Duke took her cheeks in his hands and twisted her head around so she was looking directly into his eyes.

'Okay, hon, you just concentrate on me now.'

Kim felt something wet and cold touch her buttocks. It was massaged into the fistula of her anus. A finger penetrated there, the initial resistance overcome by the greasy lubrication that had been applied. The finger circled inside her, applying more unction. She could feel it rubbing against Duke's cock. She supposed it was because she was still suffering the effects of her orgasm, still not quite in touch with the world, but even then she didn't realise what they intended. It was only when she felt the finger withdraw, and Tom's weight settling immediately behind her on the bed, his cock nudging against her buttocks, that the realisation hit her.

'No,' she cried.

Tom reached around and caught hold of the two slave chains, one in each hand, pulling them back like the reins of a horse until her hands were forced back against her chest. He transferred both chains to one hand at the back of her neck while his other grasped his cock, directing it down to the puckered hole of her anus.

He waited for Duke to give the word.

'No, please…' Kim murmured. She had never been buggered before. Not only that, but she already had one pulsing cock jammed into her body. But while her mind protested her body seemed to have other ideas. As the smooth glans of Tom's cock pressed against the little ring of muscles, her clitoris delivered a pang of sensation so intense it was almost like another orgasm. Her arousal was at such a pitch that her body appeared prepared to do anything to satisfy it.

Duke nodded. Tom pushed forward. The lubricant made the penetration effortless. For the first time in her life Kim felt a rigid cock plunging into her rear passage. She shuddered. A surge of pain coursed through her, but just like the pain from the whip, it was transformed instantaneously into an exquisite pleasure that lanced through every nerve in her body. Two cocks inside her, a voice in her head was saying. Two cocks. She could feel them both, every inch of them buried alongside each other, separated only by the thin membranes of her body.

The first surge of feeling turned into a deep oscillating wave, troughs of sensation followed by huge vivid crests. She was coming again, she knew, but it wasn't like the quick orgasm she'd had before, but like a hundred orgasms all rolled into one, an orgasm that went on and on forever, everything they did only increasing its strength. She was aware of them moving inside her, Duke pulling back as Tom pushed forward, the two cocks grinding against each other.

And there was still another level to come. Having climbed to what she thought was a plateau of ecstasy, her body so affected by pleasure it felt as if she were floating, she felt Duke's cock beginning to spasm in her cunt. In seconds it was spurting boiling semen into the deeper recesses of her sex, each jet creating a new erogenous zone as it spattered against the silky inner walls, this new provocation creating an even more intense response. And even that was not the end. Almost as soon as Duke's cock had finally ceased to twitch and jerk inside her, Tom's began to spasm just as wildly. It spat his spunk into the depths of her, where no man had ever been before, the flesh there just as sensitive as her cunt, and just as able to bring Kim yet another kick of orgasmic delight.

She wasn't sure what happened next. One moment she was sandwiched between the two men, and the next she found herself lying on her back with Candy, naked now, stroking her face. She could feel juices leaking out of both nether orifices of her body. Her hands were being freed, both the leather cuffs and the slave chains being removed.

And then she was in Candy's arms, kissing her passionately, the softness of a woman's body creating a whole new set of raging desires. Candy kissed and sucked her breasts and nipples, licked her belly, then nibbled the soft flesh of her thighs. Then she rolled on top of her, straddling her face as she crushed her mouth down on Kim's sex, as Kim raised her head to do the same...

The call had come from the hotel lobby.

'Hi, is that Kim Holbrook?'

'It is,' she said carefully.

'I'm Audrey Sanderson. I wonder if I could have a word with you.'

'In what connection?' Kim asked.

'I'm a member of the *Cul D'Or*. I understand you're trying to get in touch with Jake Ashley.'

'Yes, that's true.' Kim felt her heart leap. Last night might have taken her to new heights of erotic awareness, but it had apparently been a total waste of time when it came to getting nearer to meeting the allusive author.

'Could we talk? Can you come down to the bar?'

'Who told you where I was staying?' Kim asked.

'Candy.'

'Okay,' Kim relaxed a little. 'I'll be right down. How will I recognise you?'

'You'll recognise me,' the voice said enigmatically.

Kim put the phone down and looked at her watch. It was three o'clock and she'd only been up for an hour, the jet lag and last night's activities serving to put her into a long and apparently dreamless sleep.

She stripped off her robe and quickly pulled on tights and a skirt. The skirt fitted snugly and she winced, forgetting the stripes that now adorned her buttocks, the bruised flesh now a kaleidoscope of colours from deep purple to a dark blue. She shucked into a bra and a blouse and picked up her room key. The rather rundown bar of the hotel was not busy. Two men in crumpled suits sat on bar stools drinking cocktails from bell-shaped glasses, while the waiter served a drink to a smart looking women in a tailored red dress. Kim recognised her immediately. It was the woman she'd sat next to on the plane.

'Ms Sanderson,' Kim said, extending her hand and trying to stay calm. 'Nice to see you again.'

'Audrey, please. Can I get you a drink?'

Kim definitely needed one. 'Martini straight up, very dry,' she said to the waiter who was hovering.

Kim sat in the faded dark green armchair opposite the woman. 'So you actually know Jake?' she said.

'I told you it was a long story.'

'Why didn't you tell me?'

'I wanted to check you out first with a friend of mine who works for Reuters in London.'

'Are you a friend of Candy's?' She had lied to Candy about her reasons for wanting to meet Jake. She wondered if Audrey had told her the truth.

'Not really. But I saw you together last night and called her to get your address. From what I saw Jake would be very impressed, incidentally.'

Kim felt herself blushing. 'You were there?'

'I was watching. A very enthusiastic performance. Like Duke said, you're a natural. Is it true you'd never been whipped before?'

The waiter returned with the martini. He must have heard the last remark and gave her a long sideways glance. But Kim saw him shrug. It was New York, after all, he was probably telling himself as he left them.

'No, never,' Kim answered in response to Audrey's question.

'Jake sort of got to you, didn't he? Or was it just a performance in case he might be watching. If it was, you should get an Oscar.'

'No, it wasn't a performance,' Kim admitted. 'How well do you know Jake?'

'Let's just say I've known him as well as Candy.'

'You were one of his slaves?'

The woman nodded, then picked up her drink and sipped it elegantly.

'And what, you're here to warn me off because of what I do?'

Audrey smiled. 'Oh no, not at all. As a matter of fact, quite the reverse.'

'But I thought Jake didn't want to be found.'

'He doesn't. But I think it's time he had a little publicity. If you're still interested, I think I know a way you can get to meet him. And quite soon. Tomorrow, in fact.'

'Tomorrow?' Kim's professional interest was increasing.

'There's an auction.'

Kim remembered Lucinda asking her if she was being taken to such a thing. 'An auction?'

'You do know there's more than one master?' Audrey asked.

'Yes, I do.'

'Well, they all have scouts; people who look out for likely slaves,' Audrey explained. 'And every so often the masters organise an auction. They sell off any of the slaves they want to get rid of and look at the new ones the scouts have found. I could get you into it, if you're interested.'

'And what if Jake doesn't pick me? What if I get chosen by one of the others?'

'I'll call Jake. I'll make sure he knows all about you. I know what he likes. By the time I've told him about last night he'll be on the look out for you.'

Kim thought about it for a moment. It appeared that her night at the club hadn't been a waste of time after all. 'What will I have to do?' she asked guardedly.

'Nothing you didn't do last night. You clearly don't have any inhibitions.'

Strangely, Kim had always thought of herself as really quite inhibited when it came to sex. But all her inhibitions seemed to have been overwhelmed by lust, the images Jake Ashley had created in his books somehow burning into her sexual psyche. Last night she had allowed God knows how many strangers to watch while she had sex with two men and a woman – let alone being whipped and buggered for the first time. Even as little as two months ago at home in England just the idea would have appalled her. Now here in New York she only had to think about what had happened to start a faint pulse deep in her sex. Perhaps it was something in the air.

'All right,' she said, making her mind up. 'I'll do it.'

'Great,' the woman beamed. 'I'll pick you up at noon tomorrow.'

'What do I wear?'

'I've got something in mind. And Kim...'

'Yes?'

'Your pussy, is it shaved?'

Kim blushed, the question seeming so out of place in their surroundings. 'N-no,' she stammered, 'but I don't see—'

'You'll have to shave,' Audrey continued patiently. 'Jake loves that.'

'I... um... all right,' Kim said hesitantly, and then added, to change the subject, 'So where is this auction?'

'Babylon.'

'Babylon?'

'It's a town on Long Island.'

Kim sipped her martini, wondering what she was getting into. 'Can I ask you something now?' she said after a thoughtful silence.

'Yes.'

'Why are you doing this?'

'Because I think Jake Ashley is getting a bit too big for his boots. You've no idea who's involved, Kim. Film stars, senators, guys who run major companies. I think it would teach him a lesson if it all came out in the press.'

'But I was only going to do a profile.' Kim's mind was racing. If what Audrey said was true it looked like Jake Ashley might turn into a real story, even a front page piece.

Her editor would be delighted.

'You're a journalist, aren't you? This is a much bigger story, you'll see.'

'And why do you want to expose him?'

'I think that's my business, don't you?'

Chapter Five

'Lie down here. On your stomach.'

Kim was standing sheepishly naked in Audrey Sanderson's bedroom in a loft apartment in SoHo, the district of New York that took its initials from being SOuth of HOuston. The fact that she had shaved her glossy black pubes away made her feel even more exposed, her mons and her labia completely smooth. The skin tended to itch and she had smothered the region in moisturiser to soothe it, giving the whole area a lustrous, oiled appearance.

Audrey Sanderson had picked her up at twelve and driven her to the apartment. She had checked out the hotel and left her luggage in storage in its basement.

'I thought I was going to get dressed,' Kim said.

'You are. Trust me.'

Audrey had spread a pink towel on the bed. A little reluctantly, Kim lay on it.

'Now, keep very still,' Audrey said. She picked up an oval of thin black rubber and laid it on Kim's back. The oval covered the whole area from the top of her shoulder blades to halfway over her buttocks.

'What's that for?' Kim asked.

'Just got to tape it into position, then you'll see,' came the only reply.

Audrey picked up a reel of tape and began running it around the outside of the rubber, so it was secured to Kim's flesh.

'That's it,' the woman said when she was satisfied. 'Now

get up very carefully and stand on that towel.' She had spread another large one on the floor in the middle of the room.

'What are you doing?' Kim wasn't too sure about what was going on.

'It's a new product – spray on latex. Here, I've just got to tape this over your pussy. Open your legs.'

Kim obeyed, spreading her legs a little shyly.

'Very nice,' Audrey said. 'Shaving definitely suits you.' She applied another triangular piece of rubber to Kim's newly shaven mons and taped that in place too. 'Right, here we go.'

She picked up a spray can and, beginning at Kim's throat, began to spray her body. The substance that squirted out of the can was a thick gooey black. As it spurted against her body Kim could feel it hardening, coating her with a thick layer of latex which dried instantly.

'How do I get it off?' she asked, somewhat alarmed.

'Don't worry, it just peels off.' Audrey smiled reassuringly.

It took nearly an hour to cover her completely. She left a neat circle around Kim's throat and at her wrists and ankles, leaving her feet and hands bare. At the top of her thighs she held a piece of card against Kim's labia so as not to spray her sex. Kim watched in a large cheval mirror positioned in front of her as the latex encased her flesh, giving the impression that she was wearing an extra-tight catsuit. As the latex dried it took on a glossy, smooth sheen.

'Now that really looks sexy,' Audrey purred as she tore away the rubber oval that left Kim's back exposed. 'Do you remember *Goldfinger*? They suffocated that girl by painting her with gold. That's why you've got to leave the back bare.'

Kim turned around and looked over her shoulder into the mirror. Her back was white, the fact that the upper half of her buttocks were bare while the lower half was covered in rubber making them appear even more pouted and voluptuous. She stroked a hand over them.

'Now take off the patch at the front,' Audrey said.

Kim tore the little triangle of rubber from her mons to reveal the first inches of her now hairless labia. They were neatly framed by the black rubber.

'Seriously sexy,' Audrey added quietly. 'Jake'll go mad for you.'

Kim stepped back into her high heels. 'It feels…' She shivered. The latex plucked at her flesh, particularly her breasts, sensitising them. Her nipples were as hard as stone, the black latex gripping them tightly. The fact that her sex was totally exposed made her acutely aware of it. 'Tight.'

'You better wear this until we get there,' Audrey said, taking a long black jacket out of her wardrobe.

'Did… did you speak to Jake?' Kim asked, trying to acclimatise to the new sensation.

'Yes, I did.'

'And?'

'Don't worry, he'll be looking out for you. Come on before I forget myself.' Audrey's eyes roamed Kim's body.

'Oh…' Kim blushed, 'are you into women?'

'Darling, I've been one of Jake's slaves, remember? Even if you're not into it before you go to the house, Jake has a way of making sure you're into it by the time you leave.'

'And which were you?' Kim probed.

'I'd never touched another woman before I found Jake. Never even imagined I would. He made me realise what I was missing.'

Kim saw Audrey shudder.

'Actually, it's not just women,' she went on. 'It's the whole sex thing. It's like I was trying to tell you on the plane. Once I started reading his books, all the things he wrote, the way he seemed to be able to see into a woman's mind… I guess I'd never even thought much about sex before that. I just used to lie there wondering what all the fuss was about.' She glanced at her watch. 'Come on, we'd better go. We don't want to be late, and it's a long drive.'

Metaphorically, Kim took a deep breath. There was more at stake now than a profile piece on one of America's most elusive writers. If what Audrey had told her yesterday was true, Kim could be on to a really big story. She could see the headlines now:

American Senators Involved with Sex Slaves.

But as much as she wanted to win success on that score, she could not help wondering whether the auction would be another opportunity to explore the extraordinary sexuality she had discovered since she'd arrived in New York. She hoped she could have her cake – and eat it too.

Once they had turned off the main highway that ran through the centre of Babylon and taken a right toward the ocean, they left the rather gaudy shops and bars of the main street, over-adorned with large neon signs, behind. The houses became larger and more secluded, big clapboard buildings surrounded by white wicket fences, and standing in their own grounds.

Audrey drove her Lincoln Continental along a road that became narrower and narrower as they approached the sea, finally turning into the driveway of a beach house, the ocean no more than a hundred yards away across an expanse of white sand. The car came to a halt in front of large wooden gates. It had taken three hours to drive to Babylon and the weather had changed for the worse, black clouds hurrying across the horizon, a gale force wind whipping the waves into the shore in plumes of spray.

There was a young man standing in front of the gates with a clipboard in his hand, the collar of his red anorak turned up against the wind. 'Good afternoon,' he said, bending towards the car.

'Audrey Sanderson,' Audrey said, letting her electric window down an inch.

'Yes, Ms Sanderson, you may go straight in,' the man said. He pressed a button on the posts that supported the large wooden gates and they began to grind open.

The driveway to the house was covered in drifts of sand, blown in from the beach. The house itself was large and gothic, reminding Kim of the house on the hill in *Psycho*, except that it was immaculately maintained and painted bright white. She saw that several cars were already parked to one side of the main house as they drove up to the front door. She was surprised they were not more luxurious models. 'Not very impressive cars,' she voiced her thoughts, before she realised it.

'They're the scouts remember, not the masters,' Audrey answered.

'Aren't the masters here too?'

Audrey smiled. 'You'll see.'

At the front door another young man ran forward ready to valet park their car. Kim felt a distinct pang of apprehension as she got out.

'Leave the jacket on the back seat,' Audrey told her.

Kim did as she was told, watching the car jockey's eyes

falling on her latex covered breasts. She wondered what other sights he'd had to feast his eyes on already that afternoon.

The rubber coating that clung to her body was surprisingly warm, and she felt no chill as they waited for the front door to open.

'I'm not allowed to talk to you once we get inside,' Audrey informed her. 'And if you're selected, they'll take you off so I wouldn't see you again. Good luck.'

Kim looked at the woman. For a moment, for some strange reason, she found herself wondering what it would be like to kiss her. It was the first time she'd considered that.

'Audrey, how are you? Come in, almost everyone's here.'

A small chubby bald man had opened the door. He wore a pair of bright yellow golf trousers and a lime green shirt, the buttons of which were strained to the limit by his considerable paunch.

'Hi, Freddie.' Audrey kissed him on both cheeks.

They stepped into the hall. To the right Kim saw a gaggle of people in a large sitting room, sipping champagne. All were normally dressed, apart from a waitress who circulated with a tray of glasses. She was wearing a sheer black body made from the sort of nylon usually used for stockings. Kim could see her shaved mons and large breasts, her nipples poking through black metal rings that were somehow clamped tightly around them.

'Does she know the rules?' the man said. He hadn't even spared Kim a glance.

'No.'

'Go in there,' he snapped, as though he were talking to a dog that had misbehaved. He pointed to a door at the far end of the hall.

Audrey winked secretively at her and smiled. 'Do as he says,' she said.

'Come on, sweetie, let's get you a glass of champagne before the fun starts,' Freddie said, taking Audrey's hand and leading her into the sitting room.

Kim wasn't sure whether she should knock on the door first, and decided not to. She opened it and walked inside. A doll-like woman in a nurse's uniform sat at a desk.

'Name?' she demanded briskly.

'Kim.'

'Not your name – your handler's name,' the woman snapped.

'Oh, I'm sorry…' Kim blurted. 'Audrey Sanderson.'

The woman consulted a list, then made a tick against it.

'You will be required to have a full medical check up. Come this way please.'

The woman got up and led Kim across the room. Through the window she could see the large breakers smashing into the shore.

'Ladies and gentlemen, I think we're ready to start. Would you all take your seats.'

Freddie was standing in the middle of a large gymnasium that extended out from the back of the house. Chairs had been set up along one side of the room, and on the other side were eight circular rostrums about four feet in diameter and two feet high. Sticking up from the centre of each rostrum was a sturdy circular wooden post that came up to about waist height. Kim and five other girls stood in the middle of these rostrums, their arms bound behind their backs by metal handcuffs which were secured to a metal ring set into each post. Like her, all the girls were clad in obscene outfits, very much the sort of thing she had seen at the *Velvet Tongue*. In addition several of the girls were pierced; nipple rings and labia rings adorned with chains or decorative jewellery. Two males occupied the remaining two rostrums at the far end of the room, both completely naked.

The medical examinations had taken an hour, the blood and urine examples all processed in a special unit on the premises. No one got into the auction without a clean bill of health, the nurse told her, even though she'd had a similar examination only the day before yesterday.

In the ceiling above each rostrum was a video camera. There was a desk by the main entrance from which all the cameras were operated by remote control, a man sitting behind a bank of eight monitors. Clearly that was why there were no expensive cars; the masters were not here in person; the viewing of the slaves done from the comfort of their homes.

There were approximately twenty guests. They had already roamed the room, inspecting all the prospective slaves and commenting on their condition. Now they were sitting expectantly and the conversation reduced to a hushed whisper. Audrey sat right opposite Kim and mouthed the words, 'Good luck.'

'We'll start with number one.' Freddie walked to the girl on the rostrum at one end of the room and took a mobile phone out of this pocket. 'Any instructions for number one, sirs?' he said into the phone.

Apparently the response was negative. Freddie moved to the second rostrum in the line. The girl who stood on it was tall and skinny with very short brown hair. She wore a pair of red leather hot-pants with an open crotch, and thigh boots in the same material, but no bra. Her breasts were small but round and high, her nipples circled by the same black hoops Kim had seen on the waitress.

'Instructions for number two?' Freddie asked into the phone. He listened. 'Take the clamps off her nipples,' he said after a moment, turning to a small girl who had accompanied him since he'd started the auction. She was wearing a short black dress, black fishnet tights and high heels, and had a rather round face with long, probably false eyelashes, her black hair cut into a short bob. She mounted the rostrum. The clamps appeared to work on some sort of spring, and the girl gasped as each clamp was released.

'Anything else?' Freddie asked into the phone. 'Bend her over, Debbie,' he said, addressing his assistant.

Debbie unlocked one of the handcuffs, turned the girl around, then bent her over. Kim heard a whirling noise as the camera closed in.

'Right,' Freddie said, nodding to his assistant, who immediately clipped the girl back into the restraints. 'Number three.' He moved down the line, now only one girl away from Kim. 'Instructions gentlemen, ladies?' he said.

Kim wondered what that meant. Were there female masters too? She supposed she should not be surprised, since there were men on the rostrum too. The girl on the rostrum to her left was a blonde, her hair long and lustrous. She was wearing a tube dress in white rubber. It squeezed her breasts together and covered her pert but small bottom and the upper part of her thighs tightly, the rubber so shiny it reflected the bright lights that lit the room.

Freddie listened while instructions were relayed over the phone. 'I understand,' he said. This time he turned to the girl directly. 'The masters want to see you masturbate.

Do you understand?'

'Yes, sir,' the blonde said quietly.

Kim felt her cheeks go hot and her pulse race. The thought that she might be required to do the same thing horrified her. She hadn't hesitated when it came to the outrageous and debauched things she'd been told to do at the club or with Candy, but she could never imagine performing her most private ritual while others watched. She could not do it. That's where she drew the line.

The blonde obviously felt differently, seemingly undaunted about performing such an intimate act before so many people.

'Debbie, get her a dildo,' Freddie said.

The petite girl crossed the room to a small cupboard and took out a two-pronged rubber dildo, the long shaft of the main phallus moulded to a smaller and broader shaft at its base. She walked back to the rostrum, unlocked the blonde's right wrist from the handcuffs then handed her the dildo.

The girl wriggled the tight dress up over her hips. Her pubes were thick. Turning around so she stood behind the post, with one hand still manacled in front of it, Kim saw her brush her sex with the tip of the larger of the two shafts. Fascinated, she watched as a sheen of moisture smeared the rubber shaft.

A little electric motor whirred on the camera above as the operator adjusted its position. The girl slid to the floor, the post between her outstretched legs, the chain on the handcuffs just long enough to allow her to do this with her left arm extended in front of her. She slipped the base of the dildo against the bottom of the post and jammed the tip into her vagina, pushing herself forward so the dildo was trapped between her sex and the wooden post.

Kim saw it slide slowly all the way into her sex. As the second shaft came into play, its tip burrowing into her anus, the girl gasped loudly, bucking her hips to settle herself down on it more squarely. Then she pushed forward again until both shafts were completely buried. With her legs bent at the knee and her hands grasping the front of the post, she thrust forward, the base of the dildo crushed against the wood. She began to pump up and down so that she rubbed against the post, which in turn made the base of the dildo rub against her clitoris. She quickly pulled down the front of the rubber dress, exposing her breasts, which she also rubbed against the wood, twisting her body from side to side.

Kim could see her eyes were sparkling with excitement. They were looking around the room, taking in all the faces that were watching her, feeding on the lust she was generating among her audience, her whole body writhing, grinding her hips and rotating her shoulders at the same time, her breasts slapping against the wood.

'Oh yes… *yes*…' she cried, throwing her head back and thrusting her pelvis against the post one last time, forcing the dildo an extra millimetre deeper as her body locked, every muscle rigid, her fingers clawing at the post like talons.

'Anything else?' Freddie broke the electric silence, apparently unmoved by the spectacle. He nodded to Debbie, who pulled the girl to her feet, removed the dildo and chained her arm behind her back again.

Kim felt her heart miss a beat as Freddie walked up to her. If he asked her to do what the blonde had done she was going to have to refuse. She just couldn't bring herself to do it.

'Number four,' he said into the phone. He listened for

what seemed to Kim to be an inordinately long time, then beckoned Debbie over to his side. He said something to her that Kim could not hear.

Debbie mounted the rostrum. Instead of unlocking one of the metal cuffs from Kim's wrist, as she had done with the other two girls, she actually unclipped them from the metal ring, leaving Kim's arms bound behind her back. She then left her standing there and collected one of the chairs from the other side of the room, bringing it back and placing it on the rostrum. Debbie then sat on the chair.

'Over my knee,' she said.

Kim felt a wave of relief. Whatever the masters had ordered, it was not masturbation.

With her arms bound behind her back it was difficult to balance, but Kim managed to drape herself over the smaller girl's lap, her stretched buttocks tightly coated in shiny latex, pointing up towards the girls face.

She felt the girl's hand spreading the cheeks of her bottom apart, the camera no doubt focussing on the view of her sex that this would provide. Kim was glad she had taken Audrey's advice and shaved. If Jake Ashley was watching the picture the video camera was relaying he would, she hoped, be pleased.

'All right,' Freddie said. 'Begin.'

Before Kim realised what was happening Debbie raised her hand and brought it down hard on her right buttock, the smack reverberating around the room. It took Kim by surprise and she couldn't suppress a yelp of pain.

Smack!

A second blow made Kim's left buttock quiver, the stinging pain making her gasp again. She strained to look across at Audrey sitting no more than ten feet away, and saw her raise a single finger to her lips to indicate that she

110

should be silent.

Smack!

Smack!

Smack!

For such a slender girl Debbie was surprisingly powerful, and each blow stung Kim and made her whole body shudder. But the pain did not last long. Already she felt a familiar heat building in her bottom; a heat that radiated inwards to her sex, making it churn. All the sensations she'd felt at the club two days before began to awaken, her clitoris, trapped tightly between her labia, pulsing strongly.

Smack!

Smack!

Smack!

Debbie alternated the strokes, sharing them out fairly between each buttock. The area of Kim's bottom that was not coated in latex had turned a rosy red, and though the marks the whip had left had faded, they had not entirely disappeared, and it was these that not only prickled the most painfully but, at the other end of the spectrum, seemed to throb with the most intense pleasure too. She found herself trying to rub her mons against Debbie's thigh.

'Is that enough?' she heard Freddie say into the phone. Apparently it was not.

Smack!

Smack!

Smack!

Then suddenly Debbie's hand was smoothing against the reddened, overheated flesh; caressing it, soothing it, testing the contrast in textures between the exposed flesh and the latex coated area. Kim moaned, wallowing in this new sensation. The girl's hand worked down between her thighs, her fingers slipping into the sticky wet trough of her sex. Kim wriggled her labia against them. She wondered if this was Jake Ashley's doing, whether it was he who had ordered her to be spanked and then caressed in this way. She found herself hoping earnestly that it was.

'Go on,' Freddie said, intruding on her thoughts, 'get on with it.'

Debbie pushed her fingers downward, until they were nudging against Kim's clitoris. Another gasp escaped Kim's lips before she could stop it.

Debbie reached one hand down by her knee and gripped Kim's left breast, kneading it, then pinching the nipple exactly at the moment she slid two fingers into Kim's slippery wet cunt.

Kim felt a surge of sensation. The girl's fingers twisted around inside her, trying to screw deeper, provoking a myriad of sensations in the process. The spanking had sensitised every nerve in her sex and they were responding with vigour. As Debbie pinched her nipple for a second time Kim felt her sex clench tightly, and another jolt of pleasure erupted. She was coming now, and there was no way she could stop herself.

All eyes were turned to her, their attention rapt. She tried to ease her legs apart, wanting the camera to see her sex as she came. Was Jake Ashley watching? She liked to think she had come here and allowed herself to be used like this for professional reasons. But she knew that was only a shadow of the truth. Jake Ashley was the real reason she was here, not for her story, but to explore the extraordinary gift he had given her, the gift of sexual self-awareness. She wanted her story – but she wanted this more.

Debbie's fingers were artful. The two inside her stroked the tight tube of her vagina while another seemed to be touching the most sensitive spot on her clitoris and rubbing almost imperceptibly against it. Kim wanted to push the girl back onto the floor and kiss her. She wanted to drive the double-shafted dildo into her body, to fuck her with it then push her mouth down to her sex, though she knew she dare not do any of these things. Her body quivered, her clit spasmed and her orgasm gushed over her. In the midst of it all, in the vortex of feelings that overtook her, she could see herself, as if from above, splayed out over the girl's lap, with the camera and twenty pairs of eyes trained on her latex-coated body, her back and her sex exposed. That image gave the final twist to the long spiral of pleasure.

'Next,' Freddie said casually.

Debbie pulled a limp Kim to her feet. Quickly she clipped the handcuffs back to the post. Kim was glad of its support, her orgasm leaving her faint and breathless. She glanced over at Audrey, who clapped her hands together, lightly miming her approval.

The girl to Kim's right, like the girl at the club, had her labia pierced, and a chain ran from the gold ring implanted there to her nose, where her left nostril was pierced with a small gold ring. The chain, which was as heavy as a dog leash, was not tight, with enough play in it to loop down between her legs. She was wearing a bright red PVC body, very like the one Candy had worn at the club. Like Candy's it was crotchless, but it also had large cut-outs for her buttocks and breasts, which poked through the material obscenely. She had the air of having done all this before.

Neither her or the next girl, who wore a white chiffon slip over a white satin, quarter cup bra, and white stockings clipped to a satin suspender belt, were required to do anything by the masters, and Freddie moved down the line.

'Now the men,' he said, his eyes staring at them with much more of a glint than he'd had with the girls. 'Any requests?' he said into the phone. Again he listened.

Kim was too far away to hear what he said to Debbie, but the girl climbed onto the rostrum of the first man and took his cock in her hand. As casually as if she were shelling peas she pulled his foreskin back and wanked him until he was erect. Then she took a coil of white ribbon from the pocket of her dress and quickly wound it around the base of his shaft and under his balls, pulling it tight and knotting it. She then wound the ribbon all the way up the shaft, circling it over and over again until only his glans was exposed. She tied the ribbon in a little blow just under the ridge at the base of his glans. She licked the palm of her hand, coating it with saliva, then smeared this over the man's helmet so it was glistening.

'Next one,' Freddie called out. He moved to the last rostrum, then a broad grin spread over his podgy face as he listened to the phone. This time he stepped onto the rostrum. 'Quite a pretty boy,' he said. He stroked the man's rather lean chest, then he cruelly pinched his left nipple, using his fingernails. The man winced. 'Sensitive little flower,' he said pensively.

His hand delved lowered. He picked up the man's flaccid cock and slapped it back against the man's naked thigh two or three times. The cock began to grow. Kim heard the whirr of the motors that controlled the cameras.

Freddie made a fist and slipped it around the man's cock. He wanked it, then slapped it spitefully. 'Anything else?' he said. There was an undoubted note of hope in his voice, and his face fell visibly when it was obvious that the masters' interest had peaked.

'Well, ladies and gentleman,' he announced to the watching audience, 'that concludes the entertainment for this evening. If you would all like to return to the sitting room the results will be known in the next fifteen minutes. Then we can serve dinner.'

The audience immediately began to file out. Freddie and Debbie followed. The man on the technical console for the cameras closed down his equipment and left the room too, leaving the eight prospective slaves still chained to the circular posts, unable to do anything but stand there and wait.

'Have you done this before?' the blonde to Kim's left whispered. Debbie had not replaced the white rubber tube dress and it was banded around her waist.

'Um, no,' Kim replied, her mind racing. 'Have you?'

'No, never. It's fantastic though, isn't it? I've never been so turned on. All those people looking at me. I don't think I've ever come like that.' She shook her shoulders dreamily, making her tits wobble. 'I can still feel it. If I could get my hands on my clit I could make myself come again.'

Kim did not reply, but what the girl said was true for her too. Her whole being was still vibrating to the strains of her orgasm.

'What about you?' the bubbly blonde said, nodding towards the girl to her left. 'Is this your first time?'

'We shouldn't be talking,' the girl replied.

'No one's listening.'

'I've been with one master. This is my second auction.'

'Hey, that's great. What was it like? Did he fuck you crazy all the time?'

'It was a woman.'

'Even better. I'm really into all that lesbian shit. I love it all, as a matter of fact.'

Kim could quite believe that.

'God!' the blonde went on, 'I wish they'd get a move on and make their minds up. I'm so turned on it's driving me up the wall.' She rubbed her buttocks against the post. 'So what's it like being a real slave?'

'Like nothing you've ever felt before.'

'Did you meet Ashley?'

'Yes. Once. He came to visit.'

'And?'

'Have you read his books?'

'Of course.'

'He was like that – like the master in the books. Exactly like the master in the books.'

'Must have been one hell of a turn on then,' the blonde suggested.

'Shut up, someone's coming.'

They all heard footsteps coming down the hall. The door of the gymnasium opened and Debbie walked in. She had changed her clothes and was wearing a tight red leather jump-suit, cinched around her waist with a wide black belt. A riding crop was tucked under one arm and she carried a small nylon holdall. Two men, one of them the man who had operated the cameras, trooped into the room behind her.

Without a word she stopped in front of the rostrum where the blonde was standing.

'Her,' she said to the men, her eyes fixed on the beauty in white rubber.

Kim's heart sunk, but then Debbie moved on. 'And her,' she said, pointing to Kim.

She stepped up onto the rostrum and pulled a rubber ball gag out of the bag. 'Open your mouth, sweetie,' she said.

Kim obediently did as she was told and the girl stuffed the rubber ball between her lips. She had never been gagged before and tried to protest, but the large sphere made it impossible to form even the simplest of words. Debbie moved behind her and quickly strapped the gag in place, forcing it even deeper into Kim's mouth.

Glancing to her left Kim saw that the blonde had received the same treatment from one of the men. Then he took a black velvet bag and pulled it down over her head, closing it beneath her chin with a drawstring. Just as Kim saw him doing this she realised Debbie was pulling an identical bag down over her head. She was plunged into darkness.

The experience was surprisingly familiar. The slaves in Jake Ashley's books were frequently gagged and blindfold. She'd read about the emotions they experienced in this situation avidly; what they felt; the way being deprived of one sense seemed to increase the sensitivity of all the others; the isolation; the inability to communicate even the simplest of words – all this had excited her. But the reality, the total blackness in which she was cocooned, the actual feeling of the tight strap that held the gag in place, and the black rubber ball that forced her lips so wide apart, was a hundred times more arousing.

She started as she felt hands pushing her forward. There was a clink of metal as the handcuffs were unclipped from the post. Something cold was wound around her ankles and tightened – a thick leather belt, she thought. Another wrapped around her legs just above her knees, then a third, around her waist and back trapping her arms against her spine, binding her into a tight package. She could not move an inch.

'All right, take her to the car.' Debbie's voice sounded muffled.

Kim felt a shoulder lean against her waist and she was suddenly hoisted into the air, her body bent in two, strong hands holding her legs. She felt a thump as the man stepped down from the rostrum. He carried her out of the room.

She estimated it was no more than a few yards before she heard a door creaking open and felt the wind on her body. The man lowered her onto her stomach on what felt like the floor of a car, the soft carpeting not disguising the cold hard metal underneath. The very distinct noise of a car door being slammed confirmed her impression.

She lay still, her heart racing. She could hear the wind blowing against the side of the vehicle, rocking it, and the noise of the breakers pounding against the shore. She was so tightly bound she could hardly move, but she managed to wriggle onto her side, which was a little more comfortable than lying face down. The car seemed spacious, for though she could feel a seat at the back of her there seemed to be nothing immediately in front. She wondered if the blonde was going to be coming with her. Or was she going to a different master?

And what about her? Audrey had said she'd spoken to Jake personally, but suppose he hadn't bid for her. What if she was being taken to someone else? What would she do then? If she were kept in this sort of bondage it might be a long time before she could escape. Why hadn't she thought of that before? Audrey seemed to be so confident she would end up with Jake that she allowed herself to go along with it – but now she wasn't so sure.

Being tied up so tightly and gagged and blindfolded

had excited her. From the moment she'd been handcuffed to the post in the gymnasium her whole body had been tingling with arousal. But the idea that she might not be on her way to Jake Ashley poured freezing cold water on that. She had let her desire to explore her sexual feelings overcome her common sense. She had been a fool.

She writhed against the leather straps and tried to cry out, but knew it was hopeless. It was too late to do anything now. She'd been reduced to a neat little package, ready for delivery to whoever had paid the price. After all, she had agreed to take part in the auction of her own free will, and had let herself be bound and gagged. She was just going to have to live with the consequences of that folly.

The car door opened. She heard the key being turned in the ignition and the engine springing to life.

Desperately she struggled to sit up, trying to tell the driver that she had changed her mind. But she could not pronounce a single word and as the car wheeled around in the driveway she was tossed back to the floor.

'Settle down,' a male voice said gruffly. 'We've got a long way to go.'

Chapter Six

It was a long drive. Kim was sure she counted at least three bridges; the heavy tyres ramping on the metal structures. After that the car twisted and turned and stopped frequently for about an hour before finally getting on to what she imagined was some sort of freeway, where no cornering was required. The car's speed increased and the noise of the tyres levelled out, its forward progress unimpeded.

The car was obviously some sort of limousine as it was whisper quiet, with soft soporific suspension and, despite the discomfort of the bondage, Kim fell asleep.

She was woken with a start by the car door slamming. A moment later she felt cold air rushing in. Hands grabbed the leather straps and pulled her up and out of the vehicle. This time she was lifted by two people, one holding her ankles and the other her shoulders. She heard gravel crunching under their shoes, and a female voice say, 'In here.'

The temperature changed. She felt the warmth of a house and heard a door being closed. The noise of the feet was deadened by carpet. Her body was tilted as they descended a staircase.

'In here,' the voice said again.

Kim felt herself being lowered onto some sort of mattress.

'She's a looker,' the female said. Kim's heart sunk. Some of the masters were women. Had she been sold to one of them?

'Sure is. Had trouble keeping my hands off her.'

'You know what would happen if you did.'

'Don't worry, ma'am. I was only kidding. I want to keep my job.'

A door closed and there was silence. Kim listened intently, trying to hear anything that might give a clue as to where she was. It was clear that she was in the basement of some building. She sniffed the air, but apart from a vague hint of perfume, she could smell nothing.

Almost immediately, the door opened again.

'She's in here.' It was the same woman.

She stiffened as she felt a hand touching her thigh. It moved up to her breast and pinched the latex-coated nipple.

'Never seen this stuff before,' the woman said.

The fact that she was blindfolded did seem to have sharpened Kim's other senses, and she thought she smelt a strong musky cologne that was very definitely masculine.

Hands pulled her off the mattress. The belt around her waist was loosened and the handcuffs unclipped. After so long confined uncomfortably behind her they were so cramped and weak she could put up no resistance as she was pushed back against a wall and her arms were dragged out to the side. She felt them being manacled into new restraints, so that they were stretched out at right angles to her body.

The leather strap around her knees was removed. Hands, whether the man's or the woman's she could not tell, cupped both her breasts, kneading the flesh. Was the man her master? Was it Jake Ashley? She had no way of knowing.

'What do you want me to do?' the woman asked. 'Just

121

rip it off?'

The woman was awaiting orders from the man; she was clearly not in charge.

The man must have indicated his consent, as Kim felt a hand plucking at her neck, just above her collarbone. Fingers seized the rubber coating, pulling it away from her flesh. It puckered outward, then suddenly began to tear. The fingers worked into the hole they had created, pulling out and ripping downward at the same time. Her breasts stung and trembled as they were released through a great gash torn in the black rubber. Kim felt the latex being stripped from her belly. The gash parted at her mons and continued down her thighs.

'Mmm...' This came from the man.

The latex hung from Kim in tatters, most of the front of her body now bare. A finger traced its way down from her throat to her crotch. She heard feet crossing the room and the door being opened again.

'I'll get her cleaned up,' the woman said. 'What time do you want her ready?' Kim could not hear the man's response.

The strap on her ankles was released. The pleasure at being able to move her legs again was almost orgasmic. She shuffled them apart and bent each at the knee. The drawstring of the velvet bag was being unknotted.

'Keep your eyes closed for a while,' the woman warned as the bag was tugged off. Fingers unstrapped the gag, and Kim moaned as it was pulled away, cramp in her jaw now causing her new agonies.

Even with her eyes tightly shut the impact of the light filtering through her eyelids made Kim wince. Slowly and gingerly she opened them, but it was minutes before she could focus on anything. Eventually, through the tears that had welled in them, she could make out her surroundings. She was standing in a small pine clad room with a cord-carpeted floor. To the left was a doorway with no door, through which Kim could see a shower cubicle and a toilet. There was a wooden framed bed to her right, a wooden chair and a mirror hanging on the opposite wall. She could see herself in the mirror, bits of rubber still clinging to her flesh, her hair ragged, her face covered in sweat, with a red stripe where the strap of the gag had cut across her cheeks.

'Welcome to Shangri-La,' the woman said.

The door of the room was open and the man had gone. The woman standing in front of her was short and stocky, with razor cropped black hair. She was wearing tight leather trousers and a leather halter-neck top cut off at her midriff. The muscles of her stomach looked like the gridiron on an American football pitch. Kim's heart leapt. She recognised her immediately. The woman was Monica Montana, the major-domo in Ashley's books, which surely meant one thing: the house belonged to the man she'd been pursuing.

Kim's wrists had been clipped into metal manacles that hung from rings set into the wall. The woman released them.

'What size shoe are you?' she asked.

'Five,' Kim mumbled, her mouth dry.

'I can guess the rest,' the woman said, eyeing her closely. 'Go in there and get yourself cleaned up,' she added, indicating the tiny washroom. She took another long look at Kim's body, then walked out, closing the door behind her. Kim heard a key turning in the lock.

It had taken a long time to get the last of the latex off her. Kim sat and picked it away until she was completely clean, then showered and washed her hair with the shampoo she found in a small cabinet. She had no idea what time it was, as she'd left her watch with her other clothes at Audrey's apartment, but when she finally slumped on the bare mattress she fell asleep immediately.

She woke up next morning, if it was morning, to find a tray had been placed on the floor by the door. There was cereal, milk, sugar, and some scrambled eggs. The eggs were cold, but such was her hunger she ate them and everything else anyway. She showered again, brushed out her hair as best she could, and waited expectantly, hoping that at any moment Jake Ashley would walk through the door.

She was sure it was Jake who had been with the woman last night, eager to see his new slave. But now it appeared his eagerness had worn off, for hour followed hour with no sign of him. She heard noises and faint voices in the corridor outside, all of which, as far as she could judge, were female. But though footsteps passed the door several times, no one entered.

There was nothing to do but think, and Kim's mind roamed over everything that had happened to her since she arrived in New York. Being blindfolded again had revived memories of what Candy had done to her, and the extraordinary feeling of being touched sexually by a woman for the first time. Then there was everything that had happened in the club to play and re-play in her mind, the details so vivid it was like a video recording; each feeling, each soaring sensation etched in her memory. And she thought about Jake Ashley, too. She had assumed over all these weeks that the character of the master in his books was based on his own predilections. Everything she'd learnt from Candy and Audrey had confirmed that theory. And if it was true all the fantasies she'd had, since she'd first read one of his books, were about to come true.

Kim guessed it to be about lunchtime when the pattern of neglect was finally broken. She heard the key turning in the lock.

'Up,' the woman Kim thought of as Dolores said. She was wearing a tight short leather skirt, and a leather blouse. Her stout thighs were thick with muscle. 'You're new to this, is that right?'

'Yes,' Kim admitted as she rose obediently.

'My name is Marsha. You will call me Ms Marsha, is that understood?'

'Yes... Ms Marsha.'

'A quick study. I like that. There are only three rules here. Number one, whenever you are brought into the presence of myself or the master, or one of his guests, you must kneel until you are told to do otherwise. Number two, you must obey without question or hesitation. Number three, you must not speak unless spoken to – you must not talk to any of the other slaves. Understood?'

'Yes, Ms Marsha.' Kim lowered her gaze, already feeling intimidated by the woman.

'Good. If you break any of these rules you will be punished. If you refuse to be punished you will immediately be sent away. And if you are sent away you will not be permitted to be a slave in any of the other establishments in the system. Now put this on.'

Marsha threw a pair of denim shorts on the bed. Kim quickly put them on. They were two sizes too big and the crotch had been removed.

'Spread your feet apart,' the woman continued, dropping

125

to her knees.

She took a pair of metal cuffs from a pocket. They were like handcuffs but with a longer chain. She fitted the cuffs around Kim's ankles, then got to her feet. 'Follow me,' she snapped.

The major-domo marched out of the room. The corridor outside was narrow with a series of doors down one side, all identical to the one they had just left. There was a staircase at the far end.

Upstairs, they emerged through a wooden door into a beautifully decorated hallway, its floor covered in oatmeal tufted carpet, its walls covered with prints and photographs all framed in stripped wood.

Feeling like a member of a chain gang, with the chain clanging between her ankles as she walked, Kim followed Marsha into a large kitchen. There was another man already working there, dressed in identical shorts and chained in the same way. Kim could see his genitals hanging down between his legs through the cut-out in the denim.

'You are to scrub this floor,' Marsha said. 'Then clean all the windows inside and out. Understood?'

'Yes, Ms Marsha,' Kim said humbly.

'The cleaning materials are all here.' Marsha opened a cupboard to reveal mops, brushes, and packets and bottles of detergents.

Kim saw no choice but to obey. She had hoped she would be taken straight to Jake Ashley. But she was in his house, and now she was so close to him she could almost sense his presence, she didn't want to do anything that would ruin her chance of actually meeting him. If she disobeyed and was faced with some punishment she could not accept, she could easily be sent away without achieving either of her goals; getting her story... or satisfying her sexual needs.

So she took out a mop, ran some water into a bucket and began cleaning the perfectly clean tiled kitchen floor. The chain around her ankles made the work that much harder.

Marsha helped herself to a cup of filtered coffee, pulled up a chair, and watched her for a while. But after ten or fifteen minutes she got up and left.

The male slave said nothing. He sat at the large kitchen table cleaning a canteen of silver cutlery. Occasionally she caught him looking at her breasts, but he looked away again quickly. She needed to get a lot of background for her story, and the temptation to ask him how long he had been there, how many other slaves there were in the house, and whether he could confirm any of what Audrey had told her, was overwhelming. But Kim resisted. She didn't know how he would react. He might call for Marsha or she might come back unexpectedly. In either case, Kim might well be expelled from the house before she'd even got her feet under the table. So she decided to say nothing, keep her head down, and got on with the job.

The large kitchen windows looked out onto a stone flagged patio. To the right was a large rectangular swimming pool, and to the left a lawn and neatly tended gardens. She could see the driveway too, curling around from the front of the house to the large garage at the rear. The weather had improved again and it was a fine sunny day.

According to the clock on the cooking range it was four o'clock in the afternoon by the time she had finished the floor and the windows – both jobs, like all those assigned to the slaves in Jake's books, totally unnecessary. Marsha returned with an older woman in a flowery print dress, who put a saucepan of soup on the range, and served it to both slaves with slices of bread.

As they ate a movement outside by the pool caught Kim's eye. She glanced up and saw a tall, raven-haired woman in a tiny black bikini mounting the diving board, then executing a perfect swallow dive into the deep blue water. For a moment Kim had trouble believing her eyes. The woman looked like Nina Berry. The male slave had seen her too and was staring out of the window, clearly waiting to catch another glimpse of her. Eventually the woman pulled herself out of the pool with a straight arm lift. She reached for a towel on a nearby lounger, and for a moment was staring straight into the kitchen, her long black hair plastered back. Now there was no doubt in Kim's mind that her first impression had been correct. The woman was Nina Berry.

Kim's mind was racing. Nina Berry was probably the biggest star in the current Hollywood firmament. Her last picture had made more money than any picture in the history of movies, and it was rumoured that she was going to receive twenty million dollars for her next starring role. But despite her fame she had always refused interviews and led a secretive and reclusive life. Occasionally her name had been linked to one of her more famous co-stars, but she had never confirmed or denied any involvement with a man. Did her presence here mean she was involved with Jake Ashley? And if she was, did that lead to the conclusion that she was into the kind of sexual activities that had made him famous?

Audrey *had* been right, Kim kept telling herself. This was going to be a very big story. Just getting the news out that Nina was visiting Jake's house would be a major worldwide scoop. But if it went further, if she was actually here to slake more unusual appetites, that was mega. Kim could write her own ticket on Fleet Street after that. She would probably even be able to get a job in New York.

Nina Berry finished towelling her hair, climbed into a pair of open-toed high-heeled sandals and walked back into the house.

'All right, up,' Marsha said as they finished their food. 'Both of you, follow me.'

They trooped after Marsha with their chains rattling. Down in the basement she shut them both in what Kim had come to think of as cells. A few minutes after being locked in, the door opened again and Marsha dropped a holdall on the bed.

'Get cleaned up, then put these on,' she said. 'There's make-up, too. Just in case you're required.'

These developments made Kim's pulse race. She hurried into the shower room and stood under the powerful spray. As the water cascaded over her body she began to write the story:

It was revealed in New York today that millionaire film star Nina Berry, widely regarded as one of the most beautiful women of her generation, was having a relationship with writer and sexual guru Jake Ashley, infamous for his SLAVES OF NEW YORK books, whose themes frequently deal with bondage and the domination of women. It is not known how long their relationship has flourished or whether Ms Berry is a fan of his writing...

There was a lot Kim didn't know as yet. She didn't know whether Nina Berry liked to be dominating or dominated. Was she here to use the slaves that, like Kim, were no doubt sitting in the basement at this moment, or did she allow Jake to use her and abuse her?

But Ms Berry was seen indulging in a penchant for bondage and submission with Mr Ashley in an orgiastic scene involving several other so-called slaves. Ms Berry was reported to have been seen bound and spread-eagled against a wall where she was whipped by Mr Ashley and his guests, and subsequently made to have sexual relations with one or all of them. She was frequently seen in the bizarre rubber and leather costumes associated with bondage practises, and was said to be willing to perform in group sex with the other slaves while Mr Ashley watched the proceedings, presumably an activity that gave full range to her acting skills.

Perhaps she had come to him for advice on setting up her own establishment. She certainly had enough money to join the very elite circle of masters that Candy had referred to at the club.

But investigations have revealed that she has her own house where male and female slaves are kept to satisfy her unusual sexual demands. A woman reports having been kept in a cell in the house for over three weeks, being bound and whipped by Ms Berry and Jake Ashley on several occasions, as well as being asked to perform many sexual acts with both of them at the same time. A man, similarly, has come forward to report being held in Ms Berry's house for over three months. He was frequently bound and whipped with a riding crop and used by her and her female guests in a variety of ways, including oral sex. Ms Berry's favourite pursuit was, he claims, having him masturbate over her naked body.

Kim wasn't sure which story would play better. Not that it mattered. Either of them would be sensational.

She dried herself, then went back to the bed. She opened the nylon holdall and shook its contents out onto the mattress. There was a black satin basque with a lacy, almost transparent bra, a packet of shiny black stockings and a pair of high heels, the narrow tapering heel at least four inches high. There was a studded black collar too, with a large D-ring attached to the front, and a plastic box of make-up containing everything from lipstick and eye shadow to nail varnish, though there was no choice of colours.

Quickly Kim wrapped the basque around her body. At home she had rarely worn anything but the most functional of underwear, and the feeling of the tight garment as she clipped the hooks into the eyes at the back created a wave of arousal. She had already come to associate this sort of tight constriction with sex. Rolling the stockings up her long legs and clipping them into the suspenders had the same effect. They were so glossy they looked wet, and seemed to draw attention, by contrast, to the band of soft flesh above them.

Kim stood in front of the mirror and put on her make-up. The colours were much darker and more dramatic than she would have chosen, the nail varnish a deep red.

After she'd climbed into the shoes and strapped the collar around her throat there was nothing to do but wait. The waiting now was much more difficult, however. The corset cinched so tightly around her waist, and the taut suspenders constantly reminded her of the sexual agenda. Ever since she had put them on her sex seemed to be alive, her vagina melting and wet, her clitoris swollen and throbbing. Dolores, in *The Disciple*, had been made to

131

wait like this, dressed in only a pair of hold up stockings and high-heeled ankle boots, Kim remembered. She had waited for hours before she met the master for the first time, and Kim's feelings mirrored exactly what she had felt. Whatever Jake's other capabilities, he certainly knew how to understand and describe the emotions of the women who submitted themselves to such ordeals.

As she had no way of telling the time, it seemed to drag. Every time she heard a noise in the corridor outside her pulse quickened.

Eventually she dozed lightly, and the sound of the door being opened startled her.

'You're required,' Marsha said, with a tone of disapproval. 'Let me look at you.'

Kim got to her feet. Marsha gripped her arm and turned her around, examining her critically. 'When did you get those?' she demanded, nodding at the faint lines that still decorated Kim's buttocks.

'Th-three days ago,' Kim stammered, feeling intimidated by the overbearing woman. Or was it four? Had another day dawned?

Marsha smiled. She took a length of white nylon rope and threaded it through the D-ring on the collar, then pulled Kim's hands up to her throat, tying her wrists together so they were secured under her chin. 'All right, follow me,' she said, when satisfied with her charge.

To Kim's surprise, out in the narrow hall a man was standing in the identical bondage, his wrists also tied to a black leather collar. It was not the same man she had seen that afternoon. He was naked apart from a tiny pouch of black leather that barely covered his genitals, and had a well-developed body that suggested regular exercise. He had curly brown hair and a delicate, almost feminine face, with a sensuous mouth. She saw his eyes roaming her body, devouring every detail of the black satin basque and the silky stockings.

They were marched up to the ground floor and around to the main entrance hall. Then they were led up a sweeping staircase to a galleried first floor landing. Marsha took them along the landing to a pair of elaborately panelled double doors.

'Wait here,' she said.

She rapped twice on one of the doors then walked away, her leather trousers whispering seductively as she did so.

The man looked at Kim as though he was about to say something, but he clearly changed his mind. Instead, he bowed his head and stared at the floor. Kim decided she should do the same.

From inside the room she thought she heard a distinct moan. It was followed by a much louder cry.

One of the doors opened.

'In,' someone order sharply.

She recognised the cologne she had smelt last night... and she recognised Jake Ashley too.

He looked exactly as he did in the photograph on the jacket of his books. He was of medium height with thick black curly hair, piercing steel-blue eyes, a straight nose, bushy eyebrows and a very square chin. It was difficult to guess his age, but she thought he must be at least forty-five. His expression suggested a wry intelligence.

'My dear, how charming to meet you properly at last,' he said to Kim, and therein came her first big surprise; Jake Ashley's accent was clearly of English origin. Nowhere in all the research she'd done on him had anyone mentioned that fact. 'I'm sorry I had so little time for you last night.'

He closed the door behind them. Her second surprise was kneeling on all fours on the bed. It was Nina Berry, her head down between her arms, her long black hair trailing down to the black silk sheet that covered the mattress. She looked smaller and slightly thinner than she appeared on the screen, but there was no doubt it was her. She was completely naked with her legs wide open and a large pink dildo protruding from her sex. Above it a slightly smaller one stuck out from her anus. Both dildos were vibrating.

The room was large and luxurious; the huge double bed the focal-point. The walls were lined with cream-coloured silk, and there were two large windows draped with elaborately flounced white curtains. There was a large oatmeal-coloured sofa facing the foot of the bed.

'This is Adam, and this pretty little thing is Kim...' Jake Ashley casually introduced the woman on the bed to the two newcomers, '...another English import, so I'm told.'

Nina pulled the larger of the two dildos from her pussy. She looked up at the two new arrivals.

'Haven't you forgotten something?' Jake Ashley was also looking at them. Immediately the male slave fell to his knees. Without being able to use his arms for balance he thumped down heavily on the carpet.

Ashley stared at Kim. She remembered what Marsha had told her about kneeling, but she was so mesmerised by at last being in Jake Ashley's presence that her mind seemed unable to communicate with her body. She could not tear her eyes away from his face; his deep blue eyes like staring into the depths of an ocean. Everything he had created, all the wild sexual imagery that had plagued her since she first picked up one of his books, seemed to be crystallised there. She felt her sex pulse violently and realised she was actually trembling.

Jake Ashley had certainly used his own image to describe the master he had portrayed in his books. He was tall, his physical presence as imposing as his mental presence. He was wearing a dark blue silk robe, and Kim lowered her gaze to the carpet and felt her cheeks glow as she noticed a bulge tenting the front of it.

'What's the matter, child?' he said quietly. He touched her shoulder with such tenderness that Kim had a sudden and unaccountable desire to cry. She tried to think of something to say, but her emotions were too confused. She didn't think she'd ever had such a strong sexual response to a man in her life – but it wasn't only sexual. He had an almost hypnotic effect on her, her whole being possessed by him.

'I'm sorry,' she managed to mumble. She struggled to control herself, and sank submissively to her knees.

'Good,' he said.

'Adam, get over here – I need a good plating,' Nina said coarsely.

Kim had no idea what that meant, but apparently the male slave did. He crawled over to the bed, then climbed up onto it rather awkwardly. Positioning himself behind her, he dipped his head and pressed his mouth to the still open maw of her vagina, the juices running from it like a sticky sap. Nina moaned loudly and wriggled her hips, smearing her sex across his face, one hand holding the dildo in her arse. Kim saw him working his tongue against the fourchette at the top of her labia.

Nina pulled away. It was no wonder she'd become so successful in the movies; she was absolutely beautiful, with eyes so dark brown they were almost black, high cheekbones and a soft, sensual mouth. Her flesh, no doubt mollycoddled and pampered by expensive beauty treatments, was as smooth as the finest silk, her body lithe and supple. Her breasts were not large but had shape and substance, with dark red nipples surrounded by small areolae puckered with tiny papillae. Her pubic hair was jet black but sparse, and hid little of her labia.

'On your back,' she said, pushing Adam so he rolled over. Almost before he had settled she swung her thigh over his shoulders and planted her sex firmly on his mouth again, spreading her knees apart so it was flattened against him, the smaller dildo still embedded in her anus.

'Get your fingers in there,' she said.

Kim saw Adam straining his hands against the white rope that bound them to the collar. He managed to get two and then three fingers deep into the sticky tube of her sex. Nina moaned loudly again.

Jake Ashley opened his robe. Kim had read a description of this erection so many times in his books that it seemed familiar to her. He was circumcised, with a smooth bulbous glans the circumference of which was slightly larger than the shaft that supported it. The shaft itself was gnarled with veins, like ivy wrapped around the trunk of a tree. Kim could see his loose scrotum hanging down, his balls large and heavy.

Without a word he hooked his hand around the back of Kim's head and pulled her forward until her lips were pressed against the tip of his cock. She obediently opened her mouth and swallowed him. His erection was rock hard. She ran her tongue around the ridge at the bottom of his glans, then pushed forward until he was right at the back of her throat, the position of her hands making it easy for her to cup his scrotum as she sucked on his phallus.

'Is she good at that?' Nina asked.

'Not bad. So how about we give them a work out?'

'Why not?'

Jake held Kim's face in both hands, caressed her cheeks for a moment, then pulled his cock away. It was glistening with saliva. He went to a large mahogany chest of drawers and picked up a leather tawse, its tail split into two. At the same time Nina clambered off Adam and pulled the dildo from her perspiring body.

'Here,' Jake said. 'Take this.' He walked back to Kim and held the leather tawse out in front her. Kim didn't understand. She looked up at him dumbly.

'Take it,' he snapped. 'Don't make me have to say anything twice.'

Kim took the tawse, holding it awkwardly under her chin.

'Get up,' Jake said.

Kim struggled to her feet, the height of the heels making it difficult. Jake unknotted the rope that held her wrists to the collar. As her arms fell to her sides she felt a pang of cramp.

Nina tapped Adam on the thigh. 'Roll over,' she ordered. He obeyed instantly. He had muscular buttocks. 'Nice buns,' Nina purred. 'Come over here and warm them up for him, sweet thing,' she said, turning her gaze to Kim.

'I…' Kim was beginning to find the whole scene rather confusing.

'You mustn't refuse to do anything you're told, under any circumstances,' Jake said quietly. 'You're to use that on him.' He nodded at the tawse.

'I…' Kim stopped herself from saying anything else. After the whipping she had received at the club she was quite expecting similar treatment at Jake's hands. But she definitely had not expected to be administering the whipping.

Nina hopped off the bed. She moved to Kim and cupped her left breast, squeezing it not at all gently. She moved behind her and flattened her naked body into Kim's back, writhing from side to side, the black satin rasping against her flesh. She sucked on Kim's shoulder, making her shudder. 'Do it,' she whispered in her ear, pushing her forward.

Kim stepped over to the bed. 'I don't know what to do,' she said weakly, though she knew she should have remained silent.

'Six strokes on his backside,' Jake said, with a note of irritation in his voice.

Kim saw that she had no choice. Her adventure would end right here if she didn't obey. She raised her arm and slashed the tawse down across Adam's buttocks. The blow glanced off harmlessly.

'No, much harder than that,' Nina snapped. She grabbed the tawse from Kim's hand and cut it down across his arse. There was a loud thwack. Adam grunted, trying to suppress the sound by burying his mouth in the sheet. 'Like that,' Nina said, handing the tawse back.

Kim raised the leather again. This time she used her full strength to lash it down across his buttocks. There was another loud thwack and the firm muscle vibrated.

'Much better,' Jake said. He caught hold of Nina and pulled her into his arms, kissing her fully on the mouth. Kim was not sure whether she should stop or wait until their embrace had ended. 'Get on with it,' Jake answered her unspoken question, breaking the kiss for a moment.

Thwack! Adam grunted again.

Thwack! The sound seemed to reverberate around the room. The funny thing was that Kim remembered exactly how she had felt as the whip had landed on her flesh, and her body was reacting now as if it were her and not the prone man lying on the bed, that was receiving this treatment. Her buttocks were tingling and her clitoris was pulsing just as they had at the club.

She looked back at Jake and Nina, who were still entwined in each other's arms, Jake's left hand caressing her buttocks.

'Go on,' he said, pulling away from the brunette again.

Thwack! Kim landed the tawse on the meat of Adam's buttocks. His whole arse was already a bright red with little thin lines that had turned almost scarlet.

Thwack! The impact on his body was matched by the impact on her own. Deep inside her sex each stroke had produced a sharp contraction. She hesitated, not knowing whether the first stroke she'd muffed counted towards the total.

'One more,' Jake said, again seeming to read her thoughts.

Kim raised the tawse again, not at all reluctantly this time. She slashed it down, watching his flesh vibrate and feeling her sex contract so powerfully she gave a little gasp of delight.

The exclamation was not missed by Nina. 'It's all right,' she said, sidling over to Kim's side. 'It has the same effect on all of us. Masochism and sadism are two sides of the same coin. Flip it and this is what you get.' She snatched the tawse and slapped it down hard against Kim's bottom. Kim squealed, but the woman had proved her point; the excitement the slap caused was just as acute as the feelings she'd felt only a few seconds before when administering a beating.

'Put your hands out in front of you,' Jake said. He'd

gone back to the chest of drawers and taken out a pair of heavily padded leather cuffs. As Kim presented her hands he wrapped the cuffs around her wrists and strapped them on securely.

'She has got a lovely arse,' Nina said, stroking Kim's buttocks.

'Over here,' Jake said.

He was pointing to a spot by the wall on the other side of the bedside chest. There was a brass hook hanging from a short thick lever that projected from a vertical slit in the wall. The arm was positioned at the base of the slit, at just above head height.

Jake pulled Kim's wrists up, fastening the sturdy central link of the cuffs onto the hook, so her arms were held above her head. He operated a small switch on the bedside chest and, with a whirring of electric motors the arm began to move up, pulling Kim's wrists with it. Jake did not stop its progress until she was stretched on tiptoe.

'All right, Adam,' Jake said, smiling confidently. 'It's her turn now.'

Adam got to his feet. He had a large erection, though his foreskin was still stretched tautly over his glans. Nina handed him the tawse. 'Does it hurt?' she asked, spitefully smoothing a hand over his buttocks so vigorously it made him wince. She took hold of his cock and jerked the foreskin back, then rubbed a fingertip across the tip of it, making the turgid stalk twitch. She drew him closer, wrapped her arms around his back, then closed her legs around his phallus, trapping it between her thighs and rubbing them together. 'Can you feel how hot and wet I am?' she breathed.

'Y-yes, mistress,' he blurted.

She stepped back, unknotted the white rope from his

wrists and pushed him towards Kim.

Without any hesitation Adam raised the leather strap. He swung it down onto Kim's buttocks with all his power. She felt a line of fire erupt across her poor bottom, just as she had at the club. But then she hadn't known what her reaction would be. Now she knew exactly what to expect. What is more, her body was already primed and ready. The fiercely burning pain turned in less than seconds to a pleasure so intense she felt her sex clench and her clitoris squirm. He struck again, and was not going easy on her. Perhaps the pain she'd inflicted on him made him that much more determined. But however hard he hit her, the pain was followed by an equal and opposite sensation of ferocious pleasure. Her buttocks were alight now, the heat they were generating radiating through her body. She was trembling from head to toe, her nipples and her breasts, her belly and the soft tissue of her labia, all stinging with raw sensitivity. The steady beating continued relentlessly. The position of her arms made her shoulders and back ache, and every stroke put more pressure on them as she was knocked off her feet, hanging from the hook, until she could stretch her leg out again and get a toe to the floor. But the pain and discomfort only increased her excitement.

'That's enough,' Jake eventually ordered.

Adam stopped immediately.

'I like this one,' Nina cooed. 'Is she new?' She sidled close to Kim and hooked a finger into the leather collar, pulling her head back with it so she could stare into her eyes.

'Very new,' Jake confirmed.

'And how long have you got her for?'

'The usual six months. If you get a place of your own

141

you can bid for her at the next auction.'

'Has she been with a woman?' Nina's dark eyes were smouldering as she spoke.

'She has been with women, so I gather. But this is her first time in the system. Audrey suggested her. Do you remember Audrey?'

'Not really.' Nina was obviously too interested in the trussed girl to bother about trivialities. She leant forward and planted her lips upon Kim's, while snaking a hand down her back and over her curvaceous buttocks. Kim gasped as the fingers played over the tender flesh. 'She's such a sensitive little thing,' Nina sighed, her soft lips still lightly touching Kim's. 'She's not hardened like some of your bitches.'

'I thought you wanted to watch,' said Jake, ignoring the dig.

'I do.' With evident reluctance she broke away from the girl, opened a drawer of the bedside chest, and took out a little foil-wrapped packet. Kim strained to watch as she tore the packet open, beckoned Adam forward with a finger, then rolled the condom over his erection. The cream rubber was much thicker than usual versions, and made his phallus appear smooth and uniform.

'Fuck her, Adam,' Jake said simply and casually.

The male slave stepped forward eagerly and gripped Kim's hips from behind. She felt his erection nudging between the cleft of her buttocks. Every sexual experience she'd had since she arrived in New York had been bizarre, but this surely was the most extraordinary. That didn't mean it was any less exciting. As Adam's cock slid down between her wet labia she felt a huge surge of arousal. The whipping had created a gigantic need that was about to be satisfied.

Adam bucked his hips, directing his cock to the mouth of her vagina. It nestled into the opening, then thrust forcefully inside, so forcefully that Kim was knocked off her feet again, face and breasts squashed up against the wall, his cock buried in her so deeply she could feel his balls nudging between her thighs. Her sex spasmed, clenching around the rigid invader like a vice.

He didn't pause. He began working his hips furiously, pounding in and out of her like a power hammer, his fingers clawing at her hips, pulling her back onto him as he thrust forward.

Kim began to moan. His cock was hard and hot, and much more slippery than it would have been had it not been coated in rubber. She could feel her own juices running down the prophylactic. Every forward stroke was knocking her off her feet just like the tawse had done, so she was hanging from her wrists. But though this created waves of pain in her shoulders, it also created waves of indescribable pleasure too. His belly thrusting against her reddened bottom was having exactly the same effect. She knew she was going to come and there was nothing she could do to stop herself; the feelings were simply overwhelming. She felt her clit spasm and a jolt like an electric shock coursed through her body. She went rigid, her head thrown back, her eyes shut tightly.

'That's enough,' Jake said, a note of satisfaction in his voice.

Adam stopped at once and pulled away, Kim whimpering as his cock was withdrawn. She opened her moistened eyes and managed to get the toes of the high heels back on the floor, the relief this brought to her tortured shoulders and arms almost as great a pleasure as the climax she'd just had.

'Get over here.' Jake's voice again. Kim raised her weary head. He was lying on the bed with his legs spread apart, with Nina kneeling at his side. She was holding the small dildo that had been buried in her anus, and coating it with some oily cream from a glass jar. Satisfied that it was well lubricated she moved it down between Jake's legs, and pressed it into the little puckered crater of his arse. She straddled his hips, using her other hand to grasp his cock and direct that into the sticky wet mouth of her vagina. Then, very slowly she allowed herself to sink down on him, and at exactly the same time and with the same pace, pushed the dildo into his anus.

Kim saw Jake's face crease with pleasure. As Nina pulled her hand away from the dildo Jake drew his legs together to hold it in place. His eyes closed and he gave a little grunt of contentment.

Adam apparently knew what was required of him. He climbed up onto the bed and crouched behind Nina. Taking his rubber-covered erection in his hand, the rubber glistening with Kim's juices, he guided it down between her pert buttocks.

'Yessss,' Nina urged, peering over her shoulder at him.

Kim saw him nudge his cock into her anus. There appeared to be no resistance, but as the phallus slid forward Nina gave an odd keening yelp and shuddered.

The three-headed monster on the bed began to undulate. Jake bucked to force his cock in and out of Nina as Adam did the same, not alternating their inward thrusts, but co-ordinating them. Adam used both hands to grasp Nina's breasts, squashing them back against her chest. The film star moaned and whimpered, throwing her head back. Adam freed one hand and gathered her long black tresses in it, pulling her head back even further, like a rider trying to reign in a horse.

Kim struggled against her bonds. She felt terribly left out, her orgasm not enervating her but leaving her wanting more. Not only could she see what Nina was experiencing, she seemed to feel it too. She knew exactly what it felt like to have two cocks buried in her body, and every thrust by the men produced a wave of feeling in her own sex. But it was not only a physical torture – watching what was happening on the bed and not being able to join in – but a mental one. Jake Ashley had hardly used her at all, and apart from allowing her to suck briefly on his cock he had shown no inclination to use her either. She desperately wanted to feel that hard, gnarled phallus plunging inside her. She wanted to be his slave.

Nina's cries were reaching a crescendo, the two cocks screwing into her with relentless ferocity. She was pushing back and down on them with quite as much energy, sweat rolling down her back, the loose hairs that had escaped Adam's grasp plastered across her face. Her arms were stretched out in front of her, hands clawing at Jake's shoulders. Finally, with every muscle in her body strained and rigid, she yelled for them to stop. Instantly both men did exactly that.

Nina shook her head, freeing her hair from Adam's clutches. Kim saw Nina panting for breath, her chest rising and falling violently. She pushed down on both phalluses, but then did nothing else, her body in stasis, waiting for her orgasm to break. Suddenly she threw her head back and ground her hips from side to side, squirming against both men.

'Oh God…' she hissed. Then she gave a loud, piercing scream. Her climax raked through her body, every muscle quivering. For a long moment she stayed like that, her muscles locked, her head thrown back and her eyes screwed shut. Then the tension melted away and she collapsed on top of Jake, no energy left to support herself.

She rested for a moment, sandwiched between the two men, allowing all the little tremors of orgasm to play through her body. But it was not long before she recovered.

'Off,' she said to Adam. The male slave pulled his cock from her. The rubber was dripping with her juices. 'Cut her down,' she said.

As Adam scrambled to his feet, Nina pulled herself off Jake. She knelt at his side and kissed him full on the mouth, crushing their lips together, while she gripped his cock and wanked it aggressively. 'Having fun, sweetness?' she said, breaking away. Before he could answer she dipped her head down to his belly and swallowed his erection, taking the whole thing into her mouth so deep her lips were nestled in his pubic hair. He opened his legs so she could thrust the dildo deeper into his arse.

Adam operated the switch on the bedside chest. The brass arm descended, lowering the hook. Adam detached the cuffs from it and allowed Kim to lower her arms. They had been stretched above her head for so long they were weak and almost completely numb.

'Take the cuffs off her and bring her over here,' Nina said, straightening up.

Adam unbuckled the leather cuffs and let them fall to the floor. Kim discovered her legs were having trouble supporting her weight, and she staggered to the bed with Adam's arms around her for support.

'On your knees, here,' Nina ordered abruptly.

Kim looked at Jake. She was gratified to see that he was staring at her body, his eyes focussed on the smooth black basque cinched so tightly around her waist. She dropped to her knees on the mattress and Nina reached forward, took both her cheeks in her hands and kissed her on the mouth, crushing their lips together as enthusiastically as she had with Jake. Then, without breaking the kiss, she pushed Kim back on the bed and rolled on top of her, ironing her luscious flesh against her. Being embraced by a woman was still a new enough experience for Kim to find it overwhelming, the planes and angles of a woman's body completely different from a man. As her tongue explored Kim's mouth, Nina forced her thigh between Kim's legs, spreading them apart. She pushed it up until it was hard against her sex and Kim could feel her labia being squashed and the copious juices that leaked out of her sex smearing across Nina's smooth flesh.

The woman angled her thigh slightly and flexed her muscle so it ground against Kim's clitoris, producing a huge jolt of pleasure. Despite her orgasm, or perhaps exactly because of it, the frustration she had felt at watching Nina take the two men was extreme. Every nerve in her body seemed to be alive and crawling with need. Nina's artful body, the way she squirmed her chest so their rock hard nipples were dragged from side to side while using the same rhythm to rub her thigh subtly across her clitoris, made matters worse. Kim had never been so turned on. She could still feel the impression of Adam's cock in her sex, like a key pressed into soap, and she needed that again.

And she got it. She got more than that.

Nina rolled her onto her side. Instantly Kim felt Jake moving up behind her, spooning his body into hers, his hard wet cock butting into her bottom. Clearly he was in no mood for further delay either. He wrapped his arms around her and pushed his hands down between the two women until they were cupping Kim's breasts. She felt his fingers pinching at her nipples and moaned loudly as new waves of pleasure coursed through her.

'Sensitive, isn't she?' he murmured.

'Very,' agreed Nina, huskily.

Nina kissed Kim again, her vibrant tongue plunging into her mouth, their lips mashed together. Jake stabbed with his hips. His cock lanced between Kim's legs. With unerring accuracy it found the mouth of her vagina and thrust up into it, her natural lubrication so generous it was able to plunge right up to the hilt without the slightest resistance. It was hot, incredibly hot, like a red-hot poker. She felt her sex convulse and was sure it had produced yet another gushing torrent of juices. He screwed his hips forward as if to get it as deep as it would go.

Kim could not believe the sensations that were assailing her. Jake's body was hard; his chest and belly and legs as hard as the cock that was buried inside her. In complete contrast Nina felt soft and melting, her pliant breasts melding into her own.

Kim was already coming. Every nerve in her body was exploding with pleasure. She seemed to be able to feel every inch of Jake's cock, the bulbous glans and the jutting ridge at its base, and the long gnarled shaft, the silky wet flesh of her vagina clinging to it. Her pleasure seemed to be renewing itself from microsecond to microsecond almost as if she were having orgasm after orgasm, the feeling so intense she could not think any more – only feel.

For minutes, or was it hours? Jake stayed like this, not moving his cock at all, content to leave it inside her. But then somewhere in the miasma of sensation she was experiencing she felt it withdraw. She started to protest, but before she could actually say anything the wet glans was poking into the hollow of her anus. It was so wet here again there was no resistance and she felt him plunging into the depths of her smaller, tighter passage. This only provoked a new set of delights. The pain was intense, more intense than the last time, but her arousal was so extreme that the gap between the wave of pain and the exquisite and unique pleasure that followed was almost non-existent. She couldn't say it made her come because she was already in the throes of an orgasm, but it kicked her to new heights, her body rippling with ecstasy.

And it wasn't over yet. Grasping her body tightly in his arms, Jake rolled over onto his back, so Kim was lying supine on top of him. Her pleasure had forced her eyes closed, but this manoeuvre made her open them. Through hazy vision she saw Nina signalling to Adam, who was kneeling on the bed again. Quickly he positioned himself over Kim and directed his cock between her labia. With Jake underneath her sex was angled up towards the slave and his glans slid down to her vagina.

'No…' she cried. But she realised immediately that she didn't mean it.

'Do it,' Nina ordered firmly.

Adam thrust forward. His rubber-covered cock glided effortlessly into Kim. She didn't suppose she would ever forget that feeling. Jake's throbbing cock was filling her anus, stretching the tender flesh. And now, right alongside it and only separated from it by the thinnest of membranes, she felt another virile and demanding penis invading her. Two cocks. The words echoed in her head just as they had at the club.

Again there was pain. And again there was ecstatic

pleasure. This time the rapture she felt was not an extension of her orgasm but an entirely new one; an orgasm so sharp it made her scream, tossing her head from side to side.

She knew Jake was coming. He pumped in and out of her a few times then thrust back as deep as he could go. His penis began to spasm violently. In seconds jets of hot spunk were spattering into her. She whimpered with delight. But the orgasmic convulsions of Jake's cock squashed so closely against Adams made the slave come too. Kim felt Adam's phallus pulse just as violently, though with the thick condom covering it she could not feel his semen. But it didn't matter. The sensation of both men jerking and twitching in the tight confines of her body was enough to send her into another orgasm, as high and as deep as anything she had yet experienced.

She wasn't at all sure what happened next. Her body was so sensitised, so open and electrified every new feeling brought a cascade of pleasure so extreme her mind refused to take it all in. She felt herself being lifted and laid on the bed. She saw Nina sucking at Jake's cock, hoovering up the drops of spunk that still clung to it. Then the woman was straddling her shoulders, pressing her sex down on her lips, while she bent forward and sucked eagerly on Kim's labia.

Kim managed to look across at Jake who was kneeling now, his eyes looking back at her, staring at her, their hypnotic quality as strong as ever. She would do anything for him, she knew.

Anything.

He was her master now.

Chapter Seven

There were sixty-one panels cladding the longest walls and thirty-two on the other two. Kim had counted them all three or four times. There was nothing else to do.

She had been taken back to her cell by Marsha and stripped of the basque, stockings and shoes. Marsha had said nothing, giving her no indication of what was likely to happen next. When she left the door was locked securely. Kim had showered, curled up on the thin mattress, and gone straight to sleep.

She had no idea what time Marsha had arrived next morning with her breakfast, but again the major-domo said nothing, silently laying the tray on the floor and leaving, the door once again locking behind her.

Eating the meal had proved to be the high spot of the morning. Kim had written and rewritten her story over and over again in her head. It would undoubtedly be front page news all over the world. She sat trying to reel off Nina Berry's many credits. It seemed extraordinary that the woman she had seen in so many films, the woman who had kissed and caressed so many men on the big screen, had actually kissed and caressed her so intimately, let alone that she was involved with Jake Ashley.

But after she had mentally drafted the story and memorised every word of it there was simply nothing else to do. She certainly had plenty of time to consider her own feelings. She had never really thought of herself as someone who had any secret sexual fantasies. Sex to her had always been a straightforward business. She liked to think she had chosen her lovers well and had always picked men who were strong and able sexually, and who made sure they did not take their own pleasure first before seeing to hers. She had never entertained the least desire to indulge in games of masters and slaves with any of them, which was why she found it so astonishing that she should respond so unequivocally to such treatment.

She wondered what would have happened if she hadn't picked up one of Jake Ashley's books. Would this well of sexual desire have remained untapped? Or would it have gradually begun to assert itself. She worried that perhaps she was responding to an impulse that the books had created rather than one that had always been buried deep inside her. But she could not believe that what she had experienced last night could be based on such a superficial fancy. The fact that her responses had been so profound was surely an indication that the idea of total submission and the bondage it seemed inevitably to entail, reached deep into her psyche, though why or how it did she hadn't the faintest idea.

Being left alone with nothing to do was part of the conditioning new slaves were exposed to. She knew that from his books. Being naked she was constantly aware of her body. Her labia, her anus, her buttocks and her nipples were all sore and tingled every time she moved, making it impossible to forget the sexual agenda. That was exactly what the slaves in Jake's books had felt.

She had an almost irresistible desire to masturbate. She would have loved to stick three fingers deep into her sex while her other hand frotted at her clit, crudely and energetically. It would only have taken a matter of seconds to make her come. But she resisted the temptation. The trouble was, there was nowhere in the room or in the alcove that formed the shower room, where she could hide from the two mirrors, one opposite the door and one over the washbasin, and she had a feeling they were like eyes that watched her constantly.

They probably were.

In the books the slaves' cells had all been equipped with hidden video cameras, the master being able to observe all his slaves by switching channels on televisions in his study, and his bedroom.

But it wasn't only that. Though she'd not been told she mustn't touch herself, doing so felt like disobedience. She belonged to him now. It was up to him when and if she took her pleasure. She did not want him to see her masturbating.

Where her need to get away and file her story fitted into that scenario she wasn't at all sure. Since she'd arrived in New York her sexual agenda seemed to have taken over everything. Of course her professional mission had changed; a profile of the reclusive writer was one thing – a story involving him with Nina Berry quite another. If she was thinking purely of her professional career she should perhaps have looked for the first opportunity to get out of there. But the thought of running away appalled her. And Audrey had spoken of other prominent people; businessmen and politicians. She should certainly try to stick around for a few more days to find out if that claim was true. At least that gave her the professional excuse she was looking for to justify the fact that she had no intention of leaving – just yet.

Hopefully after a few days, she told herself, she might become inured to the effects of whatever she was reacting to so strongly, and would no longer be in its thrall. She had always thought of herself as a modern, liberated and independent woman, and the thought that she should actually allow herself to become literally enslaved to a man appalled her on an intellectual level. But her body appeared to be unencumbered by such precepts. She had to be careful not to think too much about exactly what had happened last night, for fear of provoking another bout of feelings that created an itch in her sex she would find hard not to scratch.

So instead she counted.

She counted the wooden planes, and the numbers of nails, and the buttons in the mattress. She tried to remember nursery rhymes and the plots of her favourite movies.

Eventually she heard footsteps outside the door. The key ground in the lock.

It was Marsh again, holding another tray of food and the same holdall. 'Eat this, shower and get ready,' she said brusquely, and then stared into Kim's lap. 'And you'll need to shave down there, too. Make sure you're completely smooth.' She placed the tray on the floor, dropped the holdall on the bed, then left, slamming and locking the door again.

Kim hadn't realised how hungry she was. She picked up an apple and munched it eagerly as she emptied the contents of the bag onto the bed. There was a pair of black hold ups with a black lace welt, and a lacy almost transparent body. Naturally the gusset of the body had been removed. The shoes were just as high as she had worn last night, with tapering heels. There was a pair of long black lace gloves and a thick leather belt, attached to each side of which were two short chains, each secured to a metal handcuff. The make-up case was also in the bag.

The food consisted of cold chicken, vegetables and fruit, with a large jug of water and two bread rolls. Kim eagerly consumed it all. She was so ravenous she thought it was probably later than she'd imagined, early evening rather than mid-afternoon.

Beneath the hot cascading shower she felt her excitement bringing to increase. She wasn't thinking about her story now – only what Jake Ashley had in mind for her. All the slaves in his books had one single aim; to spend as much time with the master as they possibly could, no matter what indignities he heaped upon them. Kim realised that was precisely what she felt. But she knew too, that if the way this house was run was a model for the 'chateau' in the books, she, like the fictional slaves, could be sadly disappointed.

She took the razor she'd found on the washbasin and lathered up her mons and labia, carefully shaving the delicate area. The process of doing this aroused her further.

Kim made herself up in the strong colours that had been provided, using more than the usual amount of mascara and eye-liner as well as the darker tone of eye shadow, applied a thick coat of the ruby-red lipstick, then covered that with lip gloss. She wormed into the tight body, which had been woven with lycra to give it a clinging quality, the bodice pressing her breasts back slightly though giving them no support. The black stockings were sheer, with a fully-fashioned heel and a seam. She rolled them up her long legs, strapped on the shoes, the heels increasing her height dramatically, then pulled on the lacy gloves, which reached almost to her armpits. She had noticed the effect the stockings had on her legs, highlighting the creamy flesh above them, and the gloves had the same effect on her arms, the two or three inches of flesh above them appearing as soft as the nap of a peach.

Finally she buckled the belt in place. It was tight and cinched her waist noticeably. The two metal cuffs hung down, one either side, clinking against the chain when she moved.

Inspecting herself in the mirror, she could see the outline of her breasts and her nipples beneath the lace. Though the gusset of the body had been cut away it revealed little of her mons. Only when she opened her legs was it obvious that her sex was exposed.

She sat on the bed and waited.

She did not have long to wait. The door opened and Marsha strode in. As usual, she was wearing leather, this outfit a catsuit that covered her body like a second skin. It was so tight the leather had folded itself into the crease of her sex.

'Up,' she said, pulling Kim to her feet. With what was obviously practised ease she grabbed Kim's wrists one by one and snapped the cuffs around them, making it impossible for her to raise her arms more than a few inches, either upward or outward. She pushed Kim around so she did a pirouette. 'Not bad,' she mused, caressing Kim's buttocks. 'Remember the rules tonight,' she warned. 'Now follow me.'

Out in the narrow corridor Kim saw most of the other cell doors were open. As Marsha led her upstairs she thought she could hear music and the sound of voices – like a distant party.

On the ground floor they walked through an area of the house Kim had not seen before. A wide corridor opened onto a large sitting room. There was a clock on the mantelpiece, and Kim noticed it was ten o'clock. No wonder she'd been so hungry.

There were grand French windows that opened onto the patio and swimming pool she'd seen from the kitchen. The patio had been decorated with huge terracotta pots, replicas of Roman antiquities, which were filled with all manner of exotic flowers that spilled over onto the ground. To one side an extravagant buffet had been laid out, and there were cast-iron chairs and tables adorned with white linen tablecloths and silver candlesticks, the candles flickering gently in the lightest of breezes.

There were about twenty people milling about. Most had finished eating and only a couple still sat, toying with coffee or *petit fours*. The rest had dispersed around the pool, chatting in groups or sitting on luxurious loungers. The male guests wore black tie, while the women wore the sort of outfits Kim had seen at the *Velvet Tongue*, though most wore lace, satin and silk, rather than the more outré rubber or leather garments she had seen. The costumes were nevertheless boarding on the obscene, the dresses often revealing more than just glimpses of thigh, buttocks and breasts.

Among the guests were six slaves, four women and the two men. The women were dressed in identical costumes to Kim, apart from the fact that two of the lace bodies and stockings were red, two white, and two black, though the belts to which their hands were chained were all black. Kim recognised Adam and the man she had worked with in the kitchen. They both wore leather harnesses; a series of belts which crossed their chest and followed the line of their pelvis down between their legs, but left their genitals bare. Both had large erections, their cocks strapped into another harness; a narrow strap with two thinner loops around their balls, stretching the skin of the scrotum tightly.

Marsha pushed Kim forward.

One of the women turned to face them. 'This one's new, isn't she?' she said elaborately.

'Yes, Ms Daniels,' Marsha answered. 'She only came in the day before yesterday.'

'My God, I recognise her now. She was in the auction. I wanted the blonde, but I took quite a fancy to this one, too.' The woman was nearer fifty than forty, and was wearing a gaudy black silk dress, the tight bodice pushing her breasts together, the neckline low enough to reveal the upper semicircle of her dark areolae. She raised icy fingers and stroked the back of them against Kim's flushed cheek.

'Well, she's quite something.' A man had crept up behind Kim, and pinched her buttocks hard enough to make her emit a little squeal. 'What's she called?'

'Kim,' Marsha told them.

'Lovely,' the man grunted into Kim's ear.

'Mmm...' the woman concurred.

The man examined her back appreciatively, then walked around to her front. Kim didn't have to be an expert in American politics to recognise him. Senator Tom Beddoes was one of the most influential figures in the Republican party, and was constantly appearing on television to give his views on what the current administration was doing wrong.

'If you'll excuse me.' Marsha moved quietly away.

'Of course honey-pie, you've got other fish to fry,' the Senator said after her, without taking his roaming eyes off the delicious slave standing meekly before him. He was a big man – tall with a large belly. His face was deeply wrinkled with heavy jowls. He eyed her lecherously, concentrating on her breasts.

It was a balmy night, with only the hint of a breeze, and

the air was scented by the fragrant flowers.

'She's new, Tom,' the woman said, licking her heavy lips.

'Really?' he said, his eyes still glued to Kim's cleavage. 'That's exactly what I like.' He raised a hand and stroked her shoulder. 'Maybe I'll see you later, Kim,' he added, and to her surprise, walked away. She watched as he approached one of the male slaves, who was standing with a rather gaunt woman wearing a spangle studded evening dress. The Senator wrapped his arm around the slave's shoulders and began talking earnestly to the women.

Kim was already rewriting her story for the umpteenth time. Nina Berry and Senator Tom Beddoes! It just got better and better. She looked around to see if Nina was there, but couldn't see her. And she couldn't see Jake Ashley either, for that matter.

Another woman approached. She had harshly dyed blonde hair, and was wearing a yellow halter-necked backless blouse with a pair of voluminous culottes made from black chiffon. The chiffon was largely transparent and Kim could see her belly and her legs, her pubes covered by a tiny triangle of black satin.

'Got your eye on her, have you Georgy?' she said to the other woman, who was still studying Kim with an avaricious glint in her eye. The blonde cupped Kim's chin in one hand and squeezed, so her glossed lips peeled open into an inviting O. Kim instinctively tried to raise a protective hand, but the chain on the belt thwarted her.

'Not particularly well trained, is she?' the blonde said disapprovingly. 'You've got to learn to take what's given, sweetie.' The possessive hand dropped to Kim's breasts, and manicured fingers deliberately pinched a nipple, making Kim gasp. But this time she made no attempt to defend herself.

'How's Arnold?' the other woman asked.

'Waiting for the big event, as usual,' the blonde said conversationally. 'He always hopes he'll get lucky, but he never has so far… Do you mind if I take her?'

'No, I don't mind,' the other woman replied. 'I think I'm more into men tonight – I get enough pussy at home.' She looked deeply into Kim's eyes, and added, 'But I will enjoy her… soon.'

The blonde gripped Kim's arm and guided her across the patio. As they moved amongst the guests Kim noticed that the woman standing next to the Senator had begun to play with the slave's erection. She appeared to be pointing something out, and the Senator looked down at it critically. The woman then said something to the slave, though Kim could not hear what it was. The slave dropped to his knees as the woman unzipped the Senator's flies and fished around inside. To Kim's utter astonishment she then pulled his flaccid cock out and fed it into the male slave's open mouth. As she did so she kissed the Senator full on the lips, pulling his hand up to her bosom.

But they were not the only guests who had decided to become more intimate. On one of the loungers a man was lying with his trousers around his ankles while a woman in a tight tube dress arranged a female slave on top of him, her legs straddling his body. The woman guided his standing erection into the slave's sex, the crotchless lace body providing easy access.

'Look what I've got for you,' the blonde said, interrupting Kim's spinning thoughts. 'This is my husband, sweetie.'

They had stopped in front of a tall and attractive man with a deeply tanned face and thick black hair. He was standing with a woman in a dark blue satin dress, and one of the female slaves. The slave's lace body and stockings and shoes were white.

'Mmm... very nice,' the man said. 'Is she the last one out?'

'Guess so.'

'Let's see you two together then,' he suggested.

The girl in white immediately turned to Kim, caught hold of her bound hands and pulled her close. She used her tongue to lick Kim's lower lip, then crushed their mouths and their bodies together. She had small breasts but large hard nipples, and Kim could feel them pressing against her own. Up to now she had felt detached and uninvolved in what was going on, too busy mentally writing the new version of her story to include the details of Senator Beddoes' behaviour. But the girl's mouth and eager tongue, and her sinuous body, were changing all that. She felt the familiar signs of arousal emanating from her sex.

'Come on, sweetie,' the blonde admonished Kim huskily. 'You're not supposed to just stand there.'

The truth was that Kim wasn't at all sure what she was supposed to do. She had not expected any of this. She had expected to be taken again to Jake, and perhaps Nina. But she remembered that Marsha had told her she must obey the orders of Jake's guests, so she returned the kiss with as much enthusiasm as she could muster. It was an extraordinary sensation; a few days ago she had never kissed a woman sexually, but now, standing amongst a group of strangers, she was doing it to a girl she didn't even know, wearing a costume that hid so little she might as well have been naked. But if somewhere in her mind a voice was telling her this was all terribly wrong, her body had no such reservations, responding with unequivocal arousal.

'He's here,' the man said.

Everyone on the patio stopped what they were doing and began to applaud. The lovely slave girl let go of Kim's hands and stepped back. Jake Ashley had appeared on the patio. He was wearing a white suit with a white shirt, tie and shoes. He raised his hands to silence the reserved clapping.

'I hope you're all having a wonderful time,' he said grandly.

There was a general hum of confirmation.

'Well, you're all familiar with the next event on the agenda,' he went on. He made a signal and Marsha emerged. She was holding a chain like a dog leash in one hand, attached to a leather collar around the neck of a girl who was naked apart from a skin-tight red leather helmet that had been laced tightly around her head. The girl's long flaming red hair had been pulled through the back of the lacing and flowed down over her shoulders. The helmet had holes for the girl's mouth, nose and eyes, but there were flaps over the latter that had been pulled down to make an effective blindfold. Both her nipples had been pierced and a chain was looped down between the two gold nipple rings. Her breasts were pear-shaped and pendulous and her mons was shaved.

'Some of you already know Nicole.' Jake Ashley was still addressing the gathered throng. 'And as she'll be leaving us next week, it falls to her to decide who will have the honour of performing for you all tonight.'

Kim saw the blonde glance expectantly towards her husband.

'Will those male guests who want to take part step

162

forward, please,' Jake requested. Six men, including the blonde's husband, the Senator, and the man on the lounger, moved forward, making no attempt to cover up there erections, which jutted from their flies. They formed a straight line on the patio.

While this was going on Marsha rounded up the slaves, male and female, and stood them in another line facing the men. Kim noticed that three of the girls had a small blue tattoo on their right buttock, two letters in an elaborate script fitted into the middle of the roundel: JA. They were identical to the one she had seen on Candy's bottom.

'Right, I think we're ready,' Jake announced.

Marsha walked up to the redhead, picked up her leash again, led her to the line of men, then unclipped the leash from the collar.

'Okay Nicole, you may begin,' Jake said.

The girl knew exactly what to do. She took three tentative steps forward, her hands weaving about in front of her. Her left hand came into contact with the first man and she turned to him, blindly touching his face and body. Then she groped her way down to the next. The third man in line was the Senator, and when her hands fell on his jutting phallus she gave a little mew of appreciation, taking it in both hands and squeezing it firmly. None of the men moved or said a word.

'All right, now you must choose, Nicole,' Jake said, when the girl had reached the end of the line. She fumbled her way back along the expectant queue. Kim saw the first man's face fall as she passed him and went on to the second. He too was disappointed as she passed on to the Senator. But this time she stopped.

She tapped him on the shoulder.

'I choose him,' she said clearly, staring blindly at his

chest.

'Well thank you, pussy,' he breathed. 'Thank you, thank you, thank you.' The Senator looked very pleased with himself, beads of sweat glistening on his heavy features.

Marsha moved silently forward and led Nicole over to the line of slaves. This time Nicole went down behind the line, groping their thighs and buttocks. Kim was the fourth to receive this treatment, the girl's fingers pinching her bottom and flitting momentarily up between her thighs. At the end of the line she stopped, but did not start to come back again as she had done with the male guests.

'Number four,' the girl decided.

Kim didn't realise this meant her, until she saw the sleazy Senator eyeing her with lascivious interest. 'Good choice, pussy,' he crooned, licking his thick lips. 'Good choice.'

Marsha led Kim around the pool, and the Senator followed. On the far side of the quietly lapping water was another area of patio, upon which was a raised circular dais. At its centre was a thick white mattress. The dais had a retaining wall around its perimeter, and Kim saw there were metal rings set in the brickwork at regular intervals. Alarmingly, too, there was a metal arch that spanned the dais, hanging from the centre of which, right over the middle of the mattress, was a metal hook on a sturdy metal chain. There were also two spotlights on either side of the arch, which were trained down, bathing the dais with bright light.

Marsha indicated that Kim should climb up, and she instantly obeyed, her heart beating so fast she could hear her pulse drumming in her ears. The rest of the guests, with the slaves in tow, began to follow them, fanning out around the dais in order to get a good view. It didn't take a lot of intelligence to work out what was going to happen next. Kim and the Senator were, as the blonde had put it, the main event.

The Senator and a plain woman stepped up onto the dais beside her. For some reason Kim had the feeling she was his wife. The Senator unzipped the woman's dress and pulled it off her shoulders, allowing it to fall away. She was wearing a tight black body in a slinky silk, and tan hold up stockings with a very thin welt, the elasticated rim digging a channel all the way around her thighs. The bodice of the body was lace, and struggled to contain her pulpy breasts.

Just then Marsha, apparently with little effort, lifted a wooden chest up onto the dais. The Senator's wife flipped it open.

'Oh yes, just right,' she enthused. She pulled out four leather cuffs and lengths of hemp rope.

'And you'll need this, Marsha said, taking a key from a pocket in her catsuit and handing it to the Senator. Quickly he unlocked the handcuffs, then stripped the leather belt away from Kim's waist. Kim rubbed her wrists where the metal had chaffed them, but was not allowed this opportunity for long, for the Senator's wife began buckling the leather cuffs around her wrists and ankles.

'Lie down now, sweet little pussy,' the Senator croaked, his excitement becoming more and more evident. He prodded her until she was standing by the mattress. Meekly she lay down, on her back. The Senator knelt hastily and stretched her left arm out while his wife ran a rope through the metal ring above Kim's head. Then she looped the rope through the D-ring on the leather cuff around Kim's wrist, pulling it taut so her arm was strained up and outward. She knotted the rope back on the ring again. A few minutes later Kim was spread-eagled helplessly across the dais, stretched like piano wire.

Apart from being able to raise her head or buttocks slightly from the mattress, Kim simply couldn't move. She was completely powerless. But her reaction to this bondage was unequivocal. Despite the unattractiveness of the Senator, she felt a pounding excitement as great as anything she had experienced previously. Her labia, exposed by the crotchless lace body, were stretched apart. She could feel her juices running, and was sure they were leaking out over her thighs.

But it was not only the bondage that was so arousing, she realised. It was the fact that everybody could see her tied, open and available. She had no will of her own. She was simply an object, an exhibit in a show – and for some reason she couldn't understand, that excited her as much as everything else.

'Look how wet she is, the little bitch,' the Senator's wife gloated to the audience.

'They're all like that,' Jake said. 'I thought you knew that by now.'

Kim lifted her head to see where he was.

The Senator's wife took a short leather whip from the chest. It had a tapering black lash, knotted at the tip. She trailed the knot down the length of Kim's body from her chin to her mons. When the leather snaked between her legs she gasped, even this faintest of touches enough to make her clitoris sing. She saw the Senator looming over her, hurriedly stripping his clothes off.

'Come on, Vanda, let's see some action,' he panted, as he frantically struggled out of his trousers and pants. Kim saw he had a large strawberry-shaped birthmark on the top of his right thigh. He was already erect. He took it in his fist and began to pump aggressively. His wife took a small pink dildo from the chest. Its shaft was gnarled and distressed, moulded to resemble a real penis. Extending from the flared base was a length of flex that was attached to a small rectangular box. She planted her feet on either side of Kim's head. The captive girl gazed up to her crotch, and felt a pang of desire. The woman's high heels stiffened the muscles of her calves. She opened her legs a little further and stooped to undo the gusset of the body. Kim couldn't tear her eyes from the bejewelled fingers working at the three poppers that held it in place. The delicate material peeled apart to reveal her sex, her puffy labia completely depilated of hair. They were already glistening juicily.

The Senator shuffled behind his wife. Through misty eyes Kim watched him stroke her mons. His middle finger delved down into the slit of her sex, and crooked up to her clitoris. Vanda moaned, her head lolling back onto her husband's chest.

'She's really something,' he grunted, gazing down at their trussed prize.

For a moment a silence hung over the all those gathered there, then Vanda lowered herself, squatting over Kim's face. Slowly she pressed her hairless sex down onto Kim's mouth. The supine girl instinctively extended her tongue, nudging it into the deep groove between the woman's labia, searching for her clit. It was large and swollen. Kim flicked at it with her tongue and felt it flex. Vanda stiffened and moaned.

A weight settled on the mattress by her side, but Vanda's smothering bottom obscured her sight. A hand, presumably the Senator's, began stroking her thigh, moving between the top of the stocking and the bare flesh above it. Vanda settled further and wriggled her hips from

167

side to side, rubbing her labia across Kim's mouth, her juices smearing the helpless girl's face. At the same time she leant forward slightly. Kim couldn't see what she was doing, but felt something cold and smooth slide between her sex lips. It was the tip of the dildo, she was sure of that.

Someone in the audience encouraged Vanda, upon which the little dildo thrust up into Kim's wet vagina until the flared based was pressed tightly against her labia. But it didn't stay there long. Vanda screwed the dildo around then withdrew it. She directed it down lower to the perfectly circular and puckered hole of Kim's anus. The lubrication it had gathered from her vagina made it slick, and as Vanda pressed Kim's sphincter only resisted momentarily, before allowing the dildo to slide home.

Kim moaned. Her anus contracted sharply. The muscles and sinews of her body, stretched out so tautly, seemed to give every pulse of pleasure a greater impact, her nerves on tenterhooks.

'Don't stop,' Vanda chided, settling down again.

Kim tried to concentrate on the woman's clit, her nose buried deep in Vanda's humid groin, the sticky sap of the woman leaking from it. The woman pressed down even harder, making it difficult for Kim to breathe, her face squeezed tightly between uncompromising thighs.

'Yes...' Vanda moaned, lifting her head, her eyes closed.

The weight on the mattress shifted again. Suddenly Kim saw the Senator's cock forcing its way between her heated face and his wife's sex. Vanda toppled forward, upending her vagina so he could plunge his cock into it, his balls flopping against Kim's chin.

'Suck them,' he grunted through clenched teeth.

Kim was spinning within a myriad of emotions.

'Come on,' he repeated angrily, 'suck them. Do as you're told.'

Kim closed her eyes, took a deep breath, and peeled her lips open, allowing one of his balls to nestle inside her mouth. She heard the Senator groan, his cock jerking violently and pulling against his scrotum. This in turn had a huge affect on Vanda, who reacted at once. She cried out, thrust her buttocks back against her husband so violently his balls were wrenched from Kim's mouth, and came, the muscles of her thighs clamping around Kim's head.

As soon as her crisis had passed the Senator pulled out of her and disappeared from Kim's sight. Slowly Vanda rocked back onto her heels and got up.

Kim wearily raised her head. The Senator was standing over her, his erection spearing from his belly, glistening and wet. His wife squeezed it, making the glans swell even further.

Around the dais Jake's guests were devouring the action. But he stood aloof. He stared straight at Kim, that hypnotic gaze making her heart miss a beat.

The Senator moved and blocked her view. He knelt between her legs. The effort of keeping her head raised was too uncomfortable, and she let it fall back onto the mattress. She felt the Senator's weeping cock nudging into her sex. With her legs bound so far apart there was nothing she could do to stop it.

'The little bitch is begging for it,' he wheezed, his face red and sweating from the exertions. But instead of pushing deep he held himself there, the smooth wet glans poised between her equally wet labia.

'And so are you, aren't you?' his wife crowed. She picked up the whip again, positioned herself behind the bulky mass of her husband, raised her arm, and swiped the whip down onto his naked buttocks to a buzz of approval from the onlookers. The Senator's cock was propelled into Kim's sex, impaling her with one long penetration. She moaned as the breath was shunted from her lungs.

Vanda cut the whip down again, making the Senator's large buttocks quiver. The force of the initial penetration and the vibrations in her anus had already pitched her to the brink of orgasm. However debauched all this was, however much her mind told her she shouldn't be enjoying it, her body was registering pleasure that wiped away any shame.

Vanda rained the blows down, each one making the Senator shudder and thrust his cock evermore violently. He groaned loudly and Kim felt him throb inside her. A last violent swipe of the whip drove him fully into the depths of her vagina, where the vibrations from the dildo were most extreme. Kim felt a stream of spunk jetting into her, hot and thick, and as it did so she came too. Her natural reaction was to wrap her arms and legs around him, but when she tried to do this in the throes of her climax, the sharp reminder that she was bound and completely powerless gave her such a shock she came again. Her orgasm seemed to go on forever, her eyes clamped shut by its intensity.

She was only vaguely aware of the Senator pulling away, but then another sensation made her open her eyes with shock. Vanda had dropped to her knees and was greedily sucking her sex. Kim felt her tongue lapping, licking up the sticky spending of her husband. It was all too much. Kim felt herself coming again. She pulled at the bonds, not trying to free herself but wanting to feel the constriction. This time she screamed as the force of another orgasm overcame her…

Kim was exhausted, and lay for a long time with her eyes closed, concentrating on the little shocks of pleasure that still played through her body like orgasms in miniature. When she mustered enough strength to open her eyes and raise her head, both the Senator and his wife were gone.

The other guests had dispersed too – she was alone.

Chapter Eight

Kim woke with a start. Light was flooding into her cell from the corridor outside.

'Get up.'

The gruff voice was familiar. Kim squinted against the light. Marsha stood silhouetted in the doorway.

'Get up,' she repeated irritably. She looked as if she too had been roused from her bed, her muscular body wrapped in a white towelling robe.

Kim rose wearily. Marsha grabbed her wrists and snapped a pair of handcuffs around them. She pulled her forward and out along the corridor. All the other cell doors were closed. She had been taken back to her cell no more than an hour earlier and after a shower had fallen into a deep sleep. According to the clock up in the large hall area it was now two in the morning.

They walked upstairs, Kim's heart still pumping from the shot of adrenaline being woken so suddenly had caused. But her heart rate increased dramatically as they walked towards Jake's bedroom.

'Does he want me?' she asked.

'Be quiet,' Marsha snapped.

They arrived at the double bedroom doors. Marsha rapped once on the polished surface. 'Wait here,' she said, and walked away.

Kim waited.

Eventually the door opened. Jake Ashley stood there wearing a cream silk robe. 'Come in,' he said.

172

Kim walked into the bedroom and he shut the door behind her. There was no one else present. Remembering Marsha's instructions she began to get to her knees, but Jake put his hand on her arm to stop her.

'No need,' he said. 'I haven't yet had a chance to welcome you properly. With Nina here last night, and the party...' He sat in a thickly padded armchair opposite the bed. 'Come and stand in front of me.' He pressed his fingertips together, resting them against his lower lip.

Kim obeyed. The single motivation of all *Slaves of New York* was to spend time with their master, to be given the gift of his time and attention. It was the thought that dominated their every waking hour. Kim now knew exactly how they felt. She had never felt that about any other man. Jake's eyes examined her naked body carefully. 'Raise your arms above your head, Kim.'

Once again she obeyed immediately. She couldn't remember him using her name before, and it sounded completely different on his lips; exotic and alien.

Lifting her arms tightened her pectorals and raised her breasts. For long moments he studied them minutely.

'Sit in that chair,' he finally said, indicating a wing chair in black leather with button-backed upholstery.

He had not told her to lower her arms, so she sat with them still raised. Apparently this met with approval, as he smiled and said, 'Very good.'

For a moment he did nothing. She saw his eyes moving across her body. Deep in the folds of his robe she thought she saw a twitch of movement. The effort of keeping her arms raised was already beginning to make her muscles ache.

'I was sorry you were chosen this evening,' he said quietly. 'I'd have liked to hold you back, but the rules are

173

the rules.

'Where are you from?'

'D-Derbyshire,' she stammered, her mouth dry.

'A lovely part of the country. Most Americans don't have any conception of how beautiful England is. But I could never go back there, of course. The English are rather uptight about what they perceive to be pornography.

'This is your first time, isn't it?'

'Yes,' she said, though she wasn't sure what he meant. The first time she'd been chained to a dais and fucked by a man who was having his arse whipped? The first time the man's wife had sucked her? The first time a crowd of people had watched her?

'You should call me master,' he chided.

'I didn't know... I mean, no one said...'

'I know.' He smiled warmly. 'I'm not blaming you. Just do it.'

'Yes, master.' How many times had she read that in one of his books? It was an incantation to everything she had come to find so arousing. The words seemed to echo across the room, making her tremble.

'Keep your arms up, Kim,' he said. She had allowed them to bend slightly, trying to ease the pain in her muscles. She forced them back up immediately.

'So tell me how you got into this. Was it the books?' he prompted.

'Yes,' she replied honestly. 'I didn't know... I mean.' The pain in her muscles was getting worse. She knew she dare not lower her arms again, but the effort of keeping them raised was distracting her from what she was trying to say.

'Have you always been submissive?'

'No,' she said with conviction – then quickly

remembered to add, 'Master.'

'And how did you first discover that you actually are?'

'By... by reading your books, master.'

'They turned you on?'

'Yes, master, they did.' Giving simple answers was so much easier than trying to give explanations.

'And did you masturbate?'

The pain in her arms was becoming excruciating. They drooped, but she thrust them up again purposefully, producing a new wave of pain. But the pain was exciting. Already she felt that familiar throbbing deep in her sex.

'Yes, master.'

'Because of the scenes in my books?'

'Yes, master.'

'You imagined yourself as a slave?'

'Yes, master, I did.'

Jake got to his feet. A bulge distended the front of his robe. He walked to the bedside chest and opened the top drawer. Kim heard the metallic clink of what she thought might be a chain. He stood beside her chair and took hold of the central link of the handcuffs, pulling her arms up and taking the pressure off her muscles. Her body screamed with relief – but it was only temporary. When he released the handcuffs the effort to keep her arms up seemed to have doubled.

'Keep them up,' he warned calmly.

He slipped a hand into a pocket of his robe and withdrew a thin gold chain. Attached to either end of it was a small rectangle made from surgical steel. A bar cut across the middle of this rectangle. The bar could be moved up and down by means of a screw that passed through the bottom of the rectangle and had a tiny T-bar at the end to enable it to be turned easily.

Jake stooped down in front of her. She could smell the musky aroma of cologne she had detected before. She inhaled deeply, wanting to imprint it in her brain. He fitted the little rectangle over Kim's already hardened right nipple, so the puckered bud was trapped between the top of the frame and the movable bar. The metal was cold and made her nipple stiffen still further. He began turning the screw, tightening the bar until it bit into the tender flesh.

'Very good,' he said to himself.

A sharp pain in her nipple joined the aching torment in her muscles. He stooped again and fitted the rectangle on the other end of the chain over her left nipple, in the same way.

'Pretty,' he said, standing back to admire his work. He picked up the middle of the chain, which looped down between her cleavage, and pulled it up until her breasts were stretched out and pointing to the ceiling. Then he let go and her breasts fell back against her chest, both nipples stinging with pain.

Kim gasped and shuddered. 'Please...' she begged.

'Please what?' He picked up the chain again. If anything he pulled it higher this time, the metal clamps biting into the nipples even more deeply, her breasts stretched to the limit. He let go again, the pain from the release even worse than the stretching. Kim whimpered, desperately trying to keep her arms high above her head. Jake sat down again, moving his chair around slightly so he was directly facing her.

'Lower your arms and cup your breasts,' he instructed.

Kim gratefully did as he said. It was heaven. Her muscles sung with relief. She felt as if her arms were floating as she wrapped her hands under her breasts.

'I want you to put the chain in your mouth,' Jake said,

his voice steady and emotionless.

Kim took the chain and lifted it. It was short, and pulled her breasts upward. Now the pain from her arms had disappeared her body was free to concentrate on her trapped nipples, and she shuddered as the weight of her breasts tugged at them.

'Very good, Kim,' Jake encouraged.

He opened his robe and took his erection in his fist.

'Now hook your left leg over the arm of the chair.'

Kim did as directed. She could feel the wetness from her sex had smeared against the leather seat.

'Now the right,' he said. 'Scoot down to the edge.'

She hooked her right leg over the other arm and shuffled her bottom forward. In this position her thighs were splayed apart and he would be able to see every detail of her sex. She could feel her labia trembling.

'I want you to show me what you did,' he said.

'Show you?' The words were mumbled as she tried not to lose the chain from between her lips.

'I want you to masturbate for me.'

'No…' She dropped the chain, her breasts bobbing back. Just as it had at the auction, the idea horrified her. She had never let anyone see her private ritual.

'Yes!' Jake insisted sharply. 'I won't tell you again, Kim. Put the chain back in your mouth and begin. Do you use a dildo?'

Kim's mind wasn't functioning properly. She was completely flustered, her excitement at being alone with Jake and the extraordinary affect he had on her overwhelmed by the horror at what he was asking her to do. 'A – a dildo?' she spluttered.

'Yes, to masturbate. Do you ever use a vibrator?'

'Y-yes… master,' she admitted, her cheeks glowing red.

'B-but I…'

Jake quickly got to his feet. He went to the bedside chest again and took out a large black rubber phallus. He took it over to her. 'Like this…?'

Kim felt herself blushing even more. It was ridiculous, she told herself. She had been fucked by two men at the same time, whipped, exposed to all sorts of indignities, but the idea of allowing him to watch her while she brought herself off was just too awful.

'If you don't obey me you know what will happen,' he said sternly. 'Don't you?'

'Yes…' she said sulkily. 'Yes, master, I do.'

'Then do it. Do not defy me.'

He handed her the dildo, then took hold of the chain, pulling it up until he could feed it into her mouth. She gasped as the clamps bit into her nipples once more.

Jake sat down and took his cock in his hand again, wanking gently. 'Begin,' he said, nodding once.

Kim knew she had to obey. If she did not she would immediately be sent back to the city, and she was definitely not yet ready for that. She had enough to write a good story, but that had become almost the secondary reason for being there. She didn't want to be sent away because that would mean she would never see Jake Ashley again.

Tentatively, she slid her hands down to her belly. She pushed her right hand over her mons and let her middle finger slide into the crease of her sex. Her clitoris was swollen. She gasped as she touched it, its sensitivity taking her by surprise. After all she'd been through earlier she expected to be sore and inured to more activity. Instead, her clitoris felt wonderfully receptive, responding with a surge of sensation as her finger prodded against it. She moved her other hand down between her thighs, edging the tip of the dildo into the mouth of her vagina.

'Look at me,' Jake said, his tone hypnotic.

She'd had her eyes closed, trying to pretend he wasn't there. His steady gaze met hers as she opened her eyes and looked up. He was watching her intently, his thoughts unfathomable. She felt herself blush.

Trying not to think about what she was doing, she eased her bottom right to the edge of the seat and angled her sex upward. She pushed the tip of the dildo into her vagina and felt the inner lips suck on it eagerly. Her clitoris throbbed against her finger, both sensations joining together to produce another jolt of pleasure. It was so strong it made her moan. She looked at Jake's cock, the glans emerging from the circle of his fingers. How she wished he would let her suck on it again.

Slowly she pushed the dildo into her sex, feeling the soft velvety flesh of her vagina parting to admit it. However much she disliked the idea of doing this in front of him, her body seemed to have no such inhibitions, and the tight passage was slicked with her juices. She found that the sting of pain from her nipples was beginning to generate the same sort of pleasure as when she had been whipped. By pulling her head back she discovered she could tug her breasts even higher, putting extra pressure on her nipples and making them pulse. The pain was instantly transformed into ecstasy.

Subtly she began a little routine, forcing the dildo deep into her body while her finger frotted against her clitoris. Her excitement was mounting. She concentrated on his cock, his hand gently moving up and down its length. A little tear of fluid had formed on his urethra, which was immediately wiped over the rest of his glans by his gripping fingers.

It came as quite a surprise to her to realise she was coming. She hadn't wanted to do this at all, but despite herself she began to find the idea more and more arousing. She tried to spread her thighs a little further apart, so Jake's eyes could feast on her sex. She'd seen how Vanda's cunt had pursed around the Senator's cock and imagined her own doing the same around the dildo. There was a shock of delight every time the dildo reached the neck of her womb, and another as she pulled it out again, as though it were catching on some internal contour of her vagina. These two peaks combined with pulsing sensations from her clit and the particular melange of pain and pleasure her nipples were producing, wave after wave of bliss washing over her.

'Tell me when you're coming,' Jake said.

'I think… I think…'

She was sawing the dildo in and out, the double impact generating all sorts of wonderful feelings. The fact that she had been so horrified by the idea of doing this was turned on its head, the element of breaking her own taboo giving the whole experience extra spice. She flicked her clitoris from side to side with no subtlety at all, the little button of nerves exploding with joy. All these sensations made her want to close her eyes and wallow in the orgasm that was approaching as rapidly as an express train, but she fought the impulse, wanting to savour her master's body. He was obviously equally aroused, his fist urgently working his cock.

'Tell me,' he said, getting to his feet. He took three strides towards her and stood with his throbbing erection only inches from her rosy face.

Kim jerked her head back sharply so the chain tugged hard on the nipple clamps. It was the final impetus she needed.

'I *coming*...' she hissed as her body erupted. The orgasm felt like a huge breaker rolling into the shore, rising higher and higher until finally it could resist the force of gravity no longer and crashed down on the sand and shingle, picking it up and dragging it down the beach. But as her eyes were screwed shut by the force of it, she felt a hot viscous liquid spatter over her naked body, hitting her cheeks, her chin, and her breasts.

It was a long time before their heavy breathing slowed, or either of them moved.

Time passed slowly. The next day Marsha had not brought any breakfast, as had been the routine so far. Perhaps she had orders to allow Kim to sleep in after such a late night. But at lunchtime the major-domo had collected her from the cell and she'd eaten in the kitchen upstairs, with four of the other female slaves. All, like her, were naked apart from crotchless denim shorts, and all had their ankles manacled. Whether this was intended as a symbolic gesture to emphasise their thraldom, or a genuine deterrent to escape, it was effective for both purposes; the short chain between their legs making walking difficult, the tight ankle cuffs impossible to remove without a key.

In the afternoon they were all set to work in the house, cleaning and dusting and doing other chores, most of which were totally unnecessary, the house no doubt cleaned and dusted by a professional staff. At five, according to the hall clock, they were all returned to their cells.

After showering and washing her hair Kim once again found herself sitting on the thin mattress with nothing to do but count the pine panels and think. There was no doubt in her mind that she now had a sensational story. She was sure from his ease and familiarity with everyone else at the party that Senator Beddoes and his wife were regular visitors, and clearly delighted in what was available there. Just linking his name with Jake Ashley would be enough to scandalise much of America, and with the added bonus of the gorgeous Nina Berry, editors would be clamouring for the story.

Of course Beddoes and Nina Berry might not be the only celebrities in Ashley's little circle. In fact, Kim was sure they were not. But as far as her story was concerned it didn't matter who else was involved. She had enough for a sensational scoop and if she was being absolutely professional she should now be looking for a way to escape back to the real world. This was definitely her chance to establish her name and reputation.

Unfortunately the idea of leaving the house was not appealing, especially after last night. Jake may not have touched her, but she had been alone with him and he had given her the benefit of his sole and undivided attention. He had even expressed regret that she had been chosen to be 'the main event' at the party.

The extraordinary thing about him was that not only had he been able to convince her in his books that a woman could want, even need, to be completely submissive – a penchant she would once have dismissed as a male fantasy – but that in person he had exactly that effect on her. He demanded obedience; there was simply no other way to respond to him. She wanted and needed him to treat her like a slave, to excise her free will, to take away even the simplest of choices, like what she wore or when she ate, and replace it with his own ideas of what was appropriate for her. And that is exactly what he had done. What is more, and for reasons she did not understand, it was terribly exciting. Even sitting alone in her cell with nothing to wear and nothing to do aroused her, because she knew that was what he wanted for her, and that he had ordered it.

What she had discovered about her sexuality since arriving in New York had certainly come as a shock to her. But having made the discovery she was reluctant to abandon the chance to explore it further. If she ran away from the house now she would undoubtedly never see Jake Ashley again, and that thought appalled her. And, if she were honest with herself, it wasn't only Jake himself. What had happened with Candy and at the club, let alone the proceedings at the auction, were experiences she could never forget. Her sexual world had been turned on its head. The thought of going back to London, of giving up this arcane world she had stumbled into, was deeply depressing. She wasn't ready for that yet.

She would give herself another couple of days, she decided firmly, then she would have to let professional considerations come to the fore and make a break for freedom. She had always wanted a career, and this was definitely the best chance she'd had to develop it dramatically. Not that escape would be easy. She had no idea where she was. She'd fallen asleep in the car and could only guess how long the drive from Long Island had taken. It might be miles to the nearest public transport, and she had no money. She also had no clothes, and the only time she'd not been manacled outside her cell was when Marsha was in close attendance. And she certainly did not fancy her chances of overpowering her. But as much as she wanted to escape the idea that she might not succeed for several days, far from filling her with dread, gave her a secret delight.

Kim had no idea what time it was when she heard the key being turned in the lock.

'You're required,' Marsha said briskly, and dropped the ubiquitous nylon holdall on the bed. 'Have you showered?'

'Yes, Ms Marsha.'

'Good. Stand up.'

She pulled a heavy leather harness from the bag and shook it out. She began by buckling a tight and wide belt around Kim's waist. Attached to this were two wide straps that fitted over her shoulders and down her back. At the front the straps were split in the middle so they could be forced around her breasts, pinching them and making them stick out awkwardly. Two much thinner straps hung down from the waist. They followed the line of her pelvis where, on either side of her mons, they looped around a slightly curved oval-shaped ring of bright tubular metal that was obviously designed to fit around the labia.

As Kim followed the next curt order and spread her legs, Marsha pulled the metal oval between them. At the back it was attached to a single narrow strap which the major-domo pulled up between her buttocks and buckled to the waist belt, securing it so tightly that the metal pressed forcefully into the malleable flesh between her thighs. This had the effect of squeezing her labia out through the centre of the oval ring, rather in the way her breasts were squeezed out between the split in the straps. Both were equally uncomfortable.

As Kim continued to obey and sat down Marsha gathered her long black hair into a ponytail, securing it with a little leather loop, to which a D-ring was attached.

The aggressive woman then produced a pair of sheer champagne coloured hold ups with wide, opaque welts.

Quickly Kim rolled the stockings up over her long legs, smoothing them into place and making sure there were no wrinkles.

Marsha pulled a pair of white shoes from the bag, with the usual high heels. She dropped them on the floor at Kim's feet and signalled that she should stand and put them on. Then she took out a pair of padded leather cuffs. She turned Kim away and wrapped one of the cuffs around her left arm just above the elbow. Cinching her arms together the other cuff was wound around her right arm. As the link between the two cuffs was short they forced Kim's shoulders back and her chest forward. But Marsha had not finished. She took a double snap-lock from the bag, clipped one end to the central link of the cuffs and the other to the D-ring on the ponytail, effectively pulling Kim's trussed arms upward and her head back, making it impossible for her to look down.

'Comfortable?' Marsha sneered. 'You got off lightly last night,' she went on without awaiting an answer. 'Usually it's the slave who gets the whipping. Perhaps you won't be so lucky tonight. Come on.'

Rather unsteadily, with her head held high so she could hardly see where she was putting her feet, and the usual precipitously high heels making her take diminutive steps, Kim followed Marsha out of the cell and down the corridor. One of the cell doors was open and Kim managed to glance inside. A rather chubby woman was on the bed on all fours, her grey dress hiked up around her waist, her tights pulled down so that they banded her thighs. Kneeling behind her Adam was pounding his cock into her ample buttocks, his own bottom criss-crossed with what looked like freshly acquired scarlet stripes, his fingers buried in her hips, pulling her back as he drove forward.

'Come on,' Marsha said impatiently.

The tableau in the cell gave Kim a jolt of arousal to add to the growing excitement she was already feeling. Her body had responded to her bondage with its usual ardour. She remembered in *The Disciple* that Dolores had found the tighter she was bound the more excited she became, and certainly his appeared to be exactly true of her. The unyielding and bizarre leather harness, the fact that her clit was being crushed so tightly between the forcibly pursed lips of her sex, and her breasts were sore from the leather biting into the tender flesh, made her sex throb and her nipples tingle. For whatever reason the more tightly she was bound the more her body generated unmistakably sexual feelings.

They went up to the ground floor and along to the corridor at the back of the house. Kim could see the swimming pool lit by its own underwater lights, the water appearing a deep and azure blue. Tonight, however, the patio and the pool were deserted.

Marsha piloted her along to a door that led to a long annex that had been built onto the back of the house. There was a short corridor with four black doors off it. Marsha opened the second door along.

'In there,' she said.

As Kim walked inside the door closed behind her. She recognised the room immediately. In *The Slaves of New York* books it was called the punishment room and there were four of them, corresponding, she was sure, to the four doors in the annex. Each room, if they followed the pattern of the books, was different. This one had plain white walls, a polished wooden floor and no window. Hanging from a thick wooden beam that traversed the ceiling were several hooks and rings and a pulley system.

On one of the walls was a complicated metal cross, each arm equipped with padded leather straps. Kim knew from the books that the cross could be elongated, pulling its victims limbs further apart.

In one corner was a tall metal cupboard. Though its doors were firmly closed Kim knew it contained an array of instruments of chastisement, rubber and leather garments – like specially designed spanking pants that lifted and separated the buttocks make them easier to beat – and all sorts of other things, from rope to leather harnesses, from nipple clips to every possible size of dildo and vibrator.

The other feature of the room that had been faithfully reproduced in the books was that one of its walls was completely covered from floor to ceiling with a mirror. Kim tried to lower her head to examine her reflection. She pulled her arms up as much as possible and tugged painfully on her hair, bringing tears to her eyes. She saw the leather straps of the harness had squeezed her breasts so firmly they had become a dark red, and her nipples looked bloated. She eased her head back again, slightly relieving the pressure on her arms but increasing the cramp in her neck muscles.

'Are you waiting for me?'

A man had silently entered the room. Because of the position of her head she could not see much of his body, but his face was tanned.

Kim remembered she had to kneel. Without the use of her arms it was a difficult manoeuvre, but she managed it.

The man moved closer. Now she could see him properly. He was naked and his body was lean, completely free of hair except for a thick bush at his groin. His cock was flaccid and uncircumcised.

'My name is Cantrell,' he said. 'You must call me, sir. Do you understand?'

'Yes, sir,' Kim said at once. She was disappointed that she hadn't been taken to see Jake. After last night she thought they had established a special bond. But she guessed he had sent this man, which was the next best thing. She was sure he was thinking of her, and that's what really mattered. Besides, the idea that this complete stranger was able to do anything he liked to her was so depraved, so far from what had once passed as normal sex, that it excited her as much as everything else had. It appeared that her libido now recognised no limits.

'He said you were rather special.' The man interrupted her thoughts, reaching out to stroke her hair, pulled tight by the bondage. He ran a finger around her moist lips, then slipped it between them and into her mouth.

'Suck it,' he ordered quietly. She obeyed. He slipped two fingers in, then three.

'Very good… now my cock.'

With her head pulled slightly back he had to angle his hips a little over her face, but she managed to purse her lips around the bulbous tip and suck it into her mouth. She immediately felt his semi-erect cock beginning to unfurl as he fed more of it into her moist warmth. When fully erect he pulled away to admire her handiwork.

'You're very good,' he whispered, then went to the cupboard, his glistening penis bobbing as he moved. He took a little leather harness from one of the drawers, turned so she could watch him, and wrapped it around his cock, one strap around the base of his shaft and another two twisting around his balls. With the harness in place the veins on the turgid stalk stood out prominently.

'So, what are we going to do with you?' His tone was

flat, disclosing no emotion.

Cantrell reached up to one of the pulleys. Attached to a thick nylon rope threaded over the pulley were two short metal bars, one above the other and about two feet apart. Both had sturdy snap-hooks at either end. He pulled on the rope until the bottom bar was at about ankle height.

'Crawl over here,' he ordered.

Kim moved forward awkwardly on her knees.

'Now lie flat on your front.'

With her arms tied behind her back the only way Kim could obey this order was to slide down onto her side and then roll onto her stomach. The position was extremely uncomfortable; her head still forced back and the extremely uncomfortable pull on her arms.

'I think we're going to have to lose this,' the man said, squatting down to unclip the snap-hook from her ponytail. As Kim's head was allowed to ease down she rested her chin on the floor, and the relief in her neck muscles was enormous. She lay still, feeling Cantrell clipping the snap-hook on the lower of the two bars into two D-rings on the back of the thick leather belt around her waist, the bar resting on her spine.

He straightened up and went back to the cupboard. He opened another drawer and took out two metal cuffs attached to short steel chains, and a length of rope. Again he squatted beside Kim, snapping her ankles into the metal cuffs then bending them back and clipping the chains on each cuff to the snap-hooks on either end of the higher metal bar, making sure her legs were completely doubled back, her feet poised above her thighs. Then he wound the rope around the central link of the cuffs that held her elbows together and pulled this back, tying it to the centre of the higher metal bar. Kim's body was now bent like a bow.

'A nice neat package,' he said, slapping her thigh.

He rose again and went to the door. Kim could see there was a series of round switches set into the wall. He turned one and the dull hum of an electric motor filled the air. The nylon rope creaked and tightened and Kim felt herself being pulled up, the note of the electric motor changing as it took up the weight. Her wrists, ankles and waist took the strain as she was pulled clear of the floor and started to sway a little. It was an extraordinary feeling, like she was floating but at the same time totally restricted.

Cantrell stopped the motor when she hung about three feet above the floor. The leather harness creaked. Kim was trembling, the feeling that impossibly tight constriction was causing making her clitoris throb against her grotesquely pinched labia.

After a few moments he stilled her gentle movement, putting both hands on her shoulders and moving so that her head butted against his stomach. 'Suck me again,' he said.

Kim wearily raised her head and he fed his cock into her mouth. He was still rock hard. She sucked him into her throat.

'Has she been behaving herself?'

Kim strained her eyes to see who had entered the room. She felt a jolt of excitement when she saw Jake Ashley. He, like Cantrell, was naked. His penis was erect and glistening.

'Oh yes,' Cantrell grunted huskily, as he concentrated on the mouth working so beautifully around his erection. He angled his hips slightly to bury himself deeper. 'She's very good.'

'I thought you'd like her.' The host looked pleased.

Cantrell pulled away, and Jake instantly took his place. He grabbed Kim's ponytail and pulled her face up again, pushing his cock between her lips. Kim tasted the unmistakable tang of another woman's sex. Jake had no doubt been next door with one of the slaves.

Through an inexplicable feeling of jealousy she felt her knees being spread apart, and Cantrell positioning himself between them. As he pushed forward he gripped her hips and nosed his cock between her labia. 'Nice little pussy,' he croaked.

'I'm surprised you didn't whip her,' Jake said conversationally. 'You love being whipped, don't you Kim?'

Kim wasn't at all sure that she did, the feelings of pain and pleasure too difficult to unravel, but she tried to say yes just to please him. The word was muffled on his cock.

'No, no... this is what I want,' Cantrell said, his voice strained. He drove suddenly into the depths of her vagina. It was soaking wet. As his hard cock thrust forward she felt the velvety flesh parting to admit it, another surge of desire racing through her. One part of her mind was telling her the experience was totally degrading; being hung like a side of meat and used so matter-of-factly. But the other appeared to have no such qualms; it was too busy registering undiluted pleasure. Perhaps because of her suspension and the odd leather harness everything felt completely different. The metal oval that surrounded her sex was just big enough to allow Cantrell's cock to squeeze through, but as he began to pump into her, her pinched labia were crushed against his belly and reacted beautifully. Her clit too, not stretched and exposed by the penetration, but buried deep in a velvety wet nest, was experiencing a whole new plethora of sensations.

All this, and Jake's sudden entrance, was propelling her to orgasm. As Cantrell thrust forward, pulling her back against him, Jake's cock slid from her mouth. As Cantrell pulled back she was able to rock forward and swallow Jake again – the perfect rhythm.

'Beautiful little pussy,' Cantrell mumbled.

The feeling of two erections buried in her body while she was bound so helplessly was like nothing Kim had ever felt before. However debauched, however beyond the pale of what she had been brought up to believe was decent behaviour, this was what she wanted and needed. She sucked avidly on the throbbing stalk stretching her lips and nudging her throat as her orgasm exploded, the bonds creaking as she convulsed and swayed within their grasp.

As her orgasm peaked and she began to relax, she felt Cantrell pulling himself out of her sex. His cock and balls butted into the soft pillows of her buttocks, and immediately she felt hot gobs of spunk spattering her back, the man moaning loudly. But Jake didn't pull out of her mouth. His fingers were digging into her shoulders and his hips jerked more and more erratically. She felt his cock begin to spasm. Then it seemed to recoil. For a long moment nothing happened. Kim breathed slowly through her nose, waiting – then a stream of viscous liquid jetted into her mouth. She swallowed it all gallantly, and waited until his cock had become still again, then gently ran her tongue over its tip, wanting to lick up every last drop.

'No,' Jake said, with what sounded like anger. He pulled away.

'You all right?' Cantrell asked.

'I'll get Marsha to come and cut her down,' he replied gruffly. 'Let's go and have a drink.' He held the door open.

When the man had gone out into the corridor he glanced back at Kim, and all she could see was the anger in his eyes – anger she did not understand.

Chapter Nine

She knew she was being punished, but she didn't know what for. For two days she had not been allowed out of her cell. All her meals had been delivered but she'd been given no clothes or make-up, and had spent her time reading one of three books that had been delivered with her breakfast on the first day.

Why Jake had reacted so angrily she had no idea. But whatever the reason, it had condemned Kim to forty-eight hours of boredom and frustration. From time to time she had heard the other slaves being taken upstairs, and once or twice the distinct sound of a whip coming from one of the adjacent cells. Jake and his guests were obviously indulging themselves, and to know he was deliberately ignoring her hurt more than any of the physical pain she had experienced.

Her whole body seemed to ache, but she knew her aching need was more a mental condition than a physical one. After being so intimate with the man she now thought of as her master, to be neglected so pointedly made her need that much more intense.

Thoughts of her story and her plan to escape had simply evaporated as time passed. It seemed less and less important. By the end of the second day, the passage of time only marked by the number of meals she'd been brought, she could think of nothing else but Jake and when he would call for her, every footfall in the corridor making her heart leap in expectation.

Eventually she heard the key turning in the lock and knew something was about to happen.

'Put this on,' Marsha said, with what had become her normal greeting. She threw some garments on the bed. 'Have you showered?'

'Yes, Ms Marsha.'

'And shaved?'

'Yes, Ms Marsha.'

'Make yourself up, too. I'll be back in ten minutes.'

Kim had correctly sensed her period of purdah was almost over. After so long on her own her excitement was intense. She quickly unzipped the make-up case and stood in front of the mirror to do her eyes. Of course there was no guarantee she was being taken to see Jake, but that didn't matter. Even if she was being taken to one of the guests it meant that at least he'd thought about her. But she was convinced she was being taken to see her master. He wanted her as much as she wanted him. How she hoped that was true. She put on the dark eye shadow, and used the black mascara on her long eyelashes. In the mirror she could see her eyes were sparkling again.

She went back to the bed and picked up the clothes Marsha had left. There was a red body made from shiny PVC, and thigh high boots in the same material. The body was tight. Like everything she had worn at the house its gusset had been removed to reveal her sex, and there were cut-outs in the bodice through which her breasts swelled.

She pulled on the boots. The tight PVC clung to her thighs like a second skin. She looked in the mirror and didn't like what she saw, the outfit tarty and unsubtle. She looked like a cheap whore. But it was a small price to pay if it was what Jake wanted.

Marsha opened the door again. She was wearing her

usual leather outfit of shorts and a halter-necked leather blouse. She had a leather collar in her left hand and a riding crop with a brass pommel in her right. She put the crop on the bed.

'Come here and turn around,' she said, without the slightest emotion.

Kim did as she was told. She felt the thick leather collar being wrapped around her neck. Hanging down from the back of it between her shoulder blades was another short strap, attached to which were two narrow leather cuffs, one immediately above the other. Marsha took Kim's wrists, twisted them up behind her and strapped them into the cuffs, making her elbows stick out like chicken wings. She then clipped a long thin chain into a D-ring at the front of the collar. It was attached to the chain of the manacles, which Kim had been made to wear when she was working in the house. Marsha snapped each manacle around her ankles.

As usual, bondage had added a new dimension to Kim's excitement. The position of her arms was agony, but the waves of pain were translated into a sharp tingling pleasure that made her tremble.

'Good,' Marsh said, twisting Kim this way and that. She was smiling, and Kim didn't think she'd ever seen her smile before. 'Now bend over,' she said.

To keep her balance Kim shuffled her ankles apart until the chain between them was stretched to the maximum. Looking between her legs she saw Marsha pick up the whip. She moved close and trailed the whip up between Kim's legs until the leather loop at its tip was touching her sex. It slid up to Kim's clit, the touch making her moan. Then Marsha flicked the loop between her thighs, making the flesh vibrate. It was withdrawn suddenly. Kim heard a swish then a line of pain exploded across her buttocks, like hot needles being driven into her skin, the harshest stroke she had ever received.

'What do you say?'

'Thank you, Ms Marsha,' she gasped, the pain making her pant for breath.

Almost before she had said the words another stroke landed diagonally across the first. The back of the PVC body provided little protection, the material only covering a tiny triangle at the top of her bottom, leaving most of her buttocks completely exposed.

'Thu-thank you... Ms Marsha.'

The third stroke was the hardest of them all. It set her whole backside on fire. But the needles of pain that lanced into her turned, as they had before, to sharp peaks of pleasure, her sex turning liquid. She could feel each stroke individually, and knew they had left scarlet weals on her flesh.

'All right, straighten up,' Marsha said. As Kim did so, stiffly, she saw Marsha was still smiling. 'Now follow me.'

The high heels of the thigh boots and the chain between her ankles made progress slow. They reached the ground floor and Kim was thrilled when Marsha turned towards the main stairs. Her conviction that she was being taken to see her master looked like being justified.

They climbed the second staircase and walked towards the double doors at the end of the landing. Marsha rapped on one of the doors then walked away.

Kim waited. Her buttocks were still on fire, but there was nothing she could do to soothe them. She heard voices from inside the room but could not make out any words. She supposed she could still be disappointed. It was possible the master had loaned his room to one of his guests, but that was unlikely, she thought.

The door opened. A woman stood there. She was young, probably no more than twenty, and was wearing a narrow black suspender belt, sheer black stockings and high heels. Her breasts were high and proud with puckered red nipples, and her waist narrow. She had long legs and a thick bush of blonde hair on her mons. She was beautiful, with sharp cheekbones, a straight nose, and large sparkling blue eyes, her blonde hair short but cut in layers that suited the shape of her head. She examined Kim critically, then glanced back into the room. 'What do I do now?' she said.

'Bring her in.' It was Jake's voice.

The girl took hold of the chain that hung down Kim's front, and pulled her in. She had the air of someone who had suddenly stepped into a dream and was trying hard not to be shocked by what she saw.

'Close the door.' Jake was lying on his bed, naked, his erection in his hand, his head propped up on several pillows. He did not look at Kim.

The blonde followed his instruction.

'Now bring her closer.'

She led Kim to the bed. There was a strong odour of sex in the room, leaving Kim in little doubt as to what Jake and the girl had been doing.

'She's gorgeous,' the girl sighed. 'Can I touch her?'

'Of course you can. You can do anything you want with her. I told you that.'

She raised a hand and touched Kim's cheek, then allowed her hand to fall to her breasts. She cupped one, then inquisitively tweaked the nipple. 'Unbelievable,' she breathed incredulously, her eyes wide. 'And she does this

198

voluntarily? I mean, you're not blackmailing her or nothing?'

'No, I'm not blackmailing her,' Jake said patiently. 'Have you ever been with another woman, Kate?'

'No – but I'd sure like to. I've always wondered what it would be like.'

For the first time Jake looked directly into Kim's eyes. There was a smouldering expression there that she could not read. 'Bend over,' he ordered calmly.

Kim obeyed, at once determined to show him how good a slave she could be, despite the fact she found Kate's presence disconcerting. The girl was clearly not a slave, or one of his regular guests.

'Jesus, what are those marks?' Kate asked with genuine fascination.

'She's been whipped,' came the casual reply.

'Whipped? She likes that too?'

'Of course. All submissives do. Bondage and corporeal punishment go together.'

'I'm not sure I could take that.' The lovely girl shook her head, pouting childishly.

'Then you're not a submissive,' Jake said abruptly. 'Go on then, touch her. That's what you said you wanted to do.'

'How – how many of these girls are there?'

'There are hundreds of slaves in New York. There are twelve masters with places like this. The girls come and go. Some can only take it for a few months. Others never want to leave the system.'

Kim felt the girl stroking her buttocks. She winced as cool fingers touched one of the scarlet weals.

'I've never done anything like this before,' the girl breathed, as her fingers slipped down into the cleft of

Kim's buttocks and into the opening of the PVC body. '*Jesus*, it's so wet.' She clumsily prodded one finger into Kim's sex, the long fingernail making Kim wince again.

'Now kiss it,' Jake suggested. He rose and moved closer, his erection bobbing gently.

The girl apparently thought that was a good idea. 'Get her to lie down, then,' she said breathlessly, her disbelieving eyes glued to Kim.

'She'll do whatever you tell her to,' Jake prompted.

'Really? Gee, that's cool. All right, lie on the bed with your legs open... s-slave,' the girl said, without conviction.

Kim straightened up and went over to the bed. It didn't matter what was going on, she thought, as long as she was with Jake. Upon seeing her instruction being obeyed without question, the girl giggled.

Kim sat on the edge of the bed and lay back, writhing to the middle of the white linen sheet. She could feel the warmth where Jake's body had been. With her arms twisted up behind her back, lying down was awkward and her weight increased the pressure on her tortured elbows. The weals from the riding crop also stung as they rubbed against the crisp material.

'Here, unlock the cuffs,' Jake said, picking up a small key from the bedside chest and handing it to the girl. He caught her chin in one hand and pulled her towards him, kissing her while his free hand covered her left breast.

'This – this is fun,' the girl panted when the kiss ended. She sat on the bed and put the key into one of the ankle cuffs. It snapped open and she peeled it away, leaving the other one in place. 'Now you can spread them apart, baby,' she cooed.

Kim inched her legs across the bed. She saw the girl stare at her sex, framed by the strips of red rubber that ran down on either side of her labia. For some reason she felt more naked in front of this young ingenue than she had spread-eagled and exposed to all the guests at the party.

The girl instinctively got up to her knees alongside Kim, then dipped her head to her sex. Kim could feel hot breath playing over her labia as the girl stared, taking in all the details.

'I've never done this before,' she whispered innocently.

'So you said.'

'I'm really turned on, Jake.'

'That's good,' he said.

'Do they all have to get shaved like this?'

'That's my preference,' he confirmed.

Kim turned her head to look at him. He was standing by the side of the bed looking at the blonde, but not at her. His erection jutted from his loins.

Kate stuck out her tongue and very delicately lapped between Kim's labia. She was tentative at first, but soon became more assertive, her tongue moving up to search for Kim's clit. It nudged against the little button and began to circle it delicately. At the same time Kim felt her hand moving up between her legs, her fingers spreading her labia apart as if the girl wanted to get a good look at the mouth of her vagina.

Kim saw Jake kneel on the bed beside her. He took the girl's hips in his hands and eased his erection down between her legs, rubbing it against the black welt of the sheer stockings. How she wished he was doing that to her. The girl raised her head and looked back at him. 'That feels good,' she said.

'You concentrate on what you're doing,' he replied. 'Take no notice of me.'

Kate's tongue returned to Kim's clit. She explored the

rim of Kim's vagina with her fingers, then pushed inside hesitantly. 'Will she do me?' she said, suddenly straightening up, her fingers pulled from Kim's vagina.

'I told you, anything you want.'

'Great.'

Kate bounced around the bed, straddled Kim's shoulders and pushed her sex down onto her mouth. Kim pushed her tongue into her and found the girl's clitoris. She squealed with delight as Kim flicked it from side to side.

'Oooh… that's *great*,' she purred. 'Jesus, this feels bad. Does it mean I'm turning into a dike?'

'It means you like sex, all kinds of sex, is all,' Jake said. 'Here suck on this.'

Kim felt her lean forward, then push back on her mouth again. She flicked Kate's clit and could feel the girl shudder at each contact. She could hear her sucking enthusiastically on Jake's cock. Her emotions were confused because she didn't know where Kate fitted into his life. Was he trying to recruit her as a slave? But if that were the case shouldn't he be giving her the tests of obedience he had written about so graphically in his books, not fooling around with her like young lovers?

'Oh, that's good,' Kate sighed, sitting up again, her sex pressing down against Kim's chin.

'Can you come like that?' Jake asked.

'Mmm… I think so. Feels so dirty, doing this with a woman.'

'Naughty but nice.'

'Naughty but *great*.'

A weight moved on the bed. Kim felt Jake settling behind her. His gnarled cock slid over Kim's face. As Kate tipped forward, supporting herself on her hands, Kim watched him sliding into the entrance of her vagina. How

202

much would she have given to feel him doing that to her? He pushed deep, grinding his pubic bone against her sex.

'I – I can't believe I'm doing this…' Kate panted dreamily, her back dipping in unison with his penetration.

'Does it feel good?'

'It feels fantastic.'

Kim tapped the tip of her tongue against the blonde's clit, trying to concentrate on her and exclude all other feelings. This was what Jake wanted for her and she had to prove to him that she could be a good slave. That was all that mattered. Her feelings, the terrible jealousy she was beginning to feel as this uncomplicated girl who was quite clearly right outside the system, was given what Kim wanted so desperately, had to be set aside. Perhaps after the girl had been exhausted Jake would turn to her.

The girl was moaning loudly now, Kim's tongue and the sawing movement of Jake's cock bringing her off. Quite suddenly she felt the girl's glowing face drop between her thighs and her mouth fell to her sex, her lips crushing against her and kissing hungrily. Her wicked tongue found Kim's clit and began tapping at it exactly as Kim was doing to her.

Kim could feel the blonde's orgasm mounting rapidly. Her mouth seemed to melt against Kim's sex, moulding to it, and she could feel her hard nipples pressing down against her belly. Then she reared her head up, crushed her bottom back against Jake's body, gave a piercing cry, and came, her sex clenched tightly around the rod of flesh invading it.

'Very needy,' Jake said quietly.

He pulled her back and they fell together in a heap, his arms wrapping around her, his mouth nestling against her throat.

'Oh, I'm so turned on,' Kate sighed. 'What have you done to me?'

'Just taught you what's available,' he said.

'You're still hard,' the girl giggled.

'Mmm… I've been saving myself.'

'Let me do you then,' she suggested eagerly.

'Have you finished with her?' Jake asked.

'But I want you,' the girl pouted.

Jake sat up. 'Get to your feet,' he said to Kim, emphasising the order by nudging her with a foot. 'Stand here, by the bed.' His tone was suddenly cold and impersonal.

Kim struggled to her feet, the bondage making it difficult. Was he really not even going to touch her?

'She's *really* something,' Kate said, her voice full of admiration.

'You can have her again tomorrow, if you want to stay.'

'Stay? You're not turning me into one of your little slaves.'

'Don't worry, you're not a submissive. But I have a feeling about you. Perhaps you might like to be on the other side.'

'The other side?'

'A dominant. Some of the masters like to have overseers; girls who help them keep the slaves under control.'

'And you think I could do that?'

'My instincts are usually sound,' he said, a little smugly. 'Stick around here for a couple of days and find out.'

'There's something I want to find out before that,' she said. She kissed him, pulling him back down onto the bed.

Kim had to watch as the young blonde newcomer writhed against the man she was besotted with. Then the girl rolled off him and gripped his penis in both hands, milking it with evident adoration. 'Like this?' she cooed sexily. 'Or do you want to come in my mouth?'

Jake looked at Kim, his eyes showing no warmth whatsoever. Now she knew exactly why she was there. It was to teach her a lesson. He had lost control in the annex two days before. She had made him lose control. That's why he'd been angry. But this performance with Kate was designed to teach her, like her two days of solitary confinement, that she must never come to expect any special treatment from him because of that. For a brief moment, alone with him in his bedroom, she knew she had touched him and established a special bond. What he was doing now was making sure that bond was broken. However much he wanted her, however much she had made him lose control, she was just another slave. And he was the master.

Her whole body ached with need. The pain of her bondage and of the whip was nothing to the emptiness she felt inside. How she wanted to sink onto that rigid phallus and feel it riding up inside her.

'Your hands feel good,' he said, arching his back and pushing his cock up, his challenging stare still fixed on Kim.

The blonde squeezed his shaft with one hand and ran the other down to his scrotum, cupping his balls. She worked her fist up and down. Kim watched with total fascination. She had never felt so jealous of anyone in her life. She watched Jake's cock begin to twitch, the shaft swelling even more. As Kate rubbed the ring of her fingers across the ridge at the bottom of the glans the little slit of the urethra opened and a string of pearly spunk jetted up in an arc which spattered down on Jake's belly and chest.

Kate squeezed and pumped his cock to produce a second less energetic spending, then continued until every last drop had oozed out over her fingers. She dipped her face and began to lap the spunk off her hand with the tip of her tongue, making enthusiastic moans as she did so.

He had done that, Kim knew, to show her exactly what she was missing, to point out to her that he was allowing another woman to give him pleasure, but not her.

'You know, I think you may be right,' Kate purred, straightening up.

'Right about what?' he asked.

'About being dominant. Seeing her like that, it's had a strange effect on me.'

'Like what?'

'She's into being whipped, right?'

'She's into being obedient. Part of that is being whipped, if required.'

'Can I whip her?'

'Here you can do anything you want.'

'That's what I want. I want to whip her and have her go down on me again.'

Jake laughed. 'You're getting the hang of this pretty quickly.'

'So it looks as though your instincts were right.'

'Yah, it looks that way.' Jake chuckled and reached for a tissue. 'There's a whip over there,' he nodded towards a wardrobe. 'Just tell her what to do.'

Kate rose sexily. She stood in front of Kim and gripped the long chain that still hung from the collar. She used it to pull their faces closer together. 'This is going to be fun,' she said.

It was impossible to sleep. Kim's mind turned over everything that had happened. Marsha had delivered her back to the cell at midnight, according to the clock in the hall, and had waited while she stripped off the PVC body and boots, before locking her in.

After a shower Kim lay on the bed, finding she had to sleep on her side, the weals the whip had left stinging painfully if she ventured onto her back, her bottom pink and raw from Kate's enthusiastic, if untutored use of a thin horse whip. For the first time the pain did not provoke a sexual response.

She supposed she should just accept her punishment, even though she hadn't deserved it. But it was difficult to deal with the jealousy she felt. After having shared an intimacy with Jake Ashley, it was hard to go back to realising that she was only one of many. He might show favouritism from time to time but in the end he was a master, like the others he had referred to, and would do exactly as he wished. And ultimately, if Kim was to be a slave she would have to do more than just accept seeing him with other women, whoever they were, she would have to relish it. In a sense the episode had been a test of her submissiveness.

It was a test she had failed.

It was not the whipping the girl had subjected her to. Nor the fact that the girl used her afterwards, squatting on her face while she indulged herself and came at least twice more. It was Jake's attitude; Jake's obvious pleasure in her emotional discomfort, and what she perceived as his callousness. She supposed, as her master it was up to him how he behaved, but she found it hard to accept.

For the first time since she'd arrived at the house she began to feel that she wouldn't regret leaving. Being a

207

slave was too demanding, and required a commitment she clearly didn't have. She wanted to be with Jake Ashley to do and be whatever he wanted, but was beginning to realise exactly what that entailed.

She could get back to New York and file her story, then fly back to London and resume her life. Three days ago that prospect had seemed bleak; now it was almost welcome.

Almost.

She supposed there would always be a part of her that hankered after what she'd found in New York. Perhaps there was a club for submissives in London, a place where she could go every so often to experience the sort of pleasures she had experienced here. Or perhaps the needs would just dissipate and eventually be forgotten.

Perhaps.

Of course, there was still the question of getting away. In theory all she needed to do was refuse to obey Marsha when she next came to the cell. She would then be asked to accept a punishment, which she would also refuse, and be sent back to New York. That was the theory. But though all the other slaves at the house seemed to be willing enough, it was possible that in practice Marsha and ultimately Jake might choose not to let her go until her allotted time was up. What's more, having alerted them to her lack of co-operation they might make sure her bondage was increased and confine her to the cell, making it impossible to escape. It was better all round if she said nothing, appeared perfectly co-operative, and tried to find the right moment to make a run for it.

Having made that decision, having decided she would look for a means of escape, she immediately regretted it. Forgetting herself for a moment she rolled onto her back, the sting in her buttocks reminding her of how Kate had whipped her with relish. A few minutes before the stinging in her bottom had been irritating; now it began to generate quite different feelings. She rubbed her buttocks across the sheet deliberately, producing a new wave of pain, quickly followed by a surge of pleasure...

'No!' she said aloud, rolling onto her side... but she rolled back again. If Jake was no longer her master, if she was heading for the outside world, it didn't matter if she masturbated. She pressed her sore buttocks against the sheet and snaked a hand down between her legs. She hadn't touched herself since she'd done it for Jake. Well, this time she was doing it for herself.

Kim saw Nina Berry arrive. She was driving a red Ferrari, which she brought to a halt by the front door. She got out, her lithe body dressed in a black catsuit and thigh length black leather boots, and strode to the house as if she owned it. It was just getting dark, an orange sun setting behind a bank of beech trees to the west.

Kim and two of the other slaves were washing windows on the first floor, though they were perfectly clean. She had seen Jake leaving with Kate in a black stretch limousine about an hour before, probably taking her home. So she guessed Nina's visit was not planned.

Marsha opened the front door to her in. As she was right above the hall area, Kim could hear their conversation.

'Where's Jake?' Nina demanded.

'Sorry, Ms Berry, he's just gone out.'

'Out where?'

'Back to New York, Ms Berry.' Marsha retained her cool.

'So he won't be back tonight?'

'No. Not until tomorrow.'

'All right, you'd better make the arrangements for me.'

'What arrangements?'

'Marsha, I haven't come here for the sake of my health. Jake said I could use the slaves whenever I choose. So I'm choosing now. And I need a drink. Get me bourbon rocks.' The film star strode into the sitting room. Marsha followed and Kim heard the sitting room door being closed.

Ten minutes later Marsha came out and climbed the stairs. 'Follow me,' she said to Kim.

She was led along the corridor towards the master's bedroom. Marsha opened one of the other doors on the left and ushered Kim inside. 'Wait here,' she said.

The guest bedroom was decorated in shades of toning blue and green, with flounced curtains, a thick blue carpet and a large double bed. There was a nineteenth century French style walnut wardrobe with a curved entablature, a chest of drawers in the same style and a comfortable sofa. At the foot of the bed was a chest, a bigger version of the one Marsha had produced at the party, though this had elaborately curved panels that looked as if they were Indian in origin. There was a large mirror hanging on the wall above the head of the bed, and Kim stood looking at her reflection. The denim shorts were tight and cut into the top of her thighs. Her breasts rode high on her chest, jutting proudly, her nipples for once smoothed back in the surrounding flesh.

Her resolve to try and escape was still strong. At least it was at the moment. When she'd seen Jake getting in the car it had wavered. For a moment she thought he'd looked up at her, caught her eye and smiled, a knowing smile that to her had suggested there was still something special between them, a smile that said he hoped she had learned her lesson. She sensed he had lingered a moment too long, looking at her with undisguised lust. Was she being ridiculous? Was she reading her own feelings into a blank and uncaring stare? She had no idea. But she decided, after a great deal of deliberation, that she couldn't base her actions on a single look. She wanted to be Jake's slave, but she could not face being one of many. That was the bottom line.

The bedroom door opened again and Adam shuffled in, like her dressed only in denim shorts. He was not alone. Behind him Marsha was pushing the other male slave into the room. Kim had seen him several times but didn't know his name.

'There's a bathroom over there,' Marsha said. 'Get showered, all of you.' She unlocked the metal cuffs at their ankles, then went to the chest of drawers. She took out a lacy white garment and a pair of white stockings with wide lacy welts. 'And you put these on when you're finished,' she said to Kim. 'There's shoes in the wardrobe.' She turned to Adam. 'When she's dressed put the manacles on her again – just her. Do you understand?'

'Yes, Ms Marsha,' Adam said respectfully.

Marsha picked up the other two sets of manacles and the key, and walked out. They heard the bedroom door being locked. 'Better do as she says,' Adam said. 'Did you see Nina arrive?'

'No talking,' the second male whispered, putting a finger to his lips. 'There's probably a video camera. You know Nina likes to get all her performances taped.'

They trooped into the bathroom and the men allowed Kim to shower first. Stripping off the denim shorts she caught them eyeing her body as she stepped into the glass shower cubicle and stood under the stream of hot water and lathered herself. There was nothing she could do to stop them. In any case, after what she'd been through in the last week shyness would have been ridiculous.

She dried herself on a large white towel, then walked back into the bedroom while the men used the shower. She picked up the lingerie Marsha had left out for her. It consisted of a three-quarter cup bra with a deep bodice that reached down almost to her belly. Hanging from the hem was four satin suspenders. She fastened the garment around her body. The bra cups were extremely snug and her soft breasts were squeezed together and threatened to spill from them. Her cleavage became a deep inviting shadow.

She sat on the bed and rolled on the stockings. They were woven with lycra to give them a glossy shine and were long, the lacy tops almost touching her sex.

Kim opened the wardrobe. The interior space had been partitioned into square sections. Some contained wig blocks with blonde and brunette wigs, others glass fronted drawers containing lingerie, while towards the bottom there was a selection of shoes, all with spiky heels. Kim chose a pair in white leather. As she climbed into them Adam held up the chain and the manacles. He looked regretful as he knelt in front of Kim and clipped them around her nylon-sheathed ankles. Just as he disappeared back into the bathroom the bedroom door opened and Nina Berry walked in.

'Good evening,' she said. 'There's no need for all that obeisance crap,' she added, stopping Kim from kneeling. 'I'm not in the mood.

'Now, don't you look pretty.' She raised a hand and

stroked Kim's long hair. 'Where are the men?'

'In the bathroom, Ms Berry,' Kim answered instantly.

'Playing with each other, I expect.' She strode to the bathroom door. 'Get out here now,' she ordered.

Adam appeared first, the other one following.

'I gather your master is out,' Nina said. 'But as he's always told me I could make myself right at home, I intend to do just that. You, what's your name?' She was looking at the larger of the two.

'Bill, Ms Nina.'

'Take off my boots, Bill,' she said.

The man fell to his knees. The black leather thigh boots had a long zip all the way down the inside. Bill unzipped it, then pulled the boot off as Nina raised her foot. He did the same to the other one. Nina pushed her toes into the man's lap, prodding his flaccid cock. 'Not very impressive,' she said thoughtfully. 'I hope you're going to do better than that. Look at Adam here. He clearly finds me *extremely* beautiful.'

Adam was already displaying an impressive erection.

'Perhaps you need some encouragement, Bill. Shall I get Adam here to give you a good suck?'

'No, mistress, please.' The suggestion clearly repulsed the man.

'Then you'd better get yourself hard. Come on, stand up. Let's see what you can do.'

Bill leapt to his feet and began pumping his cock vigorously. Kim saw his eyes fixing on her. His cock began to engorge and he visibly relaxed, clearly happy to have avoided the threat of having another man fellate him.

The black catsuit had a long zip running from the high neck right down to the crotch. Nina caught hold of it and slowly pulled it down, her breasts immediately spilling forth. She pulled her arms out of the sleeves then wriggled the catsuit over her hips and down her long legs. She wasn't wearing a bra and her breasts swayed firmly as she straightened up. A small pair of black satin panties covered her sex.

'Come here, Kim,' she said huskily, beckoning with a crooked finger. She lifted a hand and stroked Kim's breasts, confined within the white lace. Then she wrapped an arm around Kim's waist and pulled their bodies together. She licked her lower lip then kissed her, her tongue exploring her mouth. It was an extremely sensual kiss, and Kim responded with a surge of passion.

Nina broke away. She flipped open the top of the chest. It was full of leather straps, chains and ropes. 'We're going to tie them both up real tight,' she said. She took two coils of white rope and handed one to Kim. 'Then we can have some fun. Just do what I do.'

She went back to Adam, took one end of the rope and wound it around the top of his left arm, knotting it securely. 'Keep your arms at your sides,' she said sternly. She began winding the rope around his body, starting at his shoulders and working down over his chest and waist, enclosing his arms so they were bound to his sides. When she reached his belly she left a gap so his penis remained exposed, then started again at the top of his thighs, working the rope down over his knees and around his calves and ankles. She tied the rope off, then pushed Adam firmly in the chest. Fortunately for him he was standing right next to the bed, because there was nothing he could do to prevent himself from toppling like a felled tree, bouncing on the mattress, a neatly tied package.

Kim began to wind the rope around Bill, following exactly the same procedure, but before she reached his legs Nina moved him so he too was standing with his back to the bed. As soon as the rest of the rope was wound tightly around his legs and tied off, she pushed him in the chest too, and watched as he dropped on the bed next to Adam.

Nina took two foil packages from the top drawer of the bedside chest. She handed one to Kim. 'Put this on him. I know they've had medical checks, but condoms make them last longer.'

'Get yourselves over to the middle of the bed, I want you side by side,' she said, once their standing erections were neatly encased in rubber.

With a great deal of effort the men wriggled and writhed, obeying wisely.

'Too slow,' Nina admonished. 'That means punishment for you both.'

Kim was sure they would have been chastised however fast they moved. Nina went to the chest of drawers. She appeared to know where everything was. She opened the bottom drawer and took out a whip. It looked exactly like the whip Candy had used on Kim in her apartment. Kim saw the glint in Nina's eyes as she came back to the bed. She knelt up on it, raised her arm and slashed the whip across Adam's cock. He winced, gritting his teeth. 'This will teach you to obey more quickly,' she hissed. The whip fell again and again, viciously slapping Adam's cock from side to side. How he maintained control Kim had no idea.

'And now you,' Nina said, her breathing a little heavy from the exertions. She straddled Adam's body to get to Bill, then stroked the whip against his erection. He moaned, trying to roll his body away from the blows. But tied as he was that proved impossible and the whip lashed him as fiercely as it had done Adam.

Nina turned around to look at Kim. 'Kneel here with me,' she said, indicating the bed at Adam's side.

Kim did as she was told immediately, not wanting to risk a whipping at Nina's sadistic hands. As soon as she settled Nina leant forward, wrapped a hand around her neck and kissed her. She squeezed Kim's breasts through the bra, her fingers centring on her nipples and pinching cruelly.

'I'm in a funny mood,' she said, breaking away. 'I hoped Jake would be here; he knows how to deal with my moods.'

She lifted herself on her haunches and pushed back until she was poised over Adam's erection. The whipping had made no difference to its hardness.

'Put it in me,' Nina ordered crudely. She held the gusset of her panties and eased the damp material to the side.

Kim wrapped her hand around Adam's gnarled cock. Up until this moment she had been curiously detached, watching everything that happened but not becoming aroused. Perhaps, having made the decision that she was going to escape and leave all this behind her, she was reluctant to become involved again. But the feel of Adam's cock pulsing in her fist changed all that. She felt a surge of arousal knotting her stomach, and it soon became the familiar thumping pulse that radiated out to encompass her whole body.

She pushed Adam's cock between Nina's labia, the sparse black pubic hair plastered back against her flesh. It was not difficult to find her vagina. As she eased his cock into the waiting maw Nina dropped down, the rigid shaft stabbing up into her. She grunted and immediately began grinding her hips from side to side, so her clitoris rubbed against his pubic bone. 'Do my tits,' she said.

Kim moved around on the bed, the chain at her ankles impeding her movements, then leant forward and cupped Nina's breasts. 'No,' she chided. 'Suck on them.'

Kim fed a nipple into her mouth and sucked, then pinched it between her teeth. She felt Nina's body shudder in reaction. The American began to move up and down on Adam's cock, pressing her hands down on his stomach to steady herself. Tied as he was he was unable to do anything but lie there.

Kim moved her mouth over to Nina's other nipple. She gnawed it while she used her fingernails on the one she'd just left, nipping them simultaneously. 'Yes...' Nina moaned.

As Kim saw Adam's cock sliding in and out of Nina's sex she felt her own throbbing wildly, her juices flowing. Every time Nina dropped down, burying him in her depths, Kim felt as if it were happening to her.

'Whip them now,' Nina panted, her eyes sparkling.

Kim wasn't at all sure what she meant.

'My tits, you idiot... whip my tits.' As she said this she heaved herself up off Adam and swung her leg over Bill, facing in the opposite direction, her back to his face, this time using her own hand to jam his cock up between her legs. As his glans nudged into the mouth of her vagina she fell on him just as she had with Adam minutes before.

'Come on, girl,' she urged, thrusting her chest out.

Kim picked up the multi-lashed whip. She aimed it at Nina's breasts and slashed it down.

'Yessss... again...'

Kim cut the whip down on Nina's right breast. It flicked across her nipple.

'Again...'

She did it three or four times more, until both Nina's

breasts were criss-crossed with lines as though someone had drawn on them with a fine red pencil, but just as she was about to deliver another stroke, Nina's hand flashed out and caught her wrist. She held her arm raised, staring straight into Kim's eyes, every muscle in her body locked. Slowly her eyes closed and she let out an odd high-pitched keening noise, as she spread her legs further apart and subtly, almost unconsciously, ground herself down on Bill's phallus.

As her orgasm ebbed away she opened her eyes, releasing Kim's wrist. 'Now you mount him. Come on, I want to see you fucking him.'

Kim was not at all unhappy about that. Not only had she seen Nina's orgasm trembling through her body, but she seemed to feel it too, the sensations transmitted via her wrist. With her ankles chained together, however, it was not easy. She swung a knee over Adam so she was facing Nina, her ankles pulling against the chain which was just long enough for them to rest on either side of him, the chain stretched across his thighs. She moaned softly as she lowered onto him, his erection sliding into the silky wet walls of her vagina.

'Come on, fuck him,' Nina encouraged.

The whip had fallen between the two men's bodies and the American picked it up. She raised it, aiming it at Kim's breasts, the bra pushing them up as if presenting them for such treatment.

'No,' Kim pleaded. But she wasn't sure she meant it. As she realised Nina's intention she felt a surge of pleasure that made her sex clench tightly around Adam's phallus. The whip made a swishing noise as it whistled through the air. Suddenly little needles of pain exploded over the tops of her breasts, the pain turning instantly to pleasure.

'Come on, fuck him,' Nina demanded.

Kim pulled herself up as Nina aimed the whip again. As the lashes struck she fell on Adam, forcing his cock to stab into her again, the double impact making her cry out loud. Now Nina was moving too, riding Bill as hard as she had before, both women rising and falling at the same time. Nina threw the whip aside and reached for Kim's breasts, both hands squeezing the malleable flesh.

'Are – are you coming?' she grunted. 'Let me hear it.'

'Yes… oh yes,' Kim moaned. She rode Adam harder and harder. Her cunt was alive, her clitoris slamming down against his pubic bone. 'I-I-I'm coming…' she wailed, as a wave of ecstasy overwhelmed her.

When she opened her eyes again Nina was standing by the chest. She was holding a thick leather harness. 'Come here,' she said, her composure once more restored.

Kim eased herself off Adam, amazed that he'd not come too. But it was probably just as well for him that he hadn't; Nina was obviously not finished yet.

Nina buckled a thick leather collar around her own throat. Like the one Kim had been made to wear the night before, it had a strap that hung down between her shoulder blades, attached to which were two narrow cuffs. But there were two short chains hanging down from the front of the collar, too.

'Strap my wrists into this,' Nina ordered. Seeing Kim's puzzled expression she added, 'I told you I was in a funny mood. Sometimes I like to be bound. Why should you slaves have all the fun? Now do as I say – get on with it.' Nina held her arms behind her back while Kim twisted her wrists up and strapped them into the cuffs, one above the other. 'Now the nipple clips,' Nina instructed, turning around and indicating the thin chains that hung from the

219

front of the collar. At the end of each one there was a shiny metal bulldog clip. Hesitantly, Kim picked up one clip and opened it. She noted its jaws had been serrated into spiteful little teeth. There was not enough play in the chains to reach a nipple, so she had to lift Nina's breast before she could site the clip over the tender bud. Slowly she allowed the jaws to sink into the button of flesh. As it bit deep Nina closed her eyes and moaned. The second nipple followed, the chains held taut by the weight of Nina's breasts, the breasts angled up towards her chin.

'Mmm...' She shook her shoulders from side to side, making her breasts quiver and the nipples pull against the clips. A little awkwardly she climbed back onto the bed, swung a leg over Bill's helpless body, and straddled his hips, facing his feet. 'Help me,' she whispered.

Kim moved close. She gripped Bill's cock and pulled it up until it was vertical. Nina sank down, the wet sheath of her sex squelching as she settled on him. But apparently she had something else in mind. She squirmed deliriously for a minute or two, then lifted off him. 'Put him in my arse now,' she breathed, her eyes dancing with excitement.

Kim gripped his rubber-covered cock again. It was slimy, Nina's juices coating it thickly. She directed it up between the American's buttocks, her black satin panties still pulled to one side.

'Yes... yes, just there,' Nina encouraged. She wriggled her hips from side to side and Kim saw the hard shaft of Bill's phallus disappear into her anus. Nina moaned loudly, her eyes closed, her body trembling. 'Now get him up on his knees,' she panted, blindly indicating Adam. 'Untie the bottom half of the ropes.'

Kim did as she was told. She untied the rope and began unwinding it from his legs until they were free.

'Tie it off around his waist,' Nina ordered.

Kim did just that, then managed to roll him over onto his side, and then onto his stomach. He pulled himself up and managed to kneel.

'Come on Adam, you know what I want,' Nina said. As if to illustrate it she leant right back and spread her knees, splaying the lips of her sex apart. Kim could see her vagina, and Bill's scrotum and the base of his phallus. Adam crawled forward, straddling Bill's bound legs. It was quite clear what Nina had in mind.

'Help him,' she urged.

Kim gripped his cock. Of all the scenarios she had been involved in at the house this was properly the most bizarre. As Adam inched forward, his upper body still tightly bound, she directed his cock into Nina's open sex. As it nestled into her Adam bucked his hips and fell forward onto Nina, his cock impaled her alongside Bill's.

Nina moaned loudly. Kim could see her struggling against her bonds. With Adam's body pressing against her breasts, dragging them down against the chains, the clips must have been biting into her nipples with a new intensity. But the pain was obviously turning her on as her whole body was undulating, pushing up and down on the two men with manic energy. Kim was surplus to requirements. Nina's moaning was continuous now and rapidly reaching a crescendo, her head tossing from side to side.

Just then, for some reason, Kim noticed for the first time the small black handbag on the bedside chest. Nina must have put it there when she came into the room, but Kim couldn't remember her doing so. The bag was slightly open, and Kim could see the red fob of car keys peaking out, a rearing black horse stamped on the leather.

This was her chance, she realised, with a rush of adrenaline that made her heart race. Nina was helpless, and there was a long coil of rope trailing from Adam's body that she could use to bind them together. It would take ages for Nina to free herself or for someone to come and find them. Is that what she wanted, she thought, trying to work out her feelings? They were hopelessly confused. She wanted Jake but she could not have him – not on her terms.

'Oh yes, *yes*!' Nina screamed, grinding against both men.

Kim picked up the end of the rope and wrapped it around Nina's back. She appeared not to notice. Kim looped the rope around Adam's waist and then around Nina's – twice. Again neither of them reacted, too concerned with the orgasm that was approaching rapidly. Quickly Kim yanked the rope tight and tied it off. This only appeared to cause a new wave of ecstasy in Nina's body. She stared at Kim, and then at the rope, but clearly registered neither.

Kim got off the bed. She peered into the chest. There was a ball gag attached to a thick leather strap.

Nina was coming. She threw her head forward, burying her mouth in Adam's shoulder and letting out a long low cry that was muffled on his flesh, her eyes closed. Then gradually the hardness in her muscles began to melt away.

After a few seconds she slowly opened her eyes, and looked down at the rope.

'What have you done?' she asked, with puzzlement rather than anger.

Kim knelt on the bed. 'Open your mouth,' she said, a little gingerly.

Nina saw the gag. 'Don't be ridiculous,' she said, an uncertain smile lifting her lips.

Kim reached forward and pinched her nose. After a moment of not being able to breathe, Nina was forced to open her mouth. Kim pressed the ball inside and strapped it behind her head.

'What the hell do you think you're doing?' Adam asked incredulously.

'Leaving,' Kim told him.

'Don't be an idiot. They'll never let you back.'

'Do I have to gag you, too?'

'Of course you do – I'm not going to cover for you. You'll have to gag us both or we'll shout the house down.'

Nina tried to say something, her face reddened by the effort, but only a few grunts came out.

There was only one more gag in the chest so Kim improvised a second by tying a pair of silk panties into Adam's mouth with a nylon stocking. Now she needed clothes. She rifled the chest of drawers, but though it contained lingerie, there were no dresses or outer clothes. There was nothing in the bedside chest and with the manacles around her ankles she could not pull Nina's catsuit on either. It was too late to change her mind. She couldn't merely untie them and hope they'd understand. She'd have to go as she was.

She grabbed Nina's handbag and went to the bedroom door, opened it carefully, and crept out onto the landing. There was no one about. She thought she heard a noise as she reached the top of the stairs, and pulled back. But there was nothing.

Hesitantly she walked down the stairs, each step creaking alarmingly. At the bottom she walked on tiptoe so the heels of her shoes would not clack on the polished wood floor. She reached the front door, just as she glimpsed Marsha in the sitting room to the left. For a moment she thought she'd been seen, but she hadn't. Holding her breath she managed to open the front door without making a sound, and then slipped out as swiftly as the manacles would allow. She reached the car and ducked behind it just as she saw Marsha standing in the open doorway.

She waited. Marsha looked out, as if trying to see or hear something. For long seconds she stood there, scanning the area at the front of the house. Kim felt sick with tension; had she seen her?

Then Marsha shook her head, as if to suggest annoyance with herself, disappeared back inside and closed the large door.

The door of the Ferrari was unlocked. Kim opened it and crawled inside, keeping well down. She fished the keys from Nina's handbag and found the ignition. She had never driven a machine like this, with its H-shaped gearbox, but she was going to have to learn – and quickly.

She turned the key in the ignition and the engine sprung to life with a deep booming growl she was sure would alert the whole house.

Still crouched behind the wheel she put the car into first, then sat up, pressed the accelerator and swung the wheel round. The car skidded on the gravel, then righted itself, heading down the drive at amazing speed. Kim looked in the rear-view mirror to see the rapidly diminishing figure of Marsha again standing at the front door. She began to run after the car but quickly gave up.

At the end of the drive was a five-bar gate set into a stone wall – and it was open. Kim had no idea which direction to take, but at least she was free. The trouble was, her escape had happened in such a rush that she still wasn't sure whether she'd done the right thing or not.

Chapter Ten

Kim had no idea where she was. After driving for about ten miles on minor roads she saw signposts for an interstate to New Haven, but had no idea where New Haven was. After another twenty or so miles there were exit signs to New Haven and route signs to Bridgeport and Stamford. She recognised the name of Stamford because of the university, but still had no idea where it was in relation to New York.

She had several other problems too. She was naked but for the white lace lingerie and stockings, and her feet were still manacled. Fortunately there was enough play in the chain to allow her to drive, but she couldn't stop anywhere to ask directions or go to a diner or a bar to pee, which she desperately needed to do.

After a few more miles she decided to turn off the interstate and try to find a quiet hedgerow where she could relieve herself and search the car properly for maps. It was also possible that Nina had a case in the boot, or at the very least a coat to wear.

After a little further she noticed a gate leading into the corner of a field. The gate was set in a tall beech hedge. She hopped out of the car, opened the gate, and then managed to manoeuvre the low slung car over the tractor-rutted ground without scrapping the bottom.

Fortunately it was a balmy night. Kim got out of the car and squatted down behind the hedge, peeing a fierce stream. Greatly relieved, she walked back to the car and opened the boot. Apart from a smart tool kit it was empty. There was nothing behind the seats either, and the only thing in the glove compartment was a small leather make-up case. There were no maps and no clothes.

She opened Nina's small handbag. There was a wallet containing a platinum credit card, store cards, and about five hundred dollars in cash. That would certainly buy her fuel, but she imagined that, like in England, the bigger filling stations would be self-service, and she certainly couldn't see herself filling the Ferrari's tank and walking over to pay dressed as she was. She supposed it might just be possible that she could find a garage with an attendant, which would mean she wouldn't have to get out of the car. And if it was dark and the forecourt not too brightly lit it was possible they might just see her top half and imagine she was wearing a low cut and rather revealing evening dress.

She turned on the ignition to check the fuel. The gauge read half full. She had no idea how much fuel a Ferrari used, but was sure it was a lot. How far it would get her she didn't know, and what was worse, she didn't know how far she had to get.

She started the car again and backed out onto the top road. She drove back up to the interstate, then stopped before committing herself to the slip road. She reckoned she had a better chance of finding a small filling station with an attendant on the smaller roads. And the filling stations on the interstate would all be brightly lit. On the other hand, they would be open twenty-four hours, whereas the ones on the minor roads might not. She hesitated, not knowing what to do, then decided she had to do something and turned right onto the minor road that ran parallel to the interstate.

The Ferrari was a handful to drive. Even the gentlest of touches on the accelerator sent it shooting forward at an alarming rate, and several times Kim had to brake severely as she was going into a corner. The view of the interstate soon disappeared and she found herself in the middle of the countryside with signposts to Woodbridge, Ansonia, Derby and Huntingon – all places she had never heard of.

She wondered if Nina would have called the police about the car. It was, after all, an expensive machine. She doubted that she would, however. Trying to explain who was driving the car and how she was dressed would be much too difficult and might lead to some very awkward questions. She was sure Jake Ashley would have advised Nina to keep quiet.

There was not a single filling station, open or closed, anywhere on the road. She drove on and on, not knowing whether she was getting close to New York or further away, and watching the fuel gauge dip at an alarming rate.

At last she saw way ahead what she thought might be the lighted sign of a petrol station on top of a pole. As she got closer she saw that's exactly what it was. If the sign was illuminated, she reasoned, the garage must be open. And it was.

The filling station was small and smart, with three pumps in a row. But her heart sunk as she saw that not only was the forecourt brightly lit, but also there were signs telling her it offered all the convenience of self-service. She glanced anxiously at the fuel gauge again. It was perilously close to empty and she simply dare not drive on; there might not be another garage for miles. She was just going to have to brave it out.

She pulled the car onto the forecourt. About twenty yards from the pumps at the back was a small booth made from plate-glass. There was an attendant sitting on a stool behind the counter. He appeared to be reading a book.

Kim got out of the car, feeling more naked than she ever had in her entirely life, intensely aware that her sex and buttocks were completely exposed. She didn't even know where the filler cap was on the car and had to walk around the back bumper to look for it. The high heels clacked on the concrete and the chain on the manacles rattled.

She found the cap and inserted the nozzle of the pump into it. Unfortunately it was on the side of the car nearest the attendant, and she had to stand with her back to him, the shimmering white stockings with their deep lace welts held taut by the tight suspenders that stretched down from the cami-bra, the muscles of her long legs firmed up by the high heels that made her stand almost on tiptoe.

The car guzzled a lot of fuel and she seemed to stand there for ages. She was sure the attendant was watching her. Even if the arrival of a red Ferrari wasn't enough to attract his attention, the sight of a semi-naked woman certainly would be. But there was nothing she could do about it.

At long last the tank was full and the pump cut out. She reached into the driver's door and took a hundred-dollar bill from Nina's bag. Now came the really embarrassing part. She turned and walked towards the booth. With the high heels and the chain around her ankles she could only take tiny steps, so her progress seemed infinitely slow. She could see the attendant. He had put his book down and was staring at her, open-mouthed. He was young, perhaps no more than eighteen, with a mass of youthful spots adorning his chin.

Kim held her hands over her mons, though it was a vain

attempt at modesty. As she got closer she could see there was no window in the booth, so she couldn't pay from outside. She would have to go into the booth itself and walk right across to the counter.

She got to the plate glass door and swung it open. The booth was raked with shelves displaying oil and other car related products. To the left was a big display of magazines, with some very raunchy titles on the top shelf. But none of the girls staring out from the front pages had on anything quite as revealing as the outfit Kim was wearing.

The attendant stood up. His face was bright red. He was wearing a blue check shirt and faded denim jeans.

'H-hello,' Kim blurted, trying to remain calm. 'Look, I'm in a bit of trouble.'

'You're English,' the youth said stupidly.

'Yes, I am. And some rather cruel friends have played a trick on me. I was at this party, you see—'

'Guess that was some party.'

She pressed herself against the counter so he was unable to see below her waist. 'It was. But as you see, they thought it was funny to leave me out in the middle of nowhere – like this. I've no idea where I am. Can you help? I need to get back to New York.'

'Sure,' he said, and turned to a shelf at the back of the counter, which was filled with maps.

'And do you have something that could cut chain?' Kim went on, feeling a little more confident. 'You see what they did to my ankles.'

'I don't know. I could try. Wait there.'

He disappeared behind a small door at the back of the counter. Kim looked around in case there was anything in the shop she could buy to cover her body, but could see nothing suitable. A few minutes later the youth returned. He was carrying a bolt cutter.

'This should do it, ma'am,' he said brightly. 'Only thing is, I'm going to have to come out there.' He opened a lift top in the counter and stepped from behind it, staring at Kim's beauty. 'That's a real pretty outfit, ma'am,' he said. 'I've never seen anything like it.'

'A little too revealing,' she said, feeling uncomfortable with his close proximity and obvious interest, pressing her belly to the front of the counter so he didn't get a full frontal view. 'W-what's your name?' she asked, blatantly trying to change the subject and divert his attentions.

'Dale.'

He knelt at her feet and examined the manacles. 'You want me to cut the chain? Don't think it'll make much impression on these cuffs.' He was looking up at her, his face a few inches from the white satin suspender on her left thigh.

'That, um, that would be great,' she stuttered.

He put the jaws of the bolt cutter over the chain and pressed in on the long metal hands. The chain snapped easily.

'You've got real beautiful legs, ma'am.' A hand touched her ankle gently, stroking the sleek nylon. 'Finest I've ever seen.'

Kim knew she had to get away; she had to get away before things went too far with this youth, she had to get to New York, and for all she knew Jake Ashley and his minions might be out looking for her right now. She tried to move, but the lad rose quickly and pinned her to the counter. 'Please...' she whispered, feeling his clothed erection prodding into her hip. 'Don't do this.'

'Real beautiful tits, too,' he wheezed, his stale breath

wafting around her face, making her fringe dance delicately.

'Look—' Kim was going to try to appease him, but the words failed her as a sweaty palm cupped her right breast through the flimsy cami-bra and mauled it feverishly. The youth started to grind against her like a dog on heat, squashing her so the counter dug painfully into her waist.

'Fucking hell,' he croaked. 'You turn me on.'

Kim managed to squeeze her fists between them and tried to push against his weedy chest, but he was in determined mood. He grabbed her right wrist and forced her hand down to the lump in his jeans. He managed to open her clenched fingers and sandwiched them between his sweaty palm and the lump, moving them in a tight circle.

'Please... I... I have to go...' Kim tried feebly, but the youth wasn't going to be denied such a monumental opportunity. He sank his face to her breasts, and slobbered hungrily over their soft upper slopes and into her deep cleavage. He breathed deeply through his nose, inhaling her scent. Then Kim felt his hips convulse and a damp warmth spread against her captured fingers.

'Oh, *fuck*...' he groaned, and slumped against the counter. '*Fuck*...'

Kim managed to extricate herself from his weakening clutches, grabbed the map and dashed from the booth, and quickly reached the car and locked herself inside. She sat for a few minutes, eyes closed, gathering her thoughts and her breath, when quite suddenly a very strange thing happened; in her mind she saw Jake Ashley. He was looking at her with a stern expression, his steel-blue eyes unblinking. She shook her head and opened her eyes to rid herself of the unsettling spectre.

As she looked across the forecourt at the pathetic figure of the youth, now back behind his counter determinedly looking in any direction but hers, she seemed to hear Jake's voice in her head: 'That's not what you want. That's not what you need. You deserve more than that.' She could hear the beautifully articulated English vowels quite clearly. 'Only I can give you what you seek.'

'No,' she said aloud, and then tried to banish the chilling voice by turning the ignition key, engaging gear, slamming the accelerator to the floor, and screeching away from the forecourt in a plume of rubbery smoke.

Chapter Eleven

She parked the Ferrari outside Audrey's apartment block in SoHo. She had decided on the long trip across New York that it was better to go to Audrey than check into a hotel. Audrey would know how to contact Jake and return Nina's car, and besides, she wanted her to be the first to know that she would be filing the story implicating Nina Berry and Senator Tom Beddoes in Jake's activities. Not having slept all night Kim felt ragged. She hoped Audrey was in.

Thankfully the entrance to Audrey's apartment block was secluded, and nobody was around to observe her skimpy attire. There was an entry-phone beside the heavy steel door and Kim pressed the button next to A.SANDERSON.

'Yes?' came the metallic response.

'Audrey, it's Kim. I'm back.'

'Kim, great. Come in.'

The door lock buzzed and Kim pushed her way inside.

Audrey was waiting for her outside the door to her apartment. As Kim stepped out of the lift Audrey embraced her and gushed, 'Great to see you, sweetie. How did you get on? Come inside.'

They walked into the apartment together.

'Would you like some coffee? Jesus, you look like a refuge.'

'I've had a bad night,' Kim said non-committally. 'And I've got Nina Berry's Ferrari parked outside. I stole it.'

'Nina Berry's? The film star?'

Kim nodded.

'Well,' Audrey enthused. 'I told you there were a whole gang of people up there.'

'And Senator Beddoes.'

'You're joking, right?'

Kim shook her head wearily.

'So how did you get away?'

'It's a long story and I'm starving. I'd love to take a bath and have something to eat.'

'Of course, of course.' Audrey fussed over to the kitchen area and poured a coffee. 'Here,' she said, passing it to Kim, 'I'll do you some ham and eggs while you use the bathroom.'

'Have you any clothes I could borrow?'

'Sure, no problem. We'll sort all that out. Better get those manacles off first. I hope my key fits.'

Audrey disappeared into another room, and moments later she returned with a small key. She knelt at Kim's feet and soon had the cuffs off. She then led Kim to the bathroom. 'Help yourself to anything,' she said warmly. 'There's a robe on the door. I'll get the food.'

Kim caught sight of herself in the large mirror on the bathroom wall. For a moment she looked like Jake Ashley's slave again. Quickly she reached back and undid the cami-bra, not wanting to think of the consequences of what she had done. She would never see Jake Ashley again.

It was not until she lay soaking in the tub, the steaming water perfumed with oils she'd found, that she realised how much she missed having a bath. With no tub in her cell she'd been restricted to showers. She rested her head on the back of the bath and closed her eyes, wallowing luxuriously as the soothing water swilled all around her. In seconds she was dozing.

A knock on the bathroom door roused her.

'Come in,' she called wearily.

Audrey stood in the doorway, looking stern.

'I thought so,' she said. 'Come on, you're falling asleep. It's dangerous.' She took the robe from the back of the door and brought it over to Kim. 'Your eggs are ready.'

Her eyes examined Kim closely as she got out of the bath. She wrapped the thick white towelling around Kim's body, then used it to dry her.

'Feeling better?'

Kim nodded and smiled weakly. 'I will when I've eaten.'

And she ate everything. She finished a pile of scrambled eggs, three thick slices of ham and two slices of bread spread generously with butter.

'Mmmm... that was *good*,' she said, the sparkle returning to her eyes.

'So what are you going to do now?'

'Call my editor. But I think I should sleep first. I'd better find a hotel.'

'Don't be ridiculous,' Audrey told her off. 'You can stay here. There's a bedroom at the back that's comfortable, if you'll forgive the rather unusual décor. It's what I call my playroom.'

'I must admit I'd love to just crash out, if you don't mind.'

'Feel free.'

'Did you speak to Jake?' she asked, the man never far from her thoughts.

'No. Well, I got through to Marsha. Jake's not going to be back until tonight, apparently. But she's told Nina where she can pick up the car.

'Come on, let's get you to bed. Then maybe you'll feel like going out and getting a proper meal.'

'Love to. And if you can lend me something to wear, then we can go back to my old hotel and pick up my case.'

'Of course.' Audrey smiled warmly. 'I'll look something out.'

They got up and moved across to a door next to the bathroom. Audrey led the way inside.

The room was square with no windows. It had black carpet on the floor, walls and ceiling. There were all the accoutrements of sado-masochism that Kim had seen before; a pulley hanging from a wooden beam in the ceiling, and metal rings attached to one wall at various heights. There was a television in one corner, under which was a video recorder. In the middle of the room was a double bed covered with a black silk sheet. Leather cuffs attached to chains secured to metal rings were fastened to each of its legs. A white duvet and white pillows had been dumped on one end. They looked completely incongruous.

'It's Jake's legacy,' Audrey said, by way of explanation. For a moment Kim saw an expression in her eyes she could not read. It might have been a sense of longing; a yearning for something that had been lost.

'I don't care as long as it's a bed.' Though despite her tiredness the sight of the cuffs made her limbs tingle, a muscle memory of how it had felt to be bound and spread-eagled, stirring much deeper feelings.

'I'll wake you when you've had a good sleep.'

Kim smiled appreciatively and gave the woman a peck on the cheek.

'There's a switch here for the lights,' Audrey added. The room was lit by a bar of spotlights strung across the ceiling. There was a small table beside the bed, and a round dimmer switch on a cord that disappeared down into the floor.

'Sleep well.' Audrey closed the door. It was the first time for what seemed like an age that Kim did not hear a key turning in the lock.

She supposed Audrey having a room like this should not have surprised her. She knew Audrey had been one of Jake's slaves, and she now knew that Jake and what he represented was difficult to escape from. He had certainly stirred needs and desires in her that she would never be able to forget. As yet she had barely considered what she would do about them in the real world.

She slipped out of the robe, lay on the bed, flipped the duvet over her, and turned off the lights. She fell asleep almost before her head touched the pillow.

'Hi.'

Kim opened her eyes slowly, staring up at the spotlights above her. They were glowing dimly, the room barely lit.

'Hello,' she said, rolling over to see Audrey sitting on the edge of the bed. She was wearing a black chiffon wrap. 'What time is it?'

'Very late. You've been asleep all day. I didn't have the heart to wake you earlier. I thought it was better to let you sleep.'

Kim squirmed and smiled comfortably beneath the duvet.

'I sent out for some food, if you want it.'

'Mmm... I'm not hungry yet... still a bit sleepy.' Kim stifled a little yawn with her fingers.

Audrey reached out and stroked her shoulder. 'You're very beautiful,' she said softly.

'Not without my make-up, I'm not.'

'Of course you are.' She leant forward and kissed Kim on the cheek. 'It's just that I was feeling a little lonely, thinking about you in here. I thought you might like some company.'

'Still sleepy…' Kim murmured, turning on her side, mists of sleep drifting over her.

'Do you mind if I cuddle up with you?'

'Mmm… that'd be nice…'

Kim heard Audrey stripping off her wrap, then felt her climbing into bed beside her. She was naked. She spooned her body against Kim's.

'That feels nice,' Audrey whispered.

Kim moved back against the woman, her breasts and belly and thighs feeling deliciously soft. She felt an immediate surge of desire. Audrey's hand was moving surreptitiously down over her tummy. 'What are you doing?' Kim asked, though she knew perfectly well.

'You seem to have woken up a little.' Her fingers pushed down between Kim's thighs. 'Would you prefer that I stopped?'

'No…' she sighed, 'no, don't do that.' Kim rolled onto her back and looked into Audrey's eyes. 'I'm very new at all this,' she said humbly.

'Good,' Audrey purred. 'That's the way I like my girls. Just lie back and enjoy.'

She leant lower and her fleshy lips kissed Kim lightly. They moved down to her throat, and then, pushing the duvet aside, descended to her breasts. 'You've no idea how much I wanted you the other day when I was spraying your body with that stuff. Seeing you like that…'

Kim felt Audrey shudder. The American sucked at Kim's breast, then centred her mouth on the nipple, pinching it between her teeth. Kim's sex responded with a sharp pulse.

Having sex with a woman was still such a new experience, and still, in her mind at least, taboo, that feeling Audrey touching her provoked an inordinately strong reaction.

Audrey's mouth moved to her other breast, while her hand pressed Kim's thighs apart. As Kim spread her legs, Audrey's middle finger slid into the crease of her labia, nudging almost immediately up against her clit. Kim moaned and slowly rolled her head from side to side.

'You like that, do you?' Audrey asked unnecessarily.

'Love it.'

'You love having a woman fingering you?'

'Yes.' The admission excited Kim.

Audrey's finger was artful. Kim's clitoris was highly sensitive, but there was a tiny spot right at the tip, that seemed to be the centre of her whole sexual universe, provoking shards of pleasure so intense they were almost painful. Audrey concentrated on this spot instinctively, just rolling the tip of her finger over it with the smallest of movements.

'Kiss me,' Kim begged.

Audrey did just that, her mouth enveloping Kim's lips, her tongue pushing between them. The hotness and wetness of Audrey's mouth excited Kim quite as much as the feelings from her clit. The two sensations seemed to join together, her body arching off the bed.

'I want to watch you come,' Audrey whispered huskily. 'Will you do that for me?'

'Yes… *yes*…'

Kim felt her sex clench hungrily – but she remembered something she had chosen not to think about since she'd driven out of the filling station. She remembered the odd numbness that had taken a hold of her. And she saw Jake Ashley's eyes staring at her again.

239

'No,' she said aloud, shaking her head.

'No what?' Audrey said, looking concerned.

'It's...' In Kim's mind Jake was tutting very softly.

'Do you want me to stop?'

'No... no... it's wonderful.'

But it wasn't. Not any more.

'Harder,' she whimpered. 'I need it harder.'

Immediately Audrey increased the pressure of her finger, flicking Kim's clit back and forth. But it was no good. She closed her eyes to try and concentrate her feelings, but in the blank screen of her mind all she could see was Jake Ashley and his disapproving expression.

Kim rolled her hips from side to side, crushing down on Audrey's fingers, but nothing happened.

'It's no good,' she said quietly, pulling Audrey's hand away. 'I think I'm too tired.'

Audrey was still smiling. 'No, you're not. I know what's the matter with you.'

'You do?'

Audrey nodded. 'It's Jake. I felt the same when I left him. Every time I tried to have sex with a man or a woman it was the same. I just saw his eyes looking at me. I couldn't think of anything else. It's the effect he has on women. It's like a hypnotist not letting you out of his power.'

'Yes – yes, that's exactly it. But what am I going to do?'

'It's all right,' Audrey reassured her. 'I know what you need... Trust me.'

Audrey rolled away, then knelt beside the bed and picked up one of the leather cuffs, staring straight into Kim's eyes.

'No...' Kim said. But the sight of the restraint had caused her sex to kick back into life, a huge surge of feeling soaring through her body, like electricity. She didn't want to admit that the thought of bondage could have such an enormous effect on her – but it clearly did.

'You don't mean that,' Audrey said confidently. 'Believe me, I know. The same thing happened to me.' She sat on the edge of the bed and took hold of Kim's left arm. Kim didn't resist. As her wrist was pulled out to the corner of the bed and the leather cuff wrapped around it and buckled tight her whole body seemed to tingle.

Audrey stood up and walked around to the other side of the bed. This time as she pulled Kim's right arm out and strapped it down Kim felt a pulse of pleasure deep in her vagina.

'Feels good, doesn't it?' Audrey whispered. 'Struggle a little bit, fight against it.'

Kim tried to sit up, but her arms were stretched out so far she could barely raise her shoulders from the bed. The excitement she felt was becoming intense.

'You see,' Audrey said, obviously quite aware of what Kim was experiencing. She walked to the foot of the bed and grasped Kim's right ankle, pulling it over to the corner and securing it in the third leather cuff. 'I don't know what it is, but it's like a virus that gets into the blood. Once you've caught it, the cure is worse than the disease.'

Kim's right leg was stretched out and bound securely, her sex spread open and completely vulnerable.

'You've a very pretty pussy,' Audrey sighed. 'Did Jake tell you that?'

Such was Kim's excitement she couldn't speak, but Audrey continued anyway. She ran a hand down between Kim's legs, cupping her sex. 'You're very wet.'

'Please...' Kim managed.

'Please what? You're a slave again now, Kim. You know the rules.'

'Please don't tease me.' But wasn't being teased exactly

241

what she wanted? Her sex was pulsing so strongly now she thought she might come just like this. The strength of the feelings forced her eyes closed and she half expected Jake Ashley to be lurking there, but the only image she saw was a birds-eye view of herself, spread out on the bed with Audrey kneeling beside her. Audrey leant lower. She planted her lips firmly on Kim's sex and sucked on her clit, gathering the whole thing into her mouth where her tongue immediately went to work.

Kim moaned loudly. She struggled against the bonds, not because she wanted to escape, but because she loved the feeling that being so helpless gave her. She knew she was going to come – and quickly.

Audrey was relentless. She swung a thigh over Kim's body, sitting astride her chest. At the same time she pushed two fingers into Kim's vagina and used a third to press against her sphincter. For a moment the little ring of muscle resisted, but when it yielded and Audrey's finger slipped into the tight rear passage, Kim felt yet another explosion of ecstasy, her anus now quite as capable of delivering pleasure as her cunt.

Audrey released her clit, then found that tiny spot again, pressing her tongue against it as she had done before. Her tongue caressed it with the same rhythm that she was using to pump her fingers in and out of both nether orifices. She had tied Kim tight, her body stretched across the bed so that her muscles and sinews were taut. But rather than being painful this only seemed to increase the sensitivity of her nerves, the pleasure that was flowing through them a hundred times more potent. With all her energy she arched up off the bed, pushing her breasts against Audrey's thighs as her orgasm overwhelmed her, a colossal explosion of pleasure that left her trembling and weak.

Audrey was absolutely right; she had been through everything Kim had been through and knew exactly what she needed. Even when Kim's orgasm eventually ebbed away she could still feel tremors of exquisite pleasure simply by pulling against one of the leather cuffs.

Audrey straightened up, moving back so her sex was poised above Kim's hot face, glistening and inviting. On her left buttock Kim noticed a small blue roundel of a tattoo, the letters JA contained within it in elaborate script.

Audrey stroked her own sex, dipping one finger into her vagina right above Kim's eyes. Then she spread her fingers apart so her labia were spread too, and Kim found herself staring up into the scarlet maw. Then, slowly, it lowered onto Kim's waiting mouth.

The extraordinary texture and wetness of a woman's sex gave Kim a new jolt of pleasure, reawakening her appetites. Hungrily she lapped at Audrey, wanting to taste her juices. She probed with her tongue, running it around the outer lips. She heard Audrey moan and saw her finger flicking at her own clitoris. Seconds later the American pressed her mouth back to Kim's sex, renewing all the feelings it had created there. The circle was complete. Everything she could feel in Audrey's sex was replicated and repeated in her own. Just as Audrey's sex began to quiver as her orgasm exploded, Kim realised she was going to come again too. The feeling of Audrey's orgasm, the way her labia seemed to suck at Kim's tongue, took her to the brink, needing only the slightest touch to make her come again. She closed her eyes, overwhelmed by a myriad of different sensations.

Thwack!

Kim opened her eyes with a start. For a moment she was completely confused. She had felt Audrey jerk as if being whipped, her sex melting over her mouth with a new heat, her voice crying out in a tone she had heard before; that unique melange of pain and extreme pleasure. But her thighs and buttocks were blocking her view. Was there someone else in the room?

Thwack!

A second huge shock vibrated through Audrey's body, but this time Kim saw the whip strike, a long thin lash cutting across her buttocks and making her flesh quake. Audrey's sex clenched, her juices so copious they were dripping from Kim's chin.

Thwack!

This time Audrey screamed, a high-pitched wail, and as she shuddered she came again, her sex quivering, her head thrown back. It seemed to go on for a long time, her cry a long diminuendo.

'I know what you want.'

The voice startled Kim. She recognised it at once. It belonged to Jake Ashley.

'Yes, master,' Audrey whimpered feebly. 'You always have.'

'You've done well. Get off her now.'

'Thank you, master.'

As Audrey climbed off Kim's prostrate body Kim looked up at him standing over her. He was naked apart from a pair of black leather briefs, and was holding a riding crop. 'Whu-what's going on?' she managed. The exquisite sexual feelings that were still coursing through her were making it difficult for her to think straight.

'I would have thought that was obvious,' Jake said.

Kim looked to Audrey, who was still kneeling by her side. 'But, I thought you wanted to expose him.'

'I did, but…' Audrey mumbled, avoiding Kim's

questioning gaze.

'Audrey was cross with me,' Jake Ashley continued on behalf of the embarrassed woman. 'Actually, she was cross with herself. She didn't like the thought that her inner needs were so submissive. Like you, she escaped. Because she transferred – I think that's the correct psychological term – her anger to me, she wanted to do something to hurt me. Apparently, you were the answer to her prayer.'

'I still don't understand.' The sexual impulses were fading and Kim's mind was beginning to work. 'You told him I was here?'

Audrey nodded, her eyes still lowered.

'Why, for God's sake?'

'Isn't it obvious?' Jake said calmly. 'Audrey changed her mind. We've come to a little arrangement. Normally none of the SNY are allowed to stay with one master for longer than six months; Audrey is going to be an exception.'

'In return for what?' Kim tried to sit up, forgetting the bonds, and got a painful reminder from the muscles in her shoulders. 'Please, let me go,' she said feebly.

'In return for your silence.'

'In return for my—?'

'You have two choices, Kim,' he interrupted. 'You can write your story and return to England. You will never see me again. You will never know the sort of pleasures I can give you.

'Or you can stay with me. You can join the system. You can be one of the Slaves of New York. I'm prepared to give you a second chance. You made me lose control of myself. I can't remember another slave doing that. I want you to come back.'

'I can't do it,' Kim protested.

'Then release her,' Jake snapped immediately. His eyes darkened and he turned towards the door.

'No,' Audrey cried. 'Kim, don't you realise you're exactly the same as me. You can't live without him. You can't do without this.' She gestured at the bondage. 'Like I said, it's a disease. Once you've caught it there's no cure.'

'Let me go,' Kim insisted determinedly.

But she was looking at Jake. She wanted him. She wanted everything he represented. Could she really live without seeing him ever again?

'Let her go,' he said.

'No,' Kim exclaimed firmly as Audrey reluctantly reached to release one of the leather cuffs. It was madness. She knew it was madness. She could walk out of this apartment with a sure-fire front page story that would give her all the career opportunities she could ever wish for. She could work on any paper anywhere in the world. But at this moment the thought that Jake Ashley was going to walk out of the door and out of her life was simply too much to bear.

She didn't blame Audrey, because she knew exactly what Audrey was feeling. Ever since she had escaped from the house she realised there had been an emptiness in her life. She hadn't wanted to admit it to herself. As much as she wished she could return to her old life, when she had been independent and free, she knew she was not and would never be again until she had explored everything Jake Ashley's books and Jake Ashley in person had made her feel. That might take weeks, or months, or even years – but it had to be done. She wished she could have him to herself, but she knew that could not be and she would rather share him than not have him at all.

There would be, she hoped, other stories and other

opportunities in her career, but this was a chance she knew would never come again.

'No?' Jake echoed, raising an eyebrow.

'I'll do whatever you say,' Kim said. She hesitated, then added, 'Master.'

Jake did not smile. Instead, he knelt on the bed and caressed her cheek so tenderly she felt tears welling in her eyes. His hand ran down to her breast, handling it much less carefully, pinching her nipple. She saw a bulge growing in the briefs. His other hand snaked down between her legs and a finger nudged against her clit. Just this touch almost made her come. She gasped and shuddered.

Jake got to his feet. He pulled off his briefs. His erection jutted from his firm flat belly. He knelt on the bed behind her, his knees apart so his scrotum swayed right above her mouth.

'Come here,' he said to Audrey.

'Yes, master.'

She moved closer to him.

'Take it in your mouth.'

Audrey immediately did as she was told.

'And you,' he said, looking down at Kim, 'take my balls in your mouth.'

She lifted her head. Her shoulder muscles were beginning to cramp and her neck protested as she did so, but that was a pain she welcomed. She wanted this. She wanted this more than she'd ever wanted anything in her life.

'Yes, master,' she said softly.

Exciting titles available from Chimera

All **Chimera** titles are/will be available from your local bookshop or newsagent, or direct from our mail order department. Please send your order with a cheque or postal order (made payable to *Chimera Publishing Ltd*) to: **Chimera Publishing Ltd., PO Box 152, Waterlooville, Hants, PO8 9FS**. If you would prefer to pay by credit card, please call our **24 hour telephone/fax credit card hotline: +44 (0)23 92 783037** (Visa, Mastercard, Switch, JCB and Solo only).

To order, send: Title, author, ISBN number and price for each book ordered, your full name and address, cheque or postal order for the total amount, and include the following for postage and packing:
UK and BFPO: £1.00 for the first book, and 50p for each additional book to a maximum of £3.50.
Overseas and Eire: £2.00 for the first book, £1.00 for the second and 50p for each additional book.

*Titles £5.99. All others £4.99

For a copy of our free catalogue please write to:

Chimera Publishing Ltd
Readers' Services
PO Box 152
Waterlooville
Hants
PO8 9FS

Or visit our WebShop at:
www.chimerabooks.co.uk